D1599097

A RELUCTANT SAINT

A RELUCTANT SAINT

Tricia Fields

SEVERN
HOUSE

First world edition published in Great Britain and the USA in 2022
by Severn House, an imprint of Canongate Books Ltd,
14 High Street, Edinburgh EH1 1TE.

Trade paperback edition first published in Great Britain and the USA in 2023
by Severn House, an imprint of Canongate Books Ltd.

severnhouse.com

British Library Cataloguing-in-Publication Data
A CIP catalogue record for this title is available from the British Library.

ISBN-13: 978-1-4483-0687-9 (cased)
ISBN-13: 978-1-4483-0709-8 (trade paper)
ISBN-13: 978-1-4483-0708-1 (e-book)

All Severn House titles are printed on acid-free paper.

MIX
Paper from
responsible sources
FSC® C013056

Typeset by Palimpsest Book Production Ltd.,
Falkirk, Stirlingshire, Scotland.
Printed and bound in Great Britain by
TJ Books, Padstow, Cornwall.

ACKNOWLEDGEMENTS

First, a sincere thank you to my editor, Carl Smith. Not only is he an astute wordsmith, but also a kind and caring man; simple words on the page but to be cherished as a person. Carl revived Josie Gray from the ashes, and for that I am forever grateful.

Second, a shout out to the Labor Day crew – a group of people who covers just about everyone who has contributed plot points, characters, and shenanigans to the Josie Gray books throughout the years. See you around the next bonfire.

And, finally, a thank you to Todd, Molly, and Emily. I don't know how I got so lucky.

ONE

For mid-April in far West Texas, it had been unseasonably hot, reaching ninety-eight that afternoon, causing people to make wild predictions about the summer temperatures, climate change and the doomed world they were living in. Josie got home after an unplanned double shift, immediately changed into hiking shorts and a T-shirt, and then opened a can of fruit cocktail she'd put in the refrigerator before she'd left for work that morning. She tipped the can, wincing at the metallic taste of the fruit, but glad for the cold. Mildly annoyed at her lack of domestic anything, she tossed the can in the trash and went to the mat beside the kitchen door to slip on her hiking boots. With her foot half in the boot, she stopped, noticing that Chester's leash was gone. Her old bloodhound had died six months prior, and she still missed him, especially on night walks when he'd zipper back and forth in front of her, sniffing out animals in the brush, then circling back to check in with her. She'd left his leash hanging on the hook by the door, a sweet reminder of an old friend. She'd not noticed it in weeks, but she'd also not been looking for it. The leash on the hook was part of the house, like a painting on the wall.

She opened the pantry door off the kitchen where she stored her gun belt after work each day. The small closet had also held the dog's food and treats. After shoving around the canned goods and boxes of stale cereal, she dug through the junk drawer, the hall closet, the drawers in her bedroom, even the spare bedroom. After thirty minutes of increasingly panicked searching, she walked into the bathroom to look under the vanity and caught her expression in the mirror.

She stopped and leaned against the cabinet, facing her reflection. 'What the hell are you doing, searching for a leash for a dog that is no longer living? Get your shit together.'

She stood for a moment, wondering yet again how she'd

gotten to be thirty-something years old with no husband, no kids, no big plans for the future aside from running a border-town police department in need of everything but crime. Cursing, she flipped the light off.

Outside, she lifted her arms, tilted her head back to the galaxy and filled her lungs with the night air, still trying to push away the fact that she had not moved the dog's leash and it was now missing. She heard movement twenty feet out, just to the right of the back deck, and smiled, glad for the distraction. She had turned the kitchen light off and left the deck dark to allow her eyes to adjust to the night, lit up by a half-moon and a million stars with zero light pollution. She stood motionless until her eyes began to pick out the familiar shapes of desert scrub brush and rock, mixed with agave and cactus that she'd planted through the years. She was waiting for movement, to see if the kit fox would show herself or run for the deeper quiet.

After her dog had died, Josie was shocked when, after just a few months, a fox moved her family of three into the empty burrow of a ground squirrel, expanding the tunnels for the larger fox family. With the wide-open desert, why she would choose to move so close to a human was a mystery, but the fox, whom Josie assumed was a female, seemed to like to keep a wary eye on Josie, always taking the occasional scrap Josie would leave on the low rock wall that surrounded her deck. After a month of Josie standing quietly behind the wall each night to watch and listen, the fox began creeping closer. Josie at first assumed the fox was simply searching for scraps, but she always left them in the same place on the wall. As the fox became more comfortable, she would circle the wall, seeming not to care that most nights no food was available. But on that night, when Josie took a quiet step toward the wall, she heard scurrying and then nothing, a sign that the fox had burrowed down into her den, apparently not wanting company. Josie imagined animals were similar to people in that regard: some nights wanting nothing more than to be left alone.

Work had kept Josie late and worn her down the past several weeks. She had missed walking back to Dell's to sit by a fire and drink a beer after sundown. Dell Seapus, a seventy-some-thing-year-old rancher and Josie's closest friend, rarely talked about his love of the land, but the desert defined him as a person more than anyone she knew. She loved Dell and his ranch and the mountains beyond as one and the same.

She walked along the gravel lane back toward his cabin, feeling the tension in her shoulders and neck slowly ease. Even now, she knew that as an old woman she would be able to conjure up the smell of the desert: juniper, mesquite, creosote and pinon; pungent, oily, boiled and baked. Night-time was the best, when the least bit of moisture opened up the pores of greedy cactus ready to absorb the slightest hint of damp on the air. As the pores opened, the heady scents of the desert were released into the wind. No perfume would ever compare to the desert at night.

Dell's was the only other house on Schenck Road, and his cattle ranch led up into the foothills of the Chinati Mountains. Dell was early to bed, so at ten o'clock she wasn't surprised to see all his lights off. At the halfway point, Josie turned back home to walk the quarter-mile back to her house and up to the road to get her mail. Empty-handed, she turned back toward the house where she noticed a dark form hanging from her door.

She pulled the gun from her waistband and the small flash-light out of her pocket. After work, she had parked at the side of her house to carry a bag of ammo and cartridges in through the kitchen door. It had already been dark when she arrived home, so she might not have noticed anything, although that realization irritated her because she'd not been more aware. People assumed that being a police officer conferred on her a degree of safety that other people didn't have, but there were times in her career when the opposite was true – when her badge became the target.

Keeping her flashlight off, she approached the door and realized it was a piece of clothing hanging off the handle. She poked at it with her foot and it shifted, revealing a glint of moonlight off metal. Josie leaned forward and recognized the pin, then reached out her hand, knowing that she would feel the soft leather of the coat owned by Nick Santos.

TWO

J osie had met Nick when he was hired to investigate the ransom kidnapping of her then-boyfriend, Dillon Reese. Nick had been recommended to her by a community member as 'the best there is.' The community member, who had paid the considerable fees for Nick's services, had been correct about Nick's skills. He had tracked Dillon down to a safehouse in Mexico and brought him home physically intact but mentally ravaged. A short time after returning to Artemis, Dillon moved out of state, begging Josie to go with him, to start a new life elsewhere, free from the horrific memories, from the Medrano Cartel and their disregard for the sanctity of life.

Josie lifted Nick's jacket off the door handle and laid it over her arm, overcome suddenly with the emotion of that year. She had loved Dillon, but she'd been unable or unwilling to leave Artemis for him. She wondered what that said about her character – that she would choose chaos over love and stability. After all Dillon had endured, she had let him down when he needed her the most. Her reasons for not leaving with Dillon were complicated, but she had known that she couldn't find peace in leaving.

During the days that Dillon had gone missing, she'd grown close to Nick, enduring a horror she still avoided thinking about. Nick had lived in her home, learned her habits, her fears and vulnerabilities. Josie had never been one to share her life with others, but she had been forced to trust Nick immediately, given his need for information. He wanted endless details, and he had been the only person who under-stood the terror and guilt she experienced both during and after Dillon's kidnapping. Eventually, after Dillon moved away from Texas, Nick had become her partner. She had finally found someone who understood her devotion to the job, something Dillon had never been able to accept. What she had not anticipated was that Nick had his own devotions.

In a country where kidnappings are a lucrative business, Nick used his special forces training to specialize in victim recovery. What had started as helping two families near his home in Mexico City with cartel kidnappings had turned into a business with two teams that traveled across the country, using both negotiation and force. His success rate was high enough that his name alone was sometimes sufficient to bring victims home. Nick utilized technology and a highly trained staff, military-grade weapons and armored bulletproof vehicles. And while he missed Josie and bemoaned his lack of a family, he also admitted that he loved the speed and immediacy of his life. He had made it clear from the beginning that he would not leave Mexico or his job for anyone. And after a year of complicated visits, occasionally spending a week together and then weeks with barely a phone call, they had quietly gone their separate ways.

So why now, after months of not speaking, would he leave his coat on her front door? Was he watching out for her? Or just watching her?

Josie felt her phone buzz twice in her shorts pocket and hoped it was Nick, ready with an explanation. She pressed her finger against the security reader on her front door, listening as the lock whisked open, a daily reminder of Nick who had set up her security system when the Mexican cartel had been connected with Dillon's kidnapping. She locked the door behind her and sat on the couch, pulling up her text messages to find two from Carol, the bartender at the Legion.

Josie grinned at the messages, both begging her to come down for a beer before Carol 'passed out from boredom.' Monday nights were slow, and Carol didn't do slow. Josie texted back that it was nine o'clock and she had to be at the station at eight the next morning. Carol claimed she had 'intel' that Josie needed immediately. She sighed, knowing bed was a smarter option, but her social life had dwindled to nothing, and she decided she could use a beer and a friendly face.

*   *   *

The Legion Post #007 was located along River Road in a white cinderblock building on the outskirts of Artemis, ten minutes from Josie's house. One of the more active Legions in West Texas, the group helped veterans with medical bills and living expenses through chili cook-offs and barbecues, but mostly through profits gained from the Legion bar, which came to life from Thursday through Saturday. Six months ago, the bar transitioned from a quiet place to have a beer and stare at the TV on the wall to a rowdy poolhall full of regulars and eventually even out-of-towners. Carol Boudreaux, a Louisiana Cajun, came to West Texas to escape a past that included a 'son-of-a-bitch red-neck of an ex-husband' and a town full of people who 'couldn't handle a one-legged female with a side of sass.'

Carol ran the bar like a woman missing her command post. She gave people hell, deserved or not, could make a grown man cry tears of laughter or pain in equal measure and would help any living creature in need of a hand up. She had a soft spot for the homeless and the unloved because she claimed to have been both before she found her new forever town in Artemis.

Josie had never been one for hanging out in a bar. She found them depressing. But Carol had convinced her to stop by for a couple of special events, and Josie had recently found herself wandering in for a beer once or twice a week after work to catch the latest gossip.

She parked her off-duty Jeep Wrangler in the lot, noting two other cars, one of which belonged to Carol. Walking around to the front of the building, Josie found Carol standing in front of a massive prickly pear cactus, six feet tall and twice as wide, covering the front of the building to the right side of the entrance. A metal bucket sat on the ground beside Carol, and Josie heard the plink of items being tossed inside it.

Without turning her head, Carol yelled hello and told Josie to hold the bucket up. Carol wore shorts and a T-shirt, not the best choice to cut the fruit from prickly pear, but that was Carol.

She cursed the cactus spines embedded in her arms and the people who would never appreciate the hell she'd endured for their benefit.

She bent her prosthesis at the knee and kicked her foot up. 'See the latest on my tattoo? My nephew, the art major, came to visit over the weekend and did the next layer for my birthday. I think he did a hell of a job.'

Josie admired his work. He was drawing the muscles and bones of a leg on Carol's prosthesis; he had been working on it for several months. It was an amazing piece of work and fit Carol's personality.

With a bucket full of fruit, Josie followed Carol inside, listening to her endless chatter, something about waking up that morning to feed her cat on the back porch only to find a giant tumbleweed had blown up on to her lawn chair. 'Sitting fat and happy in my own damned chair like it owned the place.' Carol shook her head. 'Hundreds of miles of sun-scorched land that somehow produces enough water for cows and people. How does that happen, Josie? I honestly want to know. There's barely enough water out there to feed these damnable pricklies; how in God's green earth do those big old heifers in the fields survive?'

'Hells bells, Carol, I wonder how all the big old heifers survive out here, too.' Henry Laurel, a rancher from Marfa and a regular at the Double-O-Seven, as the locals called the bar, laughed at his own joke.

Carol dumped the plump red fruit into a sink behind the bar and ignored Henry.

Josie sat at the bar and sighed at the stale smell of cigarettes, knowing her clothes would stink by the time she made it home. Artemis had been a hold-out on the smoking ban, only prohibiting it from restaurants and bars five years prior. Fresh paint had done little to cover up the smell of decades of smoke that had seeped into the concrete walls, but she didn't really mind. The dim lights and veteran paraphernalia hanging on the walls always reminded her of the basement in the house she'd grown up in before her dad died when she was ten. The basement was where her dad and a half-dozen of his cop buddies and close neighbor friends would play poker and drink beer on Saturday nights. If her mom was out with her girlfriends, Josie would sneak out of bed and sit on the top step, listening to the laughter, smiling at jokes she didn't understand, but enchanted with the camaraderie. Her mom had told her a few years ago that her dad could see her little feet on the top step from where he sat at the poker table. Her mom would fuss at him for not making her go to bed, but he'd said she was learning life lessons. He claimed she was better off learning from him and his buddies than from hooligans on the street.

Carol snapped her fingers and told Josie to grab a pair of rubber kitchen gloves lying on the counter and a knife.

'I'll wash and make sure all the spines are off. You peel and halve each one and put them in that pan.'

Josie got off the barstool, and Henry rolled his eyes. 'Better you than me.'

'You ever had a margarita with fresh cactus syrup?' Carol said. 'And that pretty red color? You can't buy that in a can. Fresh cactus fruit is a delicacy.' She turned and pointed a finger at Henry who was staring down at his beer. 'Not that assholes like him deserve any of my hard work.'

'You know we love you,' he said. 'And when you're done chopping up your cactus, I could use another cold one.'

Carol jabbed her knife in his direction.

'When you're done, darlin'. No rush!'

Carol nodded toward the pan on the stove. 'We're gonna boil that down with some honey and strain it. You come back this weekend for Margarita Fest, and I guarantee you will be Ubering home.'

'I don't think we have Ubers in Artemis.'

'We do now.' She waved three fingers in the air. 'I helped get Artemis set up with three certified drivers! I should be the one running for mayor, not these assholes out to scam every man, woman and child.'

'What's that supposed to mean?' Josie asked. 'I think O'Kane has done a fair job.'

'I *bet* you do.'

Josie chose not to take the bait. She had discreetly dated the mayor over the past several months, but neither of them was falling too fast. And he was her boss, which seemed to hang over any serious conversation having to do with law enforcement or politics. She didn't think the relationship was going anywhere, but she thought he was a good person and a decent mayor.

'What's your gripe against O'Kane?' she asked.

'It's not O'Kane. It's the other ass, Mike Striker. I finally figured out his angle.' Carol dumped another dozen pieces of fruit on to the counter for Josie to peel. 'You know that son of a bitch is planning on putting a greyhound racetrack on the outskirts of town?'

Josie laughed. 'You know only about ten percent of what you hear in this place has any truth to it.'

'Bullshit. There's some embellishment, but you know as good as I do that this is where the truth is at. You want the scoop, you come to the Double-O-Seven.'

'Who'd you hear about a greyhound track from?' Josie asked.

'Smokey! And you know he don't lie.'

Smokey Blessings drove a county maintenance truck and was president of the City Council. Josie both respected and liked him, and she knew him to be trustworthy and not keen on gossip.

'He actually told you that Mike Striker is planning on building a greyhound track?' Josie remained smiling, certain that Carol had gotten the story wrong. She dealt in partial truths and exaggerations that made for a more entertaining story.

'Smokey came in here asking *me* for information! He knows this is where the facts are had.'

Josie raised her gloved hands into the air. 'I give! Tell me the story.'

Carole explained that only three states still have legal and active greyhound tracks: Arkansas, Iowa and West Virginia. It was still legal to operate a dog track within Texas, but the last track closed in 2020. Texas law only allowed three greyhound tracks, and, oddly enough, they had to be located in counties with populations over 190,000, and the counties had to include all or part of an island that borders the Gulf of Mexico.

Josie laughed. 'This is ridiculous. You don't honestly believe this crap, do you?'

Carole slugged Josie's arm and scrolled around on her phone long enough to pull up an article that supported her claims.

'What the hell does the Gulf of Mexico have to do with dog tracks?'

'Listen. That's not the point of this. Artemis clearly isn't connected to the Gulf of Mexico.'

'Let me guess. Striker wants to use our connection to the Rio Grande,' Josie said, grinning at her own sarcasm.

'Yes! That's exactly what he's doing! He's got support for some kind of legal loophole that will allow us to use the river.'

'Presidio County has fewer than seven thousand people. He's about a hundred and eighty-three thousand people short. How's he getting around that?' Josie pitched her final piece of fruit into the pot and used her hip to scoot Carol out of the way so she could wash the red juice off her hands.

'He's using some state program for rural development. I don't know. Smokey knew about that part of it. Just legal mumbo-jumbo to me. It doesn't even matter. If there's a loop-hole, Striker will find it or make his own.'

'Who would put a dog track out in the middle of nowhere? Everything he does is tied to money. How can he possibly make money off this?'

'Beats the hell out of me.'

'Think about all the dog lovers. Even if it is legal, they'll go crazy when they hear he wants to do this.'

Carol drizzled honey into the pot of fruit and turned the heat up. 'That's why you haven't heard anything about this. He wants to keep it quiet because he knows he'll lose votes if people find out.'

Josie leaned against the counter and grinned at Carol. 'What part are you playing in all this?'

'I don't even need to play a part. I just make sure the key players have the right information and then I sit back and watch it all unfold on my bar top.' She pointed toward the bar fridge. 'Grab yourself a beer. It's on me for helping tonight.'

'Why's she get a free beer? I help you all the time, and you give me nothing but grief,' Henry said.

Carol ignored him. 'Nothing encourages business better than a little trouble in the ranks. And I am more than happy to fire up the troops.'

THREE

Mike Striker slammed the door on his fully restored 1977 Lincoln Continental. He stepped back and frowned at the dust. He'd chosen silver partly because it said money, old family money, but also because it didn't show dust like the triple-black Oldsmobile Cutlass that he'd had before moving to the desert. New York City had its faults, but it showed a car at its finest. Driving that shiny black Cutlass through a shitty neighborhood had made his chest rumble with pride. Midtown at midnight – that was his favorite place and time in the entire world. Now here he was in the damned desert where sand infiltrated every nook and cranny, turning his luxe pearlescent silver to a dull greige, as his ex-wife had informed him. He'd had to search that word to find out what it meant. Cindy had pointed her bright-red dagger of a fingernail at his car and said, 'Why, that new car of yours looks just like my new couch. What a pretty shade of desert-dust greige. I hope that forty-seven-thousand-dollar reno was worth it, honey.'

It's why he'd divorced her, because if they had stayed together any longer, one of them would have committed murder. It probably would have been him, but you could never tell with her. She might have beat him to it. He'd shown her how to shoot a gun shortly after they'd married – biggest mistake of his life. She'd never let him forget her uncanny mastery of the Smith and Wesson .45 he'd bought her, and the way the other men at the shooting range had watched in admiration as her target rolled back down the lane, with the heart shot clear out of the man on the paper.

Striker took his suit jacket out of the backseat and shrugged it on to cover the gun in his waistband, cursing the noonday sun. He did not like Bobby Maiden. The man was a wise-ass with half a brain, but he had the land Striker wanted, and without the land, everything else was worthless. Striker knew the price would skyrocket if Bobby got wind of what he wanted the land for. Striker needed to get the deal sewn up fast, which had raised the hackles on Bobby's mutt-dog neck. He'd grown tired of Striker pushing him to make a deal. Bobby wanted to slow down and make sure selling was the right thing to do.

Striker stood in the dirt driveway, looking out at the scrubland pushing up against the river, and shook his head. Nothing but flat ground with clumps of half-dead bushes for miles, and this fool was worried he'd regret getting rid of the homestead.

Bobby's RV trailer looked as if it would blow away in a strong wind. Someone had obviously driven the trailer to the place it now rested in the dirt and unhooked it. And that was it. Years of junk had accumulated around its perimeter. The tires that had once made it mobile were flat and dry-rotted.

Striker banged on the aluminum screen door and waited. No answer. But Bobby's pickup truck made it obvious the man was at home. And even Bobby wasn't fool enough to be outside in the scorching heat. Bobby was inside. No doubt. After four rounds of banging on the door and waiting, Bobby finally yanked the door open.

'If I wanted to answer the door, I would have answered the first time you knocked. I do not want to talk to you.'

Bobby slammed the door, and Striker banged again.

Bobby yanked the door open. He wore a filthy white tank top that clung to his basketball-sized beer belly, and a pair of BVDs that hung loosely over his bird legs. 'There is nothing to talk about! I told you I'm not ready to sell. When I'm ready, I'll call!'

Striker pulled the screen door open and stepped into the trailer, pushing Bobby out of the way. A foot shorter than Striker, Bobby stumbled back into his kitchen. He backed around behind a small kitchen table as if the particleboard square might provide protection.

'This is illegal. You can't just barge into somebody's house. How does a man running for mayor of a town do that and expect to get away with it?'

Striker smiled. 'Surname. You know what that word means?' Striker didn't wait for a reply. 'It's a person's last name. What are you? Maiden? That's complete bullshit. What kind of benefit did you ever get from a name like that?' Striker smirked and watched Bobby grip the back of the vinyl chair he stood behind. 'Striker, though. Mike Striker? That's a man's name. White-boy hard-ass is what that name says. My daddy set me up, is what happened. I got fifty bonus points before I ever got shoved out into this shitty world. A natural-born winner.' He spread his arms wide, grinning like an East Coast mobster in a Ray Liotta movie.

Bobby's face had turned a blotchy red. 'So your last name gets you what? A booby prize in the ten-cent game? I don't much give a shit what your name is. Seems to me that I got what you want. It don't much matter what your last name is. Maybe what I got is a lot more valuable than what you're saying. Maybe that's why you keep riding my ass to sell.'

'Why do you have to be so crude? I'm trying to have a conversation with you, and you have to be crude. You got no manners?'

'OK, Mike Striker, you give me double what you offered, and we have a deal. Otherwise, we are done. We end this nonsense right now because I got better things to do than listen to you windbag my afternoon away.'

Striker turned to look out of the living-room window and saw the other car. He walked to the door and signaled before returning to Bobby. 'You don't want to play games with me.'

Striker watched the smirk disappear and Bobby's brow furrow as a hulk of a man appeared at the front door, and then terror strike as his screen door was ripped from its hinges and thrown on to the living-room floor, where the man stepped on top of it as he lumbered toward Bobby in the kitchen.

Bobby began to whimper, uttering *no, no, no* with his hands in the air.

Striker put his arm out to stop the man. 'Mr Maiden, I'd like you to meet my realtor, Mr John Smith, from El Paso. He's here to help you work through the paperwork. I think you'll find everything is in order.'

Mr Smith, whose bulk filled the tiny kitchen, pulled a manila folder from the inside of his suit jacket and stepped forward to lay it on the table. He pointed to the chair and said, 'Sit.'

Bobby looked at the paperwork and back to Striker. 'You can't do this. This is illegal!'

'Bullshit! These papers are completely legal, and you are going to sign them, telling everyone in town what a great deal I gave you. Then you're going to let my realtor here, Mr John Smith, find you a more attractive place to call home. Now sign these goddamned papers before he breaks your fingers.'

'You break my fingers and you'll have the police at your door.' Sweat rolled down the sides of Bobby's face as he appeared to calculate just how far he could push his bravado before the big guy followed through with the threat. 'Mr Politician'll be sitting in the slammer on May first instead of voting for himself.'

'This could have been so easy. Now here you are, dragging your mother into this. I didn't want to go there with you, but have it your way.' Without taking his eyes off Bobby, Striker motioned toward the realtor. 'Mr Smith, show our friend here the video.'

The man stepped forward, already holding a phone.

Bobby watched the video in silence, and Striker almost felt sorry for the guy as the tears began to fall. 'I told you, I didn't want it to come to this.'

Bobby shut his eyes finally and turned his head away from the phone.

Mr Smith dropped the phone into his jacket pocket and tapped the stack of papers on the table.

'The vice squad in El Paso? They'll love this. Won't even have to do any police work. Evidence is already here. Marie Maiden, street name Roxy, soliciting prostitution in her cute miniskirt and heels. Although' – Striker looked at Bobby as if tasting a lemon – 'those fishnet hose are not a good look on a woman her age.'

'Shut the hell up!' Bobby banged the table, then put his head in his hands. 'If I sell, you leave my mother alone. You never go near her again.'

'That's right. The video vanishes. And if you sign right now, and we don't have any more issues, the price per acre remains quite generous. Any more wasting of my time, and the price drops by half.'

Fifteen minutes later, Mike Striker walked out of the trailer the proud owner of ninety-eight additional acres of Chihuahuan desert, with sixteen acres kissing the Rio Grande.

FOUR

Josie believed the heat of far West Texas produced its own kind of masochistic delirium – burned skin, parched mouth, eyes aching, feet on fire from the hot sand – but the pain could be so intoxicating. The rich scent of millions of years of unrelenting sun and wind, and a silence so complete that the cry of a hawk felt intrusive.

But the remote desert that she loved as a citizen created inordinate problems for law enforcement. As she made her way back into town from a meeting with the sheriff, she rolled the windows down to let the wind blow through, frustrated with yet another conversation focused on increasing accountability and budgets cut for other 'more critical' priorities.

Artemis, a town of roughly 2,500 people, sat on the south end of Arroyo County, snugged up against the Rio Grande and the US border with Mexico. Piedra Labrada, Artemis's sister city, lay just across the water. The fifty-mile strip of land on either side of the river was known locally as the Territory, a stretch of land where two cultures had shared their differences peacefully for several hundred years. Citizens on both sides of the border had watched in horror as the cartels expanded throughout Mexico in the 1980s and 1990s, starting the bloody war for control of the drug corridor that had pushed its way up into and through the United States, its roads snaking into every small town in America. Josie had heard and had no trouble believing that in any town in America, a delivery of drugs could be dropped at any doorstep, any day of the year, within thirty minutes of placing a phone call. Faster than a pizza delivery; even more surprising factoring in that the coca plant used to make cocaine doesn't grow in the US. With profits of half a trillion dollars per year – greater than Walmart's – the Mexican drug cartels were not going anywhere.

Small towns like Artemis faced budget cuts in areas as remote as anywhere in the country, with crime across the Rio Grande more horrendous than most US citizens could fathom. When money did come, it was an occasional large grant that afforded the department new tricked-out vehicles or the town a state-of-the-art trauma center. But people were the day-to-day need. Grants couldn't pay for people because when the grants ended, the salaries couldn't be sustained. Consequently, Josie's three-officer department now drove state-of-the-art Police Interceptor Utility vehicles with full lights and a cage in the back, all-wheel drive, and a 400-horsepower turbo V-6, while her department was understaffed by at least two road officers, and the county sheriff's department was understaffed by even greater numbers. In a county covering 4,000 square miles, the lack of officers was a constant concern, especially when multiple officers were needed for an escalating situation but the nearest badge was fifty miles away.

Such were the facts that dominated her thoughts as she made the drive back to the Artemis PD, located in a two-story, shotgun-style brick building across the street from the Arroyo County Courthouse. Plate-glass windows faced the street on either side of the entrance door, with faded awnings hanging above the doors and windows to block the brutal afternoon sun.

Josie pulled in front of the PD at the same time Otto Podowski was walking out.

'Lunchtime, boss,' Otto said, rubbing his sagging mid-section and grinning. The sixty-something-year-old officer of forty-plus years made no excuses for his need of three square meals a day.

'Hot Tamale?'

'Let's do it.'

Josie followed him across the street to the diner owned by Lucy Ramone, a woman who saw no problem bartering food for gossip, a trait that Otto adored.

The diner had a counter with bar stools, a dozen tables and a scattering of chairs in the middle of the room, with three booths lining the windows facing the street. Otto grabbed their booth in the corner by the window facing the PD.

Lucy hollered across the busy diner from behind the order window, 'Usuals?'

Josie gave her a thumbs-up, and Lucy disappeared.

'I heard a good one today,' Otto said.

'Me, too.'

'I heard Mike Striker wants to build a greyhound racetrack,' Otto said, shaking his head.

'I heard it, too. No way can he keep his political clout by bringing a racetrack to town.'

'A dog track! People here treat their pets like kids. Cart their cats around in baby strollers. Dress their dogs in coats and glasses.'

'Those greyhound tracks have a pretty bad reputation for how rough they are on the dogs. There was one a few years ago that got busted for spiking the dogs with cocaine before a race.'

'Josie, we live in the middle of nowhere. Who in their right mind would drive to BFE on a hundred-degree day to watch skinny dogs run around a track?'

'We'll have animal protestors marching in the streets.'

Otto leaned back to allow Lucy to slide two plates on to the table.

'Burrito for my favorite cop. And a special-order garlic and pepper bologna loaf sandwich for my other favorite cop.'

'How come you never buy me special-order items?' Josie said.

'You order a burrito every time you come. Why waste my money?' Lucy slapped a bill in the middle of the table and walked off.

'You hear anything else about his plans?' Josie asked.

'I heard that Jezebel Black has taken up dog breeding.'

Josie grinned. 'My favorite stoner.'

'I'm glad you like her. She irritates me no end. She's supposedly breeding them for Striker.'

Josie shook her head. 'You think this is legitimate?'

'Let's pay Jezebel a visit after lunch. But you do the talking. She wears me out.'

* * *

On the drive out to the river, Josie filled Otto in on Jezebel's background. After working as a river guide in Terlingua for a couple of years, she got fired for losing one of her customers. Supposedly, halfway down a stretch of the Rio with a group of six out-of-towners, they stopped to explore a canyon that was part of the trip. After the scheduled fifteen-minute break, the boat loaded back up, and the woman's husband convinced Jezebel that his wife had hiked on up the canyon and was being met by a friend who was camping in the area. He convinced Jezebel to leave without the woman, a cardinal sin. It turned out that the woman either fell into a void in the canyon wall or was pushed by her husband. The woman died, the man escaped prosecution, Jezebel got fired and took up residence on her brother's ranch, and the river outfitter lost his business.

'Last I heard, she was selling fake Indian treasures at Big Bend National Park,' Josie said. 'Painted rocks and beaded bracelets. That kind of stuff. Her brother's off in Germany somewhere, so she's staying at his house.'

'Isn't she related to Sauly Magson somehow?'

'That's her dad.'

'Crazy old bastard.'

'What do you mean? I love that guy. He lives in the greatest house in Arroyo County. Built it all himself.' She could feel Otto's eyes on her as she pulled on to River Road, so she turned to smile at him. 'Let me guess. You don't like it?'

'You're kidding me, right? That house is hideous. There's no symmetry; it's just chunks and pieces added to the house all willy-nilly.'

'It's art, Otto. Artistic free expression. It's full of color and funky-shaped windows repurposed from junkyards and—'

'Junk. The operative word.'

Josie pulled down a gravel road that wound through a thickening patch of scrub brush as they headed toward the river. They finally entered a clearing featuring a sunny yellow stucco house with a bright-red front door, and a new cinderblock building located about a hundred feet east of the house.

'That's new,' Josie said. 'Must be the kennel.'

As they exited the SUV, they heard dogs barking and a female voice yelling something. They walked across hard-packed desert sand toward the block building, shaded on all sides by live oak trees as wide as they were tall. The temperature dropped by ten degrees as soon as they walked under the shade.

Behind the building was a long stretch of chain-link fence enclosing dog runs, where they found Jezebel shouting commands to two dogs.

Jezebel Black, born Karen Magson, looked like what her name change would suggest: a hippy with a flair for the supernatural. After her rugged river-guide phase ended so abruptly, she changed her name and regained her flower-girl vibe. She was the kind of over-the-top person that Josie tended to avoid, but she'd always liked Jezebel. Josie thought her talents ran deep, but she'd not had the opportunity to figure out where she fitted in the world. She never seemed to catch a break.

Jezebel stood at the end of the dog run, calling out commands to a dog running in circles in front of her, while several others barked from inside the kennel. She wore a flowing white skirt and a gauzy top that hung loose over her thin body. Her long black hair was pulled up in a bun, and she looked at one with the graceful greyhounds surrounding her.

Josie waved from outside the fence and caught Jezebel's attention. She broke into a smile and put her finger up. A few minutes later, the barking stopped, and she joined Otto and Josie outside.

'What a nice surprise! I never have visitors out here. Well, I don't know. I haven't found out the reason for your visit. I hope it's a nice surprise. Dad's OK, right? I'm not being carted off to jail?'

Josie smiled. 'No worries, I'm sure your dad is fine. We're here on a friendly visit.'

'In that case, let's go around to the other side. Daddy built me a picnic table to sit out here with the dogs.'

On the other side of the kennel under dappled shade was a

picnic-style table with bench seating on all four sides. Josie watched Otto gingerly lift a leg over the bench, wincing at the pain, a reminder that retirement was looming.

'I didn't realize until today that you'd taken up dog training,' Josie said, sitting next to Otto.

'Breeder, actually. I'm just experimenting with the training now, trying to figure out the basics. I've been working with a trainer from Florida, exchanging videos. We've talked on the phone for hours. He's been absolutely wonderful, so patient with all my questions.'

'You're only working with greyhounds?'

'Oh, definitely. One breed is enough to learn.' She reached across the table to put a hand over Josie's, her expression somewhere between love and pain. 'They are so smart and gentle. I know your sweet bloodhound passed away. You should think about getting one of these beauties. You would love them.'

Josie raised her hands in the air to escape the hand-holding. 'I'm not ready for that yet.'

'You know they can run forty-five miles per hour in short spurts? They're amazing dogs.'

'Don't they get hot in this desert heat?' Otto asked. 'Lord, I can barely take it and I'm not running around a track.'

'They don't have a layer of fat to keep them warm like we have, so they're actually more comfortable here than up north. It's easier for me to keep them cool with fans than trying to warm and train them in cold climates.'

'Why greyhounds?' Josie asked.

Jezebel dipped her head and gave Josie a coy grin. 'Come on, you know the answer to that or you wouldn't be here.'

'I assume you're breeding them for Mike Striker's big project, but so far all we've heard is rumor. That's why we're here. Hoping you'll give us the skinny.'

'Fair enough. I don't know why he's keeping it such a secret. I think it's a great thing. I love these dogs. They've been bred as sighthounds for hundreds of years, so running is in their blood. They love the training. My problem is staying up with their needs. The grooming alone is overwhelming with this bunch. Their coat and nails, their teeth and ears. I'm brushing dog teeth on a daily basis,' she said, laughing. 'But they're so sweet about it. Do you want to see them?'

'I'd love to,' Josie said.

'They love rewards and hate punishment, so they naturally take to training. But they're a bit stubborn. I swear they know they're working, and they expect their payment or they won't respond. Willful little buggers.'

The building was the size of a two-car garage with individual bays situated around the perimeter, each bay separated by a cinderblock wall on either side. Jezebel took them to a middle bay where a beautiful dog with markings a bit like a cheetah sat patiently waiting for Jezebel's attention.

'She's beautiful,' Josie said.

Jezebel grinned like a proud parent. 'Very exotic, aren't they? People think all greyhounds are gray in color, but they come in all different shades. This brindle is my favorite. She's a little diva. Her racing name is First Up, but I call her Bella.'

She opened the cage, and the dog approached Josie first, sniffing her all over, then allowing her to stroke her sleek coat. She considered Josie carefully, and Josie was struck by the dog's expression of intelligence.

Jezebel took them through the kennel, focusing on the great care they were getting, explaining that her first batch was a kind of trial run and they probably wouldn't make it as racers because they couldn't get the proper training in place until the track was built.

Josie finally steered her outside, keeping the conversation light and with no hint of confrontation over the dogs. 'How'd you end up connecting with Mike Striker over this?'

'He came to me! I had no interest in being a dog breeder. He was out here poking around our property one day, so I stopped and asked if he needed something. I didn't know who he was that first time. He tried on multiple occasions to get me to sell my land to him, but there was no way. My ashes are going right into the Rio one day. And it's actually my brother's property, but who knows when he'll be back! Anyway, it was maybe the third time he'd come out here trying to get me to sell when I finally got him to share his big dream, about bringing a track to West Texas. I told him how I loved animals, and pretty soon he'd convinced me to take on a breeding program. He flew me to Florida for training and had the kennel built. He's a great guy. I hope he has your vote. I think he'll make a great mayor.'

'Why breed dogs before you even have a track?' Otto asked.

She shrugged. 'The chicken or the egg? You have to start somewhere.'

'Has he purchased the land?'

'I don't know. I can't keep up. He was in negotiations with someone but that's not my interest. The dogs are my focus.'

Otto drove so Josie could make phone calls. She tracked down Mike Striker's phone number as a state senator and tried the government number first. She listened to a recorded message from a staffer asking her to leave a detailed message because her opinions were important to Mr Striker. She also tried the number of the gas station that he owned in Artemis, but a bored cashier didn't have any idea when he might be in.

'How does a guy like that get voted into the senate?' Otto said. 'I don't know anyone who doesn't think he's a scoundrel.'

'If nobody else is running, that makes it pretty easy.' Josie pointed ahead to the lone traffic light that led to downtown Artemis and the PD. 'Turn up here. Let's drive by the gas station to see if he's in. I checked the website, and the senate schedule says district work, so he might be in town.'

'You ever see yourself getting into politics? Maybe running for mayor?' Otto asked.

'Can you seriously see me shaking hands and small-talking? Politicking? Trying to make everyone happy?' Josie pointed to the back of the gas station. 'I see that mammoth old car he drives. Pull around back so he doesn't hide from us.'

'I'll give him that. He's got good taste in cars,' Otto said.

'I bet that thing gets ten miles per gallon. I think it's ugly.'

'What are you, a millennial? Have you no soul? Those old cars are classic,' Otto said.

She rolled her eyes. 'Give me five minutes. I'm gonna see if he'll talk to me.'

Josie walked past the cashier who was probably told to tell anyone who asked that Mr Striker was not in at the moment. Josie walked down a short hallway with a filthy door with *Men/Women* on it, and tried a door that was locked, and then another door that opened. Striker, sitting at a desk in a room the size of a janitor's office, turned around in surprise and frowned at Josie.

'Restroom's up the hallway,' he said and turned back to the pile of papers spread across his desk.

'Actually, I've been trying to track you down, Mr Striker.'

'Most people knock before tracking somebody down. I happen to have a very good reason for not answering your repeated phone calls. I'm a busy man.'

'This won't take five minutes. People are talking around town about a racetrack being built. A dog track. I'd like to be able to answer people's questions.'

He turned in his chair to face her more fully. He wore a button-down shirt and tie that appeared to be strangling him, and the anger in his expression intensified the red in his cheeks. He was the kind of suit-wearing, gray-haired, angry-looking man that could have been anywhere from forty to sixty years old.

'Since when is the police chief charged with answering questions? You running for mayor now, too?'

'Some people are worried crime will increase if pari-mutuel betting comes to town. They're concerned about what a track will do to a community this small.'

'Then they can come talk to me in person.'

'Trouble is, they can't reach you. No one returns their calls.'

'To be honest, it's none of your business what I may or may not be looking into.'

'I think your constituents would disagree. Most voters would think the racetrack you want to build in our town is very much their business.'

'And if and when I decide to move forward with any kind of racetrack, I will share it with the voters who elect me. Until then, I have work to do. And I assume you do, too.'

'What about Jezebel Black? Why would you pay her to raise greyhounds if you weren't planning to build a racetrack?'

Striker stared at Josie. Watching his jaw flex she had no problem imagining his rumored temper.

'Have you purchased the land yet?'

'This conversation is over, Ms Gray. If you have additional questions, leave a message with one of my staffers and I'll be sure to get back to you in a timely manner.'

FIVE

Over the next few days, talk of the racetrack exploded. Animal cruelty and pari-mutuel betting were topics that generated little moral ambiguity. It was all people talked about because everyone had an opinion and a stump speech. Someone had taped poster-board signs with photos of greyhounds with broken bones and gauze-taped heads; one picture showed a dog that had been savagely attacked in a kennel. There were no words on the posters, just photos. The posters would disappear and then reappear the next morning. Someone had taken out a full-page ad in the paper that said simply, *Vote against animal cruelty.* Other flyers had been posted on phone poles and bulletin boards reading, *BRING JOBS and MONEY TO ARTEMIS! DON'T LOSE THIS CHANCE!* And *Vote Striker* and *Re-elect O'Kane* signs were everywhere. Josie had never seen an election so hotly debated.

Once Striker's plans had been outed, it was obvious he couldn't hide from the facts, so he decided to use the racetrack as his running platform. A week after refusing to answer her questions about the track, Josie heard an interview with him on Marfa Public Radio where he stated, 'This is one of the few options for gambling in the state of Texas. As I've talked to the people of Artemis about running for mayor, the one common complaint I hear is that our area is neglected, forgotten about because of our remote location. We don't generate the tax dollars or revenue that other cities in Texas get. I'm tired of West Texas being the forgotten stepchild. I want our town to thrive. And giving people a place to gather, a destination point for people throughout the region, is what we need. I have statistics from all over the country that show the amazing economic growth that can happen from organized betting. If run responsibly, which I absolutely support, the racetrack could support programs like we've never seen.' The interviewer grilled him about community concerns about bringing crime to the area, and he laughed them off. 'That is just not true. It hasn't happened anywhere else. Why would it happen here? I've never seen so many people want to focus on negative lies and ignore the positives. Have you seen where our high school band kids practice? It's a dirt lot! Those kids deserve better than that! We don't even have a football team! Not because our kids don't want to play, but because we don't have the money to build and maintain a field. Twenty percent of the proceeds from this track, right off the top, would go directly to the schools. Who else has ever offered that kind of support to the kids in Artemis?'

Josie was in her office getting ready for a seven forty-five a.m. meeting with the voting commissioner to prepare for May first when she received a call from a sobbing Jezebel Black.

'They've taken two.' She repeated the phrase multiple times, her breath so erratic she couldn't speak more than a word or two at a time.

Josie put the woman on hold to call Otto. 'Can you head toward Jezebel Black's place?'

'I'm working an accident. Oil rig nailed a car.'

'Just head her way when you're done. I'll call you back with details.'

With her breathing more under control, Jezebel was finally able to tell Josie that someone had spray-painted *Animal Killer* in red across her kennel, had tossed food and supplies all over the floor, and had taken two of her dogs.

'They took Bella, my little diva. And they took Iggy. They spray-painted filth at my home, terrorized my dogs. I treat those dogs like family. I would never hurt them. They're the criminals, not me!'

'Jezebel, whoever did this doesn't care about the truth or the care of your dogs. They don't want the track, and you were an easy target.'

'You have to find those dogs. I can't imagine how scared they are. And when I find out who did this—'

'You won't do anything. You'll let the police handle this so you don't end up in trouble over someone else's crime. Yes?'

Josie listened as Jezebel continued to control her breathing, but she didn't answer the question.

'Officer Podowski is finishing up with another issue, then he'll be on his way to your house. Stay away from the kennel for now. That's a crime scene. You don't want to clean up the mess and cover up something that might help us figure out who did this. OK?'

'I just need to check on the other dogs.'

'You just need to stay out until Otto gets there. I'm sure they'll be fine for a few more hours. You give Otto all the information you can think of. We'll do everything we can.'

Josie watched as Mark Jackson, head of the Arroyo County elections board, entered her office, frowning. He pitched a folder on her conference table and sat down while Josie finished up with Jezebel.

'Good morning,' Josie said. She pointed toward the coffee pot at the back of the office. 'I just brewed coffee. Would you like a cup?'

'No, thank you.'

Josie noted his tight response. She poured a cup and made her way past the three desks shared by Otto, Marta Cruz and herself, to the front of the room and the long conference table. The space looked more like a large room in an old schoolhouse than a police station, but it served their purposes. The large bank of windows across the back wall provided a great scan over a downtown neighborhood of small family homes and the desert mountains beyond, but the windows also heated up the room in the summer to unbearable levels that their window air conditioner could never touch. Otto complained daily about the heat.

Josie sat across the table from Mark and tried for a bit of small talk about the weather, but he had no patience for restraint. He was the kind of man whose concerns were always more important than those of anyone else around him.

'Do you have any idea how nasty things have gotten over this election? It's turned into the gamblers versus the anti-gamblers. The dog lovers versus the dog racers. I talked to Tim Shilling the other day, and he said his wife hasn't talked to him in days because she thinks they ought to carry picket signs for the dogs. He told her he couldn't wait to have a place to go to actually do something. He thought it would be fun to follow the dogs. And he didn't see any difference between dog racing and horse racing.'

'I'm not sure what this has to do with the police,' she said.

'That's just one example! People are fighting mad over this track. I guarantee we'll have people arguing at the polls. They'll be picketing and passing out flyers. Polling rules will be broken. We can't have the results of our election called into question.'

'Sure we can. People call into question the presidential race every four years. I don't know why our mayoral race should be any different.'

'Don't make a joke of this!'

'I'm not joking in the least. You could do everything perfectly, but the losing side will find a reason to dispute the results. That's just life.'

Mark's face had grown red, and he'd crossed his arms over his chest. 'I want officers at each of the polling stations to help control this nonsense. That is not too much to ask.'

'We don't have the officers available to do that.'

'That's funny because when some big traffic accident happens, I see dozens of cop cars and ambulances and fire department trucks on the highway.'

Josie sighed. 'That's for a disaster. Officers come from other towns when we need them. Election day does not qualify as a disaster.'

'So you *can* get extra officers, is what you're saying.'

'This is why you have poll watchers. They are appointed specifically to observe the conduct of an election. You call my officers in if a crime has been committed.'

'That sounds typical. Let's wait until disaster strikes before we do something.'

'That's exactly right. Artemis has three officers, myself included, to take care of every crime, big and small, that takes place in this town every day. Often, we're called to take care of crimes in the county as well because the sheriff's office is as undermanned as we are. I don't have the officers to sit and wait for crime to happen. We're already out on the roads dealing with theft and burglary, with husbands beating their wives, and kids overdosing in the Value Dollar parking lot. I will not use taxpayer money to park my butt in a chair for eight hours to watch people enter a voting booth.'

'This is not a normal year! I haven't even brought up the voter fraud allegations.'

'Mark, you can have as many poll watchers as you want. You can sign up ten at every site in town if you want. They will do a fine job.'

'I'll be lucky to find one for each location!'

'Then you feel my pain.'

He stood up and pointed a finger down at her. 'When your town ends up in the news as being a hotbed for voter corruption, you take the blame.'

Josie remained unruffled. 'No, that's actually what you're charged with. I'll just clean up your mess if things go bad.'

He narrowed his eyes, and his features became pinched like a small angry bird. She kept her own facial expression neutral.

'Your town is going to shit, and you sit there like you don't have a care in the world. You wait until this racetrack comes to town and all the sleazebags that come with it. You think poverty and border crime are rough? You wait until illicit money starts flowing through your coffers, and politics goes from trying to convince Uncle Joe to run for coroner to outsiders realizing there is significant illegal money to be made in this little spit-gob of a town. It'll make your mayoral race this year seem like a church social.'

'I'm not sure what any of this has to do with you – or why you've decided to lecture me today,' Josie said.

He pointed at the pad of paper that lay in front of Josie, untouched. 'I want it noted that I came here today requesting for men to be stationed at the polls and was denied. So when things go to hell—'

'Hold up. Just to make sure we're both living in the same reality. How many *men* do you think work in the Artemis Police Department?'

He clamped his lips shut in a tight line.

'One, Mark. There is one man who works as an Artemis

police officer. So I'll be sure to put it on the record that the police chief denied sending that one man to all of the voter polls in Arroyo County on May first. I'll be glad to document that for you.' Josie stood and noticed Officer Marta Cruz standing in the doorway, grinning. She gave Josie a thumbs-up and walked into the room.

'Morning, Chief,' Marta said. She put a hand out to Mark, and Josie walked out of the office before she said something she would regret.

Josie stopped by dispatcher Lou Hagerty's desk to pick up phone messages and let her know she would be at Junior Daggy's Realty if needed. The two-block walk to Junior's street-front office allowed her to enjoy the morning sun, nodding to the other locals out getting errands done before the temperature crested on another ninety-nine-degree day – high for April but not unheard of. Josie felt as though most people remained unfazed by temperatures under a hundred, but once they hit the three-digit mark, the entire town seemed to take on an edge. The narrow-eyed squint from the sun became narrower, patient people snapped, animals burrowed underbrush for deeper shade, kids abandoned their bikes for TVs in air-conditioned living rooms, bosses shut their doors to nip at the secret bottle and hoped for a quiet afternoon.

Junior Daggy was one of the few people Josie knew who seemed capable of snagging any curveball West Texas cared to throw at him, until the current bust of the Permian Basin oil boom had sat him down hard on the bench. Even before the pandemic shut the world down for a year, the oil boom had started to slow, and with it, housing sales had all but stopped. Junior lived in a one-room apartment above his office, so he had remained open even during the quarantine. Josie would stop in and check on him over the shutdown and found him with no business and no contact with others for weeks on end. For a socialite who loved people and lived on gossip, the year had taken a hard toll on him.

She found him sitting in front of his computer, looking bored and a bit disheveled. His gray hair hung low over his shirt collar. The button-down shirt and khakis were both in need of an iron. He stood when she entered and came at her with hand extended – and a big grin. Josie thought Daggy would benefit from a nice partner to share his life with. She wasn't the woman for the job, but she wished he would find someone.

'Chief! It is damn good to see you.'

Josie pointed to a stack of house flyers he appeared to be ready to tape on the windows of his office. 'Business picking up?'

'Are you serious? We went from boom to bust in ten minutes flat. Houses selling for three hundred thousand last year are selling for a hundred today.'

'What do you think about the racetrack? Think it'll spark the economy?'

'That racetrack isn't going to draw house buyers. People don't buy a house to be near a racetrack. They sell a house to get away from one. It'll bring money into Artemis, but will it be the right kind of money?'

'That's the big question. What's the word on location? All I've heard is down by the river.'

'You know Bobby Maiden?'

'Owns a house trailer out on River Road?'

'Word is, he sold his land to Mike Striker.' He flopped down on the couch in his sitting area. 'Can you believe Striker went and used a realtor out of El Paso? He claims he wants to bring business to our area and then didn't even talk to me about representing him. I think the guy's a blow-hard. He's out for number one. And that sure ain't me or you.'

Josie left Junior to drive out to Bobby Maiden's place, now too curious to let it drop. She couldn't figure Striker's angle on the dog track and the run for mayor. There had to be significant money at play or he wouldn't be wasting his time. She'd heard rumors that his wife was miserable and threaten-ing to move back to San Antonio without him. Until he'd thrown his hat in for mayor, Josie hadn't known much about the couple. They had moved to town two years prior after buying the gas station and convenience store. She was certain they were making decent money on the venture, but not enough to draw them away from the city life they claimed to adore and miss.

A quarter of a mile from Bobby's trailer, she slowed to watch a semi-trailer lumber on to the road hauling a doublewide. Bobby lived on a stretch of land with no houses for at least a mile on either side of his trailer. His closest neighbor was a ranch hand who had dreams of running his own ranch one day and had been slowly buying up land as he could afford it. Josie wasn't sure who owned the land on the other side of Bobby, but she was fairly certain a dog track wouldn't be a welcome sight.

The land was flat, with the road following the curves of the shallow-banked Rio Grande. Josie could see the river from her car, a rarity in much of the county where invasive salt cedar had grown so thick it now crossed from bank to bank. The state was paying landowners to clear the river banks and having some success, but for a region already struggling with water and wildfires, the spread of the water-draining invasives was a major concern.

Josie pulled off the side of the road to allow the wide load passage and drove on back to the lot that once held Bobby's house. All that remained were piles of trash and tires and rusted-out appliances. As she started to pull out of the driveway, she noticed a new black F-250 pickup truck parked back amid a cottonwood grove. Since the truck cost more than the house trailer, she doubted it belonged to Bobby. She drove back through the desert scrub, dodging mesquite and creosote clumps. She parked next to the truck and looked inside the tinted windows but saw nothing but several suitcases and a hanging clothes rack in the back of the crew cab.

The truck was pointed toward the river, so she took a guess that the driver had headed that way. A few hundred feet from the truck, she saw a man standing several feet into the river with the current rushing past his waist fast enough that both his arms were extended to help him maintain his balance. He wore a T-shirt and cargo shorts, and had sandy-blond hair and a trim, muscular build. He looked a bit like a tourist experiencing the Rio for the first time.

'How's the water?' Josie called out.

He turned, surprised at the voice, and smiled when he saw Josie.

'The current is deceiving.' He waded to the edge of the river and made his way up the sandy three-foot bank. 'Thought I'd take a quick swim and cool off, but that water is moving pretty quick.' He held a hand out and pulled it back. 'Sorry. A bit wet at the moment. My name's Jack Striker.'

'I'm Josie Gray. Police Chief. You the new owner?'

'No, my uncle, Mike Striker, bought this. I came out to help him get things settled.'

'You're part of the racetrack development team, then?' She watched his expression. He didn't seem put off by the question.

'Land development, not the betting end of things. I'm a mining engineer. Mike's not from the West Texas area so he asked me to come out and assess the land, offer input on track placement.'

'You don't sound like you're from around here either.'

'I was born in New Jersey but spent the past ten years in the Congo.'

'As in Africa?'

'That's the one.'

'Isn't that one of the poorest countries in the world?'

He nodded.

'So why would a mining engineer spend ten years in a third-world country?' She grinned. 'Not that it's any of my business. But it's not every day that you meet someone from the Congo hanging out in the Rio Grande.'

'No, fair question. The Congo is worth trillions of dollars in raw mineral ores. It's also probably the most corrupt place on earth. Kids bathe in mud puddles while companies like the one I worked for make billions. It's a sick place.'

'So your uncle enticed you out of the Congo into this little piece of desert nirvana?'

'It wasn't quite like that.' He smiled and pointed toward his truck. 'How about a water?'

Josie followed behind him, eying his wide shoulders and narrow waist. He was an attractive man with an interesting past. With a population of 2,500 people, single men fitting that description who she'd not had a run-in with were hard to come by.

He pulled two waters out of a cooler in the back of his truck. 'Is this heat typical for the end of April?'

'It's a bit early for upper nineties,' she said.

'This is the kind of heat I left. But more humid.'

'How does the Congo take you to a West Texas greyhound track?'

'I was already back when Mike called. He and my dad own a shipping business together in Manhattan. It's that company that took me to the Congo. I finally said I'd had enough. Rather than quit, my dad convinced me to come back to Manhattan. Then Mike called with this side project.'

'Are you close to your uncle?'

He leaned his head back and grinned, taking a moment to answer. 'We're family. Enough said?'

She laughed at the evasion. 'Enough said. Any timeline on breaking ground on the track?'

'The sooner the better, according to Mike. When he's got a new project, he runs with it. He wants a land report by next week. But he wants everything by next week. Whether it's doable or not.'

'Are you clear on the controversy surrounding the track?'

'Just what Mike's told me. He says the tree huggers are in full force.' Jack looked around at the obvious lack of trees in the desert environment. 'That's his generic term for any kind of rights advocate. Animal rights groups, human rights groups – they're all tree huggers.'

'Sounds like you don't always agree with your uncle's assessment of things.'

'It isn't that I don't agree so much as I come at things with a different perspective. He's a businessman. I'm an engineer and a geologist. I frame my opinions on facts and science. He forms his on risk and profit. You need both sides, but we don't always see eye to eye. Could be why my family sent me across the world to work.' He gave her a disarming grin. She liked that he didn't seem to take himself too seriously, wasn't the self-important politician that his uncle seemed to be. 'What's your story? Have you been in law enforcement long?'

'Since I got out of college. I grew up in Indiana. I graduated and opened up a map and looked for the place least like where I grew up. That's how I ended up here.'

He raised his eyebrows. 'So no family here?'

'My mother decided to follow me here a few years ago.' She shrugged, not wanting to go down that twisted path.

'Enough said?'

She laughed. 'Exactly.'

He looked around, kicked at the dirt, seemed to be choosing his words. 'Would your voters think you'd crossed over to the dark side if you were seen having dinner with me one night?'

'The sheriff is elected. The police chief is appointed. Actually, the mayor is my boss. It might actually be your uncle thinking *you* crossed over to the dark side.'

The grin again. 'Nothing would make me happier. Could I buy you a sandwich and beer tonight?'

'That sounds good. Where are you staying?'

'The little one-story motel downtown.'

'Manny's. He's a good man. Nothing fancy, but he'll take good care of you.'

'I could pick you up around six?'

Josie gave him directions to her house and drove off, realizing she'd just made a date with the nephew of the man running against her boss: Simon O'Kane, the man she'd been dating off and on for the past several months. And she realized she didn't care. When she and Simon met for a date, they always met at his house for dinner. She assumed that was to keep the community from commenting about a relationship between the mayor and the police chief. It had been a long time since a man had driven to her house to take her out on a proper date, even if it was just a sandwich and a beer in downtown Artemis. Propriety be damned; Josie was ready for a good time.

SIX

O tto finished working an accident between an oil rig and a woman in a Prius who collided over the center line. The woman had been taken to the trauma center but would most likely need to be life-lined to a proper emergency room for surgery. She had slammed on her brakes when she saw the semi drift into her lane and had fishtailed, swinging the back end of her car around. The semi effectively cut her car in half, sending the front half of twisted metal over the guard rail and into a mound of rocks and boulders. Otto had been first on the scene and was amazed the woman hadn't been killed instantly. As a practicing Catholic, he believed firmly in angels, and he had no doubt that the woman in that car had been protected by a fleet of them that morning.

Once the ambulance had carried her away and the tow-truck drivers and state troopers were busy processing the scene and cleaning up the debris, Otto left for Jezebel Black's to find out what kind of drama she'd managed to get into the middle of. Josie liked Sauly and his daughter, but Otto found the pair of them to be too much. They were the kind of people who not only drew conflict but drew *weird* conflict. And Otto had less and less tolerance for weird.

He pulled his patrol car down the lane to Jezebel's house and decided he needed an attitude adjustment. Even her name annoyed him that morning. Who changes their last name to Black? She had a perfectly good name. What was wrong with Magson? And then he remembered the woman who'd died on her watch during the rafting trip and decided maybe a name change had indeed been in order.

When he curved around the drive and the kennel came into view, his internal rant was replaced with a stab of sorrow. After so many years on the job, the cruelty evident in so many people still managed to surprise him. Someone had spray-painted, in large red letters, *Animal Killer* and *Dog Hater*, and a slew of filthy language. He parked his car in the grass, well away from the house and kennel, to maintain any tire tracks that may have been left.

Jezebel walked out of the kennel as Otto approached. She wore another long, flowing skirt and tank top, but her hair hung limp around her face, which was blotchy red and swollen from crying. When she saw Otto, her demeanor changed to instant anger.

'They stole my dogs! Two of them! They call me the animal abuser and yet they come in and trash my kennel and terrorize my dogs. I can't imagine how scared Bella and Iggy are. When I find out who did this, I'll spray-paint their own house and break windows and steal their babies out of their beds. How do you think they'd like that?'

'Let's hold on. Nobody's going to steal any babies.'

'They stole *my* babies!'

Otto told her how sorry he was for what had happened to her and promised that the police would do everything in their power to return her dogs unharmed. 'Why don't you tell me what happened? From the minute you realized something was wrong.'

Her expression fell into misery again. 'I didn't know anything until this morning when I got up. I sleep with a fan on in my bedroom, so I didn't hear anything last night. I got up at six to start a pot of coffee and wandered out at around seven to feed and water them, and found this.' She gestured at the red spray paint but turned her head away from it. 'I ran inside the kennel and saw the dog food all over the floor, the water bowls flipped and my supplies thrown around. Then I saw two of the cages opened, and Bella and Iggy gone. That's when I called Josie.'

'Do you think they could have escaped? Maybe run off?'

'No way. Bella is such a baby. If they'd let her out, she'd have run straight to the house. She'd have been terrified. And Iggy would have followed her.'

'Do you have any security cameras?'

'Out here? I don't even lock my doors. Obviously, I will now.'

'And you didn't wake up in the middle of the night to the dogs barking?'

'I take Ambien. I could sleep through a tornado.'

Otto looked down at her shoes. 'Are those slippers the same shoes you've been wearing since you first went into the kennel this morning?'

She looked confused at first and then nodded.

'This fine dirt will hold a good print. Have you driven your car anywhere this morning?'

'No. Josie told me to stay out of the kennel and inside until you got here. I was just sitting on the floor talking to the other dogs, trying to calm them down. But I didn't really touch anything. Picked up a few things. I guess I did touch the doorknob when I went in. But I couldn't just leave them alone in there with that mess. The poor things are terrorized.'

'OK. Here's what I need you to do. Go inside your house and write down everything you can think of that might relate to this. Things people have said to you in the community. Any strange phone calls you've gotten, cars you've seen drive by. Make sure that you include names. If you've seen or heard anything around your property over the past few days that seemed odd, then write it down. Any detail at all. I'm going to start outside with pictures and fingerprints and so on. I'll come get you when I'm done.'

Otto started outside the building and found several footprints intact on the side of the building. Laying his measuring tape beside each, he snapped photos and took close-ups of the tread. He guessed it was a man's hiking or work boot, a size ten or eleven. He found only one type of tread and tracked it all the way down the driveway where it disappeared on the gravel road. Otto assumed the man had driven to the property and parked on the side of the road. As remote as the area was, and as few houses as there were on the road, Otto doubted any other cars had made it past the house in the middle of the night to have seen him.

He did wonder about the dogs. It made him think the person might be familiar enough with the dogs to know he could get them from the kennel to his own vehicle without getting bitten or attacked. Otto knew greyhounds were typically docile animals, but after their kennel was ransacked in the middle of the night, Otto couldn't imagine the dogs allowing a stranger to cart them off without a fight.

He also wondered at the noise. He felt fairly certain that the person who took the dogs had to have known that Jezebel wouldn't wake to the noise of the dogs. Someone had assumed they had the time to spray paint, trash the kennels and steal two dogs while Jezebel slept through it. There were another eight dogs in the kennel, and they'd all started barking and jumping up against the cage doors as soon as Otto had walked in. He couldn't imagine the ruckus they must have put up the previous night. He'd never taken Ambien, but he found it surprising that Jezebel hadn't woken up to the sounds of her dogs in distress.

Josie scheduled the three officers in the department to work Wednesdays in order to keep the small team abreast of the current caseload. The sheriff scheduled an extra man on Wednesday third shift so that the city had some coverage. Josie and the sheriff had a good working relationship and made the best of their shorthanded staff.

The three officers met back at the PD that afternoon to wrap up a hit-and-run investigation that Otto had led. The car-versus-bicycle accident had taken place across from the courthouse in broad daylight, and three witnesses had three very different accounts of what had taken place. Josie was finally ready to take the case to the prosecutor's office that afternoon.

The conversation finally turned to the mayor's race and the vandalism at the Black residence.

'I hear Mark Jackson got under your skin,' Otto said to Josie.

'Did you hear he demanded a police officer at every polling station on May first?' Josie looked at Marta, who put her hand up.

'Hold on. There's more to that. After you left, Mark calmed down and finished telling me why he'd come. He claims Mike Striker is rigging the election.'

'Oh, come on,' Otto said.

Marta laughed. 'I know, everyone has a conspiracy theory. But Mark isn't a bad guy. He cares about his position. He wants this election run right, and he feels like it's spinning out of control and he can't get anyone to take him seriously. He feels like the police, the final group he can go to for help, are brushing him off.'

'What the hell am I supposed to do, Marta? There are three of us barely getting by as it is. I'm not going to waste a day guarding the schools and churches while people stand in orderly lines waiting to vote. Which is what happens every year. We've never once had an issue in May, and I can't imagine we will this year either.'

'Throw a peace offering. Put Otto and me on a polling station on May first. If you need us, pull us off. But at least give Mark that.'

Josie frowned.

'Tell him you reconsidered.'

'What makes him say that Mike Striker is committing voter fraud?' Otto asked.

'I guess he's been showing up on the days they're installing the machines and inspecting them. He's telling people that he's on some congressional commission on voting oversight, and part of his job is to monitor electronic voting machines. But Mark said he's made calls to several members of congress, and no one knows anything about Striker serving on any oversight committee. No one has said he's *not* serving, but they also haven't been able to confirm that he is.'

'He's inspecting the machines, as in actually touching them, getting into the machines?' Josie said.

'That's what Mark said.'

'Why didn't he tell me that?' Josie said.

'He said he didn't get the chance. You got defensive and walked out.'

Josie took a deep breath to keep from making an angry retort. 'You and Otto, work with Mark to choose a polling station and start your day there. This isn't worth the fight. Striker is the bigger issue, though. He can't be inspecting the same machines people will be using to vote on in his own mayoral race. That's absurd.'

'Let me work on that end,' Marta said.

Josie nodded.

'And I'll let Mark know you're posting Otto and me at the polls unless something else comes up that day.'

Josie ignored the comment, which she knew would be taken as affirmation. 'How bad was Jezebel's place vandalized?'

Otto filled them in on the spray paint and missing dogs, and the fact that she had slept through the kennel being trashed. 'I asked her if she had any ex-partners who might have known about her living situation and that she takes a sleeping pill and would have slept through it. She informed me she's been celibate for eighteen months, and that she has two close friends who know her routines, neither of whom would do such a thing.'

'Could also mean it was someone who was willing to confront Jezebel if she came out and tried to intervene. Maybe someone figured a single woman living out in the middle of nowhere wouldn't put up much of a fight,' Marta said.

'Based on the size of the boot print, and the fact that I only found one variety of boot tread, I'd say we're looking for one male. I sent a couple of emails this morning to a greyhound association and some Texas dog breeders about where someone might sell a dog with no papers.'

'Any idea who might have done it?' Josie asked.

'There's a group on Facebook bashing her. They have a name . . .' Otto scrolled through his phone until he found the group's name. 'Citizens Against Animal Cruelty. I used my fake Facebook page to request to join the group. Most of the posts focus on photos of starving dogs and greyhounds with broken legs, filthy kennels, dogs chasing live rabbits and so on. Some of the same photos have been posted around town. But the comments are more about destroying the reputations of Jezebel Black and Mike Striker. Many of the posts were made by a man who goes by the name Dugout.'

'Any idea who this Dugout is?' she asked.

Otto grinned. 'I know him. He and Mina were friends.'

'I can't picture Mina hanging out with someone like that,' Josie said.

'He wasn't a bad kid. At least, twenty years ago he wasn't.'

'So he's, what, late thirties now?'

Otto nodded. 'That's about right. They called him Dugout because that's where he spent all his time. He loved baseball. Played through high school and spent more time on the bench than anyone on any team. He didn't care. He just wanted to be a part of the game. Everybody liked him. Coaches and players alike.'

'Looks like a loudmouth to me,' Marta said.

Otto shrugged. 'Probably. He's the kind of person that gets sucked into every cause. Thinks if he talks loud enough, he'll make people believe. I'll follow up with him tomorrow.'

Josie shared a few additional details on other open cases and wrapped up the meeting. She stood from the conference table and gathered up her folders and paperwork.

'What's the rush?' Otto asked. 'You got a hot date tonight?'

She looked at him, shocked that he could have found out, and then realized he was kidding. She tried to recover, but he'd already seen her expression.

'You do have a date! Who with?' he asked.

'None of your business,' she said.

Marta smacked Otto on the arm. 'Mind your own. She doesn't owe you any kind of explanation.'

Josie waved and walked out of the office, wondering if her cavalier attitude about a date with Striker's nephew might not serve her well.

SEVEN

Two hours later, Josie had showered and slipped on a pale-blue, open-backed dress she rarely found the opportunity to wear and pulled her hair up into a loose bun. She played Bruce Springsteen to ease her nerves and missed Chester. The dog had been a great companion. His old hound-dog eyes showed instant compassion and understanding for all of life's complexities. Chester would nose his way out of the front door to greet each visitor from a respectable distance, standing a few feet from their vehicle to check out the novelty. No one drove down Josie's road without the sole purpose of finding Josie or Dell, so Chester wouldn't miss the excitement, but he watched with amazing restraint, especially as he'd gotten older. Once the guest had fawned over him and patted his head, he'd lumber back up to the porch and lie down for a nap. He had been the perfect companion.

Josie saw the truck pull into her drive and watched from her living-room window as Jack got out of the truck and took his time looking around the house. She tried to imagine her home as he might see it: a small white adobe at the base of the Chinati Mountains. How would that translate to a world traveler who originated from Manhattan?

She stepped out on the front porch. 'Did you have any trouble finding me?'

He laughed. 'No. What an amazing place. I'm guessing you don't have too many uninvited visitors out here. From the main road, I would have never guessed this little gravel road led to two homes and a cattle ranch.' He gestured to Dell's place. 'Your lone neighbor. I hope you get along.'

'Dell Seapus. One of the finest people you'll ever meet. He had some prize horses stolen when I first moved to Artemis. I worked the case and got his horses back. As a thank you, he deeded me ten acres to build my house on.'

'I feel like I stepped back into some old Clint Eastwood western.'

She grinned. 'My namesake. Josie Wales?'

Jack laughed. 'Seriously?'

'My dad watched *The Outlaw Josey Wales* on Sunday afternoons. Some people watch golf or football. He watched Josey Wales.'

She gave him a quick tour of her house, pointing out the knobby wood posts on her front porch that had been cut from the pine on Dell's ranch. They walked around the desert scrub and cactus off her back patio, looking at the animal signs in the sand: prints from jack rabbits, ground squirrels and her fox. They finally wound their way back to his truck where he opened the door for her and drove them into Artemis, where they had decided on the Legion for a hamburger. She felt the same nervous energy as she had as a high school girl on a first date. It had been so long since she'd been excited about spending time with a man that the nervousness actually felt good.

She watched as he drove down the deserted road back toward the Legion, chatting about his first impressions of the wide-open space with one hand draped over the steering wheel, pointing out a low mountain range in the distance, and the eggplant purple streaks of color in the folds of the rock. He had an easy confidence that made him even more attractive.

'It's the colors out here that surprise me the most,' he said. 'I've seen the flat midsection of Texas, Dallas and Houston, but this is a surprise. I'd pictured more flat land, just drier and dustier. This land at sunset looks like camel-colored suede, like you want to reach out and run your hand across it.'

'I'm always curious to hear a person's first impressions. Some people are amazed at the beauty. Others can't imagine living in a place so void of color. To me, the colors are everywhere; they're just more subtle.'

By the time they reached the Legion, they had settled into easy conversation, realizing they had more in common than Josie would have thought, at least in their love of the outdoors.

She introduced Jack to Carol, who said she would need his essentials in order for him to be served. 'I got your name. To drink at the Legion, I need to know your political affiliation, date of birth, religious preference and criminal history.'

Jack glanced at Josie who shrugged.

Carol grinned and patted him on the back. 'I'm just shitting. First beer's on me.'

Jack pointed a finger at her. 'I need to watch out for you.'

During dinner, Carol joined them for a beer and filled Jack in on the benefits of drinking at the Legion and described other hot spots in town, such as the Hot Tamale and Tiny's Gun Club. After Carol left, the conversation turned to Artemis and Josie's take on the West Texas mindset, which boiled down to *You do your thing and let me do mine.*

'I don't know about that,' Jack said. 'It seems like everyone in town has an opinion about the racetrack. They either want it shut down or raking in the money. I don't hear many people saying do your own thing.'

'The problem with the track is that it hits on our other mindset: *Change is never good.*'

'So, you do your thing, as long as you don't *change* my thing?'

She laughed. 'That's it! You figured us out in no time.'

Carol sat two fresh beers on the table, and Josie changed the topic.

'When your uncle called and asked you to check out the land for a dog track, were you shocked?' she asked.

'What do you mean *shocked*? As in gambling is a vice and I can't believe Uncle Mike wants to do this?'

She grinned. 'No, I'm not shocked your Uncle Mike has a vice. I think part of why the community is in such an uproar is because nobody saw it coming. We thought your uncle was just another politician, caught up in the West Texas dream. People come out here to disappear into some dusty hole in the mountain. Not to race dogs for profit.'

Jack nodded slowly as if he was putting it all together. 'Mike has been misunderstood his whole life. I still don't think his current wife gets him either. I actually laughed when I heard about the racetrack. I think it fits him perfectly.'

'Mike's a gambler?'

'Not in the sense you mean. He's not one to blow money in a casino. But a longshot business? It's not so much a gamble as a challenge. He hasn't said this to me, but I can guarantee that Mike has studied the sport of greyhound racing and decided there's room for a comeback. I'm guessing he's read up on the track closures across the US, how it's a dying sport, and he's decided he's the man to bring it back.'

'But it's a dying sport because people have changed. Animals are part of people's families. I'm not lying when I tell you there are people who get more upset over animal cruelty than they do child abuse. They'll look the other way at a kid taking a beating but carry a picket sign for a dog on a chain.'

Jack leaned forward to make his point. 'The pendulum. Ever hear of it?'

She grinned. 'I don't know if the animal cruelty pendulum will ever swing back.'

He laughed. 'Of course it will! It always does. And the swing always comes back to money. Look. Twenty years ago, when someone took their dog for a walk down the street wearing a coat, you rolled your eyes. People said, "It's a dog, for crying out loud. They belong outside." Right? Today, you wouldn't say that. People would look at you like you were a cold-hearted son of a bitch for sticking your dog outside in the cold. So what caused the shift?'

She considered the question. 'We're more compassionate.'

'Bullshit.'

She laughed, knowing she'd not believed it when she said it.

'Look at the way people attack other people on social media. The way politicians and the media will destroy someone if it benefits their polls or their ratings.'

'I get it. You're right. So what caused the change?'

'Money! It started with dog food. Remember when Iams first came on the market? I remember my mom wanting to buy the expensive stuff for our own dogs and my dad coming unglued. "They're dogs, Margaret! We're not spending more on the damned dogs' food than our own."'

'I get that.'

'Look at cops! One year you're loved. Next year you're the devil's spawn. How many reality cop shows used to be on TV? Cops busting the bad guys as we cheered them on. Then, in a matter of a year or two, cops had turned into racist, violent criminals. Pot used to be bad; now it's OK. Cigarettes, on the other hand, used to be OK, but now they're bad. You see? You get the right group of people with the right message and you can change society. That's pretty heady stuff.'

'Changing society is a pretty tall order.'

'You clearly were not raised in a business family,' he said.

'Good guess. Dad was a cop. Mom stayed home.'

'Changing society isn't a tall order; it's a challenge. It's what think tanks and the media and advertisers live for. It's what motivates my uncle.'

'And you?'

He shrugged. 'Honestly? I couldn't care less what motivates society. I'm more black and white than my dad and uncle. It's why I went into geology and engineering. Makes more sense to my simple brain.'

Josie thought that if this was a simple brain talking, then she'd hate to see his complicated side. 'Speaking of geology, have you been to Big Bend?'

'That was one of Mike's enticements. He said it's a great national park.'

'If you like to hike, it's one of the best in the state. But by the end of April, the heat is a killer,' she said.

'How about an early-morning hike on your day off?'

She hoped she didn't look as eager as she felt. 'I could do that. I'm off on Saturday.'

'Then it's a date.'

Jack drove her home and walked her to the door where he reached out for her hand. 'I know I'm just a traveler wandering through town, and I don't exactly come from a well-loved family around here, but I sure look forward to getting to know you.'

'If well-loved families were my requirement, I'd never get out of my house. I'm looking forward to Saturday, too.'

He dropped her hand and stepped closer until they were almost touching. In the moonlight, with a sky full of stars, she could see his expression clearly – the smile playing at the corner of his lips, the intensity of his stare. He ran his hands up her arms and whispered, 'You stop me at any time.' He ran his thumb along her jawline and kissed her lightly, pulling his head back to study her expression. This time she leaned into him. He placed his hand behind her neck while his other skimmed over her skin through her open-backed dress. Josie felt her body hum in response. Her body felt like silk under his hands, and the kiss melted away all thoughts of racetracks and rigged elections.

Josie felt her handbag buzz against her leg and ignored it. After thirty seconds, it buzzed again and she pulled away, apologizing. 'It's a second call. I have to check.'

It was a call from Juan Ramos, a Texas Ranger located in Marfa. She listened to the voicemail.

'Josie, this is Juan. Give me a call when you get in range. We've got a suspicious death up on Pinto Canyon Road. One of the deputies says it's a local. Jezebel Black. She was found about an hour ago by a hiker in the area. Head this way. We'll be here a while.'

Josie listened to the message again, shocked at what she'd just heard.

'I'm sorry. I have to go,' she said. Jack had walked away to give her privacy on the phone.

'Everything OK?'

'A police matter I need to deal with. I'll see you Saturday, though?'

He grinned. 'If not before.'

EIGHT

K nowing the terrain she was headed toward, Josie put on an Artemis PD T-shirt, hiking pants and boots rather than her uniform. She grabbed her duty belt and equipment, and was out of the door in less than ten minutes. Once she was on River Road, it didn't take her long to pass Jack on his way back to Manny's Motel. She hit the siren as she passed and smiled when he flashed his lights behind her. She was on the way to a death, possibly a murder, but damned if she wasn't excited about life for the first time in a long time.

She put Jack and his quirky grin out of her head and called Ramos.

'Josie, thanks for calling back.'

'Yes, sir. I'm headed that way. Fifteen minutes out.'

'Hunt me down when you get here, and I'll catch you up.'

Juan Ramos was a first-rate officer, one of seventeen Texas Rangers located in the El Paso region of the state, which included Arroyo County and Artemis. In the state pecking order, Texas Rangers were at the top, then Highway Patrol, then everyone else. And anywhere that a pecking order existed typically followed egos and the staking of territory. Juan's wide-shouldered stance and loud voice gave him a reputation for being arrogant, but he worked hard and never asked something from another officer that he wasn't willing to do himself. If Josie had to work with a state cop, Juan was at the top of her list.

She took Farm to Market Road 170 to the town of Ruidosa to pick up the gravel Pinto Canyon Road. It didn't require a high-clearance vehicle, but one was always advised. With the surprise inch of rain that had fallen north of town the night before, there would be washouts. The county road eventually bisected the private ranch for a good ten miles before finally ending up in Marfa fifty miles later. The two-hour drive was one of Josie's favorites, winding through mountainous terrain, deep canyons strewn with boulders, past the 7,700-foot Chinati Peak and into the Marfa highlands. At night, the mostly single-lane road wasn't advisable, and Josie could imagine the mess of police cars perched along the gravel road with drop-offs into the canyonland. Since Juan hadn't mentioned the location specifically, she hoped the body had been found along a stretch of flat land, but if someone had taken the trouble to take her to Pinto Canyon, they wouldn't leave her out in the open.

Eight miles into the drive, she had her answer as a string of headlights wound up and around a curve in the mountain. She stopped her vehicle about an eighth of a mile before the first car, where there was a four-foot shoulder, wide enough that she could maneuver her SUV around and face it toward home. She radioed her location to the dispatcher at the sheriff's department and locked her car up to begin the hike into the chaos.

With all the traffic on the mostly dirt road, the air was filled with dust so thick she could taste it and see it floating in the headlights from the cruisers. She counted a half-dozen spotlights fifty feet down into a ravine, where she assumed Jezebel's body was located. As she snaked her way in and out of the cruisers, she asked around for Ramos and finally found him standing on the road, immediately above the spotlights, directing another highway patrolman to move cars back out of the ravine.

'One hell of a mess,' he said, turning to Josie.

'Have you confirmed the identity?'

'One of the Presidio County deputies recognized her. No cell phone or ID on her.' He pointed toward the lights, and Josie could see three deputies pointing up the steep grade on the side of the mountain toward the road. 'Her body is just beyond the officers down there. Until we get a hold of the coroner, we're stuck, but it'll be a hell of a chore getting her up out of those rocks.'

'You couldn't reach Cowan?' Josie asked.

'All I had was his office phone. One of the deputies was trying to track down a number.'

'I've got his cell.'

'Call him. He's top priority. I'll be back in five to check in.'

The local cops referred to County Coroner Mitchell Cowan as Eeyore after the old gray donkey with the droopy eyes. A sagging midsection and sloping shoulders added to the effect, but his plodding ways made for a first-rate coroner and medical examiner. He worked hard and rarely complained. Given the nature of his job, Josie thought that counted for quite a bit.

She glanced at her watch. At ten o'clock, she worried from recent experience that he might be too far into a bottle of the hard stuff to make the trip. He answered on the first ring.

'Cowan.'

Josie gave him a rundown on the situation, and he said he would head that way. She told him to call when he reached Pinto Canyon and she would come to get him to avoid one more car stuck in the mess.

'What shape is the body in?'

'I don't know yet. She's probably fifty feet down the canyon.'

He sighed. 'I don't suppose there's an easy path down to reach her?'

'Not a chance. Bring your video equipment. Maybe I can take it with me and you can walk me through the steps from the road.'

'That would certainly expedite the process. This is not the body of a mountain climber. I should be there in less than an hour.'

Ramos found Josie and offered to take her down to the body before Cowan's arrival. As they walked down the road to an area that Ramos described as 'slightly more accessible,' he explained what they knew so far.

'This is on John Edward's ranch. He's got "No trespassing" signs up, but a young couple pulled their car off on the side of the road about a half-mile up and hiked down the side of the mountain here to reach what the girl had thought was a pool of water. The kids are from the area and know the road well. She said she saw something shiny and was sure she'd found a creek. She convinced the boy to hike down and check it out. What they found was the white shirt and skirt worn by Jezebel Black. Her body was a mangled mess. The kids called it in, thinking she had been hiking and fell from the road above, tumbling down to the bottom.'

Before he stepped down off the rocky path, Ramos turned to face Josie. 'You OK with making the trip down? It gets rough after the first ten feet or so.'

'I'm fine. I'll follow your lead.'

Josie was glad she'd opted for her hiking boots. The trip down was littered with basketball-sized rocks and loose sand and pebbles, as well as piles of boulders the size of a small car that required some maneuvering and hoping for a foot purchase on the other side in the dark. About halfway down, one of the other officers shone a light on the rocks, which helped with the remaining climb, but the deep shadows made judging depth difficult.

Josie stepped down on to a flat patch of loose rock, and Ramos put a hand out to stop her, pointing to a streak of blood on the rock just above them. She caught a glimpse of Jezebel's body and had to turn her head for a moment and take several deep breaths before she could face her again.

Ramos guided Josie a few feet back from the body, where a small ledge provided about eighteen inches of foot space. She steadied herself by pressing her hand against the side of the mountain and looked up. The spotlights illuminated the mountain, throwing deep shadows toward the night sky. They were approximately forty feet from the road above them, with a steep grade and almost sheer faces at several intervals.

Ramos gave her a minute to take in the scene. Jezebel had landed with her right leg bent back up under her at the hip joint in a grotesque pose that Josie's brain did not want to accept. Her face and head were battered and bloody, her long black hair fanned out around her, matted with dried blood. Her features were almost indistinguishable, but the flowing white skirt and a leather bracelet that wrapped around her wrist with silver greyhound charms left little doubt about who Josie was looking at.

In the small space on the ledge, Ramos stood next to her, their shoulders touching as he pointed to a white spot on a rock twenty feet above them that had been identified as part of Jezebel's skirt. 'We're ruling this a homicide. There aren't any vehicles anywhere on Pinto Canyon Road, and given the distance to her house, there's no way she could have hiked here.'

'You have an estimate on time of death?'

'We need the coroner to weigh in, but I'd say recently, probably a few hours ago.'

'Have you confirmed the location of her car?'

'Deputy Caldwell called about ten minutes ago to say he found the car registered to her in her driveway. The keys were on her kitchen counter. Nothing out of place. All her doors unlocked.'

'I interviewed her a few days ago to talk about the kennel and the racetrack. She didn't mention then that anyone had been harassing her or giving her a hard time.'

'I had to pull Caldwell off the house. He's headed toward Presidio for a home invasion call. Since you have background at Black's house, can your office take care of processing? Get prints, photos, check for calendars or notes about where she was supposed to be tonight. I'll get an open warrant to the judge so you can log her computer, phone and so on.'

'Will do.'

'Caldwell will make sure the house and property are locked and cordoned off. You can work with him to get the keys.'

She nodded.

'Tell me about the vandalism,' Ramos said.

'Took place in the middle of the night. Just her kennel, not the house. Someone painted "dog hater" and "animal killer" on the exterior of the building, then trashed the inside. Two dogs were stolen. They're still missing.'

'You said someone. Meaning one person?'

'We believe so. Otto Podowski took the case. He found one

boot tread, like a hiking boot. A men's size ten or eleven. He found the tread around the kennel and out to the road.'

'Photos?'

'Yes. Several clear shots of the tread with a measuring tape.'

'Good. The first officer to arrive tonight did a good job securing the area on the road. We've got a clear tire print, most likely a pickup truck tire. Different tread from the kids who found her. The tire veers off the gravel road for ten feet, then there's a smudge in the print where I believe the truck stopped and then started again.'

'It's a start,' she said.

'I'll have him go back over the area with the boot tread in mind.'

'I'll text you the photos. I don't think Otto had anything conclusive on tires. She lives on a gravel road, right off River Road near the water.'

'Where Striker's planning on putting the track?'

'Yeah, it's her brother's place,' Josie said. She watched Ramos shake his head and look away. 'What's that look for?'

'I think that guy's a snake. I heard Striker's had some shady dealings with the state attorney's office. They were looking into him for misusing campaign funds for personal expenses.'

'I heard the rumor,' she said.

'I think it was more than rumor, but that's just my opinion. I also think he's got a lot more going on than misusing campaign funds.' Ramos glanced back to the body and said, 'First priority, let's get this woman off this mountain. ETA on Cowan?'

Josie pressed the light on her phone. 'I'd say in the next fifteen minutes.'

'He'll be OK to make it down here?'

'No, sir. I worked with Cowan on a similar off-road situation. I talked to him about me taking his equipment down. I could use a deputy to livestream, and Cowan can walk me through the necessary steps before we move the body. Are you good with that?'

'He's the boss. If he's OK with someone else doing his

work, it's OK by me. I don't know how a jury might view that, but . . .' He shrugged, obviously put out by the fact that Cowan wouldn't be hiking down to the body himself.

Josie made her way up the mountain and down to her car where she drove down to pick Cowan up from the county hearse. Larger counties would have deputy coroners in charge of investigating the scenes, leaving the coroner to perform the autopsies. Arroyo County wasn't large enough to fund such a luxury. Most law enforcement officers realized how fortunate they were to have Cowan, a trained medical professional, who referred to himself as a doctor for the dead.

They transferred his kits and bags to the back of Josie's SUV, and Cowan took the passenger seat.

'I don't know why they don't make hearses with four-wheel drive for remote areas,' he said.

'You'd look good driving a Subaru. Shiny black and decked out with lights.'

'Looking good has never been high on my priority list,' he said with no trace of humor. 'Have you seen the body?'

'I have. There's no vehicle in the area, so it looks as if someone brought her out here to hide the body or pushed her and assumed she would die from the fall.'

'Anyone touch or move the body?'

'No. Juan Ramos is working the case. He said a couple of high school kids found her but didn't get close. They called it in as soon as they saw her.' Josie pulled up photos on her phone and handed it to Cowan as she began the drive back toward the scene. 'Flip through there and you can see what you'll be dealing with.'

'Any obvious cause of death prior to the fall? Bullet wound, knife marks or so on?'

'With the location of the body so close to the edge, there's very little we can see. I can get video and I can do a cursory look, but there's no chance we can flip the body. With the way her leg is torqued behind her body, it'll be a mess getting her loaded on a board to get her up the side.'

Cowan grunted in disgust. 'I need the body intact, with the

leg as is. If they start moving her leg around, it will be hard to confirm if she was killed pre- or post-fall.'

'What a gruesome sight that'll be coming up the mountain.'

'You want to talk gruesome to the county coroner?'

Josie put the SUV into low and dipped down into an arroyo that had washed out with the recent rain.

'Good Lord, don't turn this thing over,' he said, pressing one hand on the dash and the other on the arm rest.

'Have you ever driven Pinto Canyon?'

'No, for good reason.'

'It's going to get worse. Just trust me. I've driven this road many times.' Josie wrapped the SUV around the first of the larger mountains, zippering up the side.

'My God, there's no guardrail.' He tentatively put his head out of the passenger window and looked down. 'Roll these windows up. There is a sheer drop off the side. Is this a one-way road?'

She laughed as she hit the button on her windows. 'No one-way roads out here.'

'And if a car comes toward us?'

'Then one of us backs up.'

'On the side of a mountain. In the dark.'

'That's right,' she said, still trying to decide if he was being overly dramatic or serious. 'We'd just take it slow. Although you might need to get out of the car and be my spotter.'

'I will not get out of this car. There's no road on my side to step on.'

Josie drove in silence for quite some time, finally getting them back on a straight path for a stretch before they rounded another bend to see the flashing lights of the emergency vehicles up ahead. It became apparent to her that Cowan's fear of the mountainside was not something he was putting on. His hands were still pressed against the dashboard and window. 'Josie, stop.'

She rolled the car to a stop and turned to him. 'What's going on?'

'I have a fear of heights. Of falling. I can't do this.'

'You'll be fine. You don't have to climb down—'

'I'm not talking about climbing down! I can't do this. I can't walk between those cars. All those people.'

'Mitchell, I will stay right beside you. I'll get you set up in a safe place with your equipment.'

'Not in the dark. I can't do this in the dark. I can't see over the side. If I trip, I won't be able to stop myself.'

They had stopped on the roadside, but his hands remained pressed against the dash. She'd never seen this side of him.

'Take me back. I'll come out in the morning.'

'Mitchell, listen to me. It will be worse in the morning. Right now, I can get you set up in a place that's pushed up against the mountain. I promise you will be safe. If you wait till daylight, you'll have to deal with the officers, with some smart ass wanting to know why you aren't hiking down the mountain. Let's get this over with. Then we can get her transported to you in the morning.'

He said nothing.

'I promise. You will be fine.'

He still said nothing, so she slowly put the car back into drive and found the same wide shoulder where she'd turned around before. She maneuvered her car around and backed down the road to get him closer to the scene, so he didn't have to walk. He moaned quietly several times, mumbling what she assumed was a prayer.

Josie helped him out of her car and positioned him next to the side of the mountain, where he kept his eyes averted from the edge.

'Keep one hand on the rock. You'll feel more stable. And keep your eyes on the rock, too. If you're worried about not talking to people, just put your phone up to your ear until we can get you settled in a car.'

Cowan nodded, grabbing the rock and staring at it as she spoke.

She saw Scott Philips, one of the Arroyo County deputies she knew well, and asked if Cowan could use his car to set up for the examination.

'He can't get all his equipment down that mountain. I'd like to set him up here in your car. Then I'll take the camera with me and he can direct the initial examination from here.'

'Sure, no problem.'

Philips moved the seats forward and his tactical gear out of his backseat and into the trunk to give Cowan room. While Philips arranged things, Cowan turned his back on the rays of halogen light streaming up from the canyon below and talked Josie through the basic steps of what he needed her to do.

Once he was seated in the backseat with the overhead light on, he looked at Josie with real gratitude. 'You are one of the good ones,' he said.

Josie patted him on the arm and set off down the mountain with his black medical case strapped to her back. Philips agreed to take care of the filming and took off first to scout the best route, given the large case on Josie's back. The first twenty feet were fine, but a large boulder just ten feet before she reached the ledge where the body was located proved difficult. The boulder was large enough that it required her to crawl on to the rock, then lie flat on her stomach with her feet pointing down. She had to slide down the back side of the rock with the black medical case on her back, causing her to slip faster than she had anticipated down the sheer face of the rock. She dropped two feet before landing in loose gravel where Philips was standing to steady her landing. There was a terrifying few seconds between leaving the rock and hitting solid ground. The blackness beyond the spotlights didn't help the dizzying freefall.

Once they reached the body, she opened up the medical examiner's kit, and Philips set up the camera and connected with Cowan, taking a trial recording to ensure all was working. Josie had been drawn into a court case years before where another police department hadn't documented physical evidence in a sufficient manner for the prosecutor, and a rapist had walked free. She learned in that case that an officer's word was not sufficient. Evidence and the chain of custody were crucial.

With Philips filming, Josie positioned herself to the right of the body, on the far side of the ledge, and kneeled to begin taking samples of soil. She took hair samples and, using her flashlight, made a careful survey of the ledge for any items that were not there naturally. The only additional evidence was the torn piece of skirt several feet above them. She took photographs of the position of each of the limbs, describing what she was seeing so that Cowan could ask additional questions to clarify.

'The current time is eleven fifty-two p.m.,' he said. 'I need you to cut away the skirt and blouse to get close-up photographs of her skin and any lividity that may have set in.'

Josie used scissors from the kit to cut away Jezebel's skirt. She stopped suddenly and had to stand and hold on to the rock behind her. She felt her peripheral vision begin to fade and heard Philips asking if she was going to pass out. His voice sounded far away, as if it was in a tunnel.

She took several deep breaths and felt Philips's hand on her shoulder and him saying something about her falling. After several minutes of deep breathing, the dizziness passed and she forced herself to face the body again.

Philips gave her a water bottle he pulled out of his backpack. 'You need to switch places? Do the filming for a while?'

She heard Cowan asking if everything was all right and she assured him she was fine. Josie kneeled again beside the body as he continued, 'Josie, it's critical that you get close-up photos of her skin. Since she is lying on her back, be sure to lift her leg and have Philips film the skin. We're looking for the blueing from lividity or blanching. This will help determine both time of death and whether she was killed elsewhere and moved.'

The process took a full hour before Josie was able to pack up the kit and strap it back on to her back to make the climb back up to the road. At the top of the mountain, she stored the kit in her car and found Ramos to let him know Cowan had released the body for transport.

'I appreciate you coming out and working with him,' Ramos said. Josie ignored the dismissive tone he used in reference to Cowan. 'I think we've got it from here if you want to head out. Just let me know ASAP on the house tomorrow morning.'

Josie started to walk away and thought of Sauly. 'Next of kin?' she asked.

'The sheriff should be at her dad's house now. Were you aware of any boyfriends or partners she might have had?'

'No. She told Otto she'd been celibate for quite some time. She could still have a partner, but I'm not aware of anyone. I'll get the specifics from Otto and let you know.'

NINE

'Sixty-seven years old, Otto. You're too old for this nonsense. Waking up to phone calls at the crack of dawn to go look at dead bodies.'

'The body isn't even there, Delores. I'm just going to the house.'

'That's not the point and you know it.'

'It's early. You're grumpy. Go back to bed. I'll try to make it home for lunch today.'

Otto drew the razor down his face, attempting to ignore Delores standing in the doorway of the bathroom in her nightgown, glaring at him in the mirror.

'I had pancakes with fresh blueberries planned for breakfast this morning. Those blueberries cost a fortune at the grocery, and they'll go bad if we don't eat them today.'

'Did you not just give me fifty kinds of hell last night for eating a bowl of ice cream before bed?'

'It was two bowls of ice cream that you ate. And I was making the pancakes healthy with blueberries. I found a sugar-free syrup we were going to try this morning.'

Otto ran a washcloth over his face to clean off the shaving cream and turned to kiss her on the cheek as he walked by. 'Come eat a piece of toast with me. I'll fill you in.' He knew that would appease her, at least through breakfast. She had wanted him to retire for years, but there was no doubt she would miss the excitement of police work. Delores liked to be in the know.

She poured him coffee while he buttoned up his uniform shirt and told her the few facts he knew about Jezebel's death.

Delores handed him toast smeared with peanut butter and said, 'You know, I always liked her dad.'

'Sauly? How do you know him?'

'There's twenty-five hundred people in this town. Of course

I know him. We'd chat at the grocery store. I sat on one of
the benches at the courthouse one afternoon and had the nicest
talk with him. Sauly has a good heart. I think he tried his best
with her, but maybe it was too late.'

'What was too late?'

'Sauly was in the Vietnam war. He was there for the fall of
Saigon.'

Otto put his toast on his plate and stared at Delores. 'How
in the world would you know that?'

She sighed. She hated to have her stories interrupted, and
Otto had been doing it to her for forty years. 'I just told you,
I talked to the man, Otto. He settled here in Artemis after the
war ended. But my point is that he got a girl pregnant while
he was in Vietnam. Jezebel didn't come to live with him until
she was thirteen. You know Sauly is about your age. He's been
retired for years.'

Otto stood and grabbed his remaining toast. 'I love you,
Delores. I vote for blueberry pancakes for supper tonight.' He
pecked her on the cheek and put the rest of his toast in his
mouth on his way out of the door.

Josie had dropped Cowan off at his hearse and then driven
home for a quick shower before meeting Officer Downey at
Jezebel Black's home at five a.m. He gave her the keys
and said he had just done a quick walk-through of the
house that morning before heading to Pinto Canyon. 'Nothing
indicated a struggle, but her keys were left on the kitchen
counter.'

That detail told her little. She could have been outside and
gotten in the car with someone she knew. Or someone could
have put a gun to her head and caused her to leave without a
struggle.

It was still dark out, with another two hours before sunrise,
so Josie skipped the outside of the house. Downey had said
he'd stuck his head in the kennel, and the dogs were jumping
and barking at the sight of him, but none appeared hurt, and
all but two cages contained dogs. Josie had already left a
message on Marta's cellphone asking her to start looking for
foster homes for the remaining greyhounds. She assumed Mike

Striker would have something to say about that, but he wasn't her immediate concern.

Jezebel's living room looked as if someone had tossed a handful of confetti in the air and let it stay where it landed. The walls were painted a sunny yellow with bright green trim, and a pink couch was centered under a large picture window that faced the kennel. Plants and candles and framed photos and pictures lined the windowsills and end tables. Brightly colored scarves were hung in layers from the ceiling in each corner. Claustrophobia would set in fast for Josie.

She quickly sorted through stacks of art books on top of old *Rolling Stone* magazines and found a few pieces of mail that appeared to be junk. The room was neat and tidy and offered little in terms of her personal life.

Josie walked through each room of the house to get an overall picture of who Jezebel was in her private space, and to determine where Josie needed to focus her time. The bedroom gave the same bohemian vibe as the living room, but the dominant color was white. Josie saw no fewer than ten white flowing skirts hanging in her closet. Boxes held clothing and shoes and household goods but offered little information.

The office gave the most promise. An old wooden teacher's desk took up most of the space in the small room, along with two filing cabinets and a bookshelf lined with binders. Given Jezebel's work history, Josie was surprised at the amount of paperwork stored in the small space.

The binders included one for each of the past ten years with her tax forms and receipts for the year hole-punched and neatly filed away in plastic pouches. Another shelf held books and pamphlets on greyhounds: training, grooming, betting, breeding and so on. Several books had post-it notes sticking out from the pages. Josie flipped through the breeding book and saw where Jezebel had highlighted and taken notes in the margins. The front of the book had a phone number and Mike Striker's name beside it.

She pulled the binder off the shelf for the current year and found flyers for plots of land for sale in Florida. Several of them appeared to be the kind that might show up randomly in the mail with titles like *Incredible Land Sale – This Is Your*

Opportunity! Prices ranged from $150,000 to $500,000 for plots from one-tenth of an acre to half an acre. The flyers were for land only, and most showed photos of waterfront property. Josie couldn't imagine how Jezebel could come close to affording that kind of property and then still have money to build a home. Josie flipped through other binders and didn't see any mention of property, so it didn't appear to be some long-term dream to purchase land in Florida. She hoped Sauly would be able to shed some light on the Florida land sales. Or the finances that Josie might be unaware of. Sex, drugs and money were the leading causes of homicides. Jezebel had stated she was celibate, and Josie wasn't aware of her ever using illegal drugs, so money initially made the most sense.

After snapping photos of the binders and contents, and then doing the same with the desktop, she sat down to page through the messy pile of paperwork. A cork bulletin board was hung directly behind the desk and was filled with scraps of papers with quotes and notes, as well as a dozen photographs tacked on the board. Given Jezebel's appearance in the photos, most appeared to be recent.

Josie smiled at a photo in the bottom corner of the board of Jezebel as a teenager holding Sauly's hand. The two were standing side by side, knee-deep in some muddy river, grinning at the camera. Sauly was bare-chested, wearing cutoff jeans, and Jezebel wore a white swimsuit that glowed against the dirty brown water. But their smiles were what stood out the most. They both looked proud to be in each other's company.

Josie pulled the photos down to scan the groups of people Jezebel was with. Most photos were of Jezebel smiling at various functions. One appeared to be at a racetrack with leaderboards in the background. She was holding a glass of what looked to be champagne; holding her glass aloft with a group of five other smiling people, one of whom was Mike Striker. Josie flipped the photo over and found the following written in someone else's handwriting: *It's a deal! Here's to many more!*

Josie saw headlights out of the window and glanced at her watch. She walked outside to meet Otto.

'Sorry for the early-morning call,' she said.

'Lord, you need some sleep. You look like somebody smudged ashes under your eyes.'

'Thank you, Otto.'

'Anything new?'

'Not much. Nothing new from Ramos. Cowan released the body. They're planning on lifting her out at daybreak.'

'Cowan hiked down into Pinto Canyon?' Otto asked, eyebrows raised.

'Did you know he's afraid of heights?'

'Not exactly a surprise to learn that.'

'He was terrified to get near the edge of the road.'

'I won't judge. You wouldn't have seen my fat belly sliding down that mountain either.'

Josie led the way into the house and filled Otto in on the land acquisition papers she'd found in the office.

'Isn't Florida one of the other states that still has legal dog betting? Maybe she and Striker were working together to purchase more land for another track.'

'No, Florida just outlawed it in 2021. I think most people believe it will be outlawed across the US in the next five to ten years. So why would he pursue something that is so obviously on its way out?'

'And of all people, how did Striker end up in partnership with Jezebel? That's a pretty unlikely pair.'

Josie took him into the office and showed him the photo of Jezebel and Mike at the dog track.

'Check this out,' she said. 'I just found this in a stack of paperwork Jezebel had been reading and highlighting. This is from the official Texas Racing Act, Article Six Racetrack Licenses. Carol was right about tracks being located on the Gulf of Mexico, but the rules state that the commission can waive compliance.'

(c) The commission shall not issue licenses for more than three greyhound racetracks in this state. Those racetracks must be located in counties that border the Gulf of Mexico.

(d) In considering an application for a class 4 racetrack

license, the commission may waive or defer compliance with the commission's standards regarding the physical facilities or operations of a racetrack.

Otto skimmed the rules. 'I just don't see her as the type of person who would sit around reading racetrack laws for loopholes.'

'Money's a good motivator.'

'True enough. Maybe she's making enough off this deal with Striker that she's looking at buying waterfront property in Florida for half a million dollars.'

'But what skill could Jezebel bring to the table that's worth that kind of money?' Josie said. 'And, along those lines, what makes Striker figure that a dog track in the desert in a town the size of Artemis is going to make him money?'

Otto pointed to the laptop bag lying next to the desk. 'Have you looked on any of her electronics yet?'

'No. I'm taking her laptop back to the office. Her phone hasn't been found. Her purse was lying on the kitchen counter, but her phone wasn't in it. And no phone has been found on Pinto Canyon. Obviously, it could have fallen into the rocks when she fell, but they'll have people search the mountain this morning.'

'How about her car?' he asked.

'I haven't gotten there yet. You want to start there first?'

Otto set up a portable spotlight to pull prints off the handles on the driver and passenger doors of the two-door Honda Accord Coupe. He got one partial that he assumed belonged to Jezebel. Both doors were unlocked and revealed a car in need of a vacuum and airing out. Dog hair clung in a thick mat to the black fabric on the backseat. Several gnawed-on rawhide bones lay on the floor. Her registration was current and located in the glove compartment with some receipts for oil changes. Nothing more than lip balm and change and receipts in the front seat.

After he finished the car, Otto helped Josie load the filing cabinet files into boxes that she moved to her SUV. Back at the office, Otto spent the day pouring through her files and checking bank accounts and credit card accounts for balances. As he was wrapping up for the day, he discovered a savings account containing $239,000, with the last deposit of $100,000 made only the month prior. The check was issued from a company based in Switzerland, so tracking down the specifics was going to be complicated.

As he was cleaning up the files at the end of the day, he received a call from Billy Hanson, a rancher who proudly told people he had never cared about 'book learning' but could tell you anything you wanted to know about a cow. Billy's lack of education hadn't kept his ranch from earning profits in the millions, a feat that he thought gave him special status and community standing.

'Have you seen the internet today?' Billy said.

'No. I have not seen the internet today. What does it look like?' Otto asked, already annoyed with the conversation.

'There's a group of morons that formed a Facebook group to protest the dog track. They have photos they claim show dogs being abused by Jezebel Black. I am here to tell you those photos are fake. They aren't even taken on her property! I am filing defamation charges and a cease-and-desist order. Jezebel won't do it, so I'll do it for her.'

Otto sighed heavily into the phone. 'Billy, you can't file charges against Facebook.'

'That's fine. Then I want to file charges against RiverRider.'

'Billy, I don't have time for this.'

'You can't tell a citizen that pays your salary that!'

'Call back when you have a serious complaint,' Otto said.

'Now you hold up! This is legitimate.'

'RiverRider?' Otto said.

'It's the bastard's username. He spouts lies nonstop and there ought to be something you can do about it. He says terrible things about Jezebel. It's slander.'

Otto didn't tell him that Jezebel had been murdered. 'Do you know who this person is?'

'No. They're too cowardly to put their real names.'

'Then you need to take this up with Facebook. You get on the internet and figure out how to post a complaint.'

Josie walked into the office, and Otto hung up the phone.

'I'm telling you, Josie. This job is wearing me down. All this technology makes life ten times harder than it should be. How are we supposed to file charges against people who have names on their Facebook page like RiverRider and LibbyKittyLover?'

Josie shuddered. 'We've had other complaints about LibbyKittyLover. She's the neurotic ER nurse from the trauma center. Calls herself a keyboard warrior. She's out to make the world a better place by spewing hate across the internet. Who's complaining about her now?'

He told her about his conversation with Billy.

'See if you can track down who RiverRider is. Did you talk to Dugout?' she asked.

Otto glanced at his watch. 'No, but I'll head that way. What happened with the body?'

'It was a five-hour job, but her body is now with Cowan. There wasn't enough room on the road to get the hoists set up properly to lift her up the side. They ended up lifting her out with a helicopter.'

'Poor woman. Any belongings or cell phone show up?'

'No cell phone. Once the cars cleared out, I drove back to Pinto Canyon to check out the place where her body was found. There are plenty of places it could have been disposed of, but where her body was found was protected. I drove both ends of the road, and you can't see that side of the mountain from either end. The chances of her being found so fast were really slim.'

'So whoever killed her knows the area well,' he said.

'That's my bet. And one more thing. The only personal information found on her was a folded sticky note that was inside the pocket of her skirt. She was wearing one of those flowing gauze skirts and the pocket wasn't obvious. Cowan found it when he prepared her body at the morgue. It had the name Kip Esposito and a phone number on it.'

Otto narrowed his eyes as if he hadn't heard right.

'The name's familiar, but I can't place it,' she said.

'He was the political operator behind the scandal in El Paso. I think that's where he lives. They tried to get him for voter fraud over their mayoral election a few years ago, but he's too slippery. He comes in for a fee, organizes an election and moves on before he's ever implicated. He's been involved in some major races all over the country. He's a shark.'

'What the hell? Why would someone like that be involved in our speck on the map?'

'This won't sound kind, but I also never saw Jezebel as having the brains to get caught up in something like election rigging,' Otto said.

Josie frowned. 'People underestimated her. She didn't mind playing the part of a ditz if it got her what she wanted, but that wasn't who she was.'

'Then who was she? River guide, dog breeder, hippy? Pretty flakey if you ask me.'

'She was a chameleon. She could be whoever she needed to be to get the job done. I don't think she'd found her niche yet.'

'You might be wrong there.' Otto flipped through the papers on his desk to find his notes on the bank account in Switzerland and gave Josie a rundown. 'Her niche landed her a quarter of a million dollars in a savings account.'

Josie shook her head, stunned at the number. 'I'd have guessed she was barely making grocery money.'

'A Swiss bank account sounds like better motivation for murder than breeding a few greyhound dogs.'

'Any contact from Senator Striker on any of this?'

'No. I tried his office several times, but he's not returning calls,' he said.

'He's on my list for tomorrow morning. Marta's working on Mark Jackson today. She's meeting with him to talk about election-day plans. Hopefully, he'll fill her in on Striker. I'm headed to talk to Sauly now.'

After Josie left, Otto took the laptop and a box of the files down to the evidence room to lock them up for the night. His knees popped and cracked on the way down the stairs, each step causing him pain. He set the box on the counter while Lou unlocked the door to the storage area. He logged the box and computer and pictured the three other boxes up in the office, dreading two more trips up and down the stairs to log them in. Glancing at his watch, he saw it was already five o'clock and he still hadn't checked in with Dugout. Delores would be angry he was going to be late again for supper. So instead of locking up the other boxes, he signed off on the evidence logbook and wished Lou a nice evening.

TEN

Marta Cruz finished her walk up and down the courthouse stairs and sat down on the bench outside to catch her breath. Day two of her new life plan to get into shape, and she felt somewhere between disgusted with herself for panting like a dog and proud that she had actually followed through this time. The first week was always the worst, or so she told herself. She worked a shift from three-thirty p.m. to midnight, so she had committed to walking up and down the two flights of courthouse stairs twice at the beginning of her supper break. She would do this each day for a week and then add something else to her routine the next week. She usually attacked a new workout like a rabid dog and was exhausted by the end of the first week, hating life, and never made it to week two. Her new plan was to ease into it. Sneak up on it. The weight would come off because she wouldn't be obsessing over it as she usually did.

Marta had celebrated her thirty-ninth birthday alone, ruminating about her lunatic ex-husband in Mexico, her daughter in college who still liked to live life on the wild side, and a smattering of friends and family who had all forgotten her birthday. At noon that day, after she acknowledged she would be spending the day by herself, she drove to the grocery store and bought a round birthday cake with the thickest layer of chocolate icing she could find, along with a gallon of vanilla ice cream. She'd taken it home and sat in front of the TV, watching her mother's favorite telenovela for hours on end, intermittently crying and eating cake and ice cream throughout the day. She woke up the next day red-eyed and sick to her stomach and drove to the courthouse to make her first trip up the stairs.

Marta thought about that day a few weeks ago and knew other changes were needed. She had to quit living in the past. Her ex-husband was never going to change. She loved him, but he was a mess: an angry, alcoholic man bent on self-destruction. She could not save him, but she could save herself.

She saw Mark Jackson round the corner and she sat up straight, sucked in her stomach, tucked the stray strands of hair behind her ears and wiped the sweat off her forehead with the back of her hand. She had thought the shady bench away from the office would be a nice spot to chat, but it was still close to ninety degrees, and she'd just huffed up and down two flights of stairs. She hoped she didn't smell.

Mark smiled as he approached her and held out a brown paper bag. 'This is your supper break, right?'

'It is,' she said, smiling back and patting the bench beside her.

'I brought you a treat. Have you ever had the cannoli at the Hot Tamale? She uses mint chocolate chips. They are my absolute favorites. I got us each one if you're interested.'

'I'd love one! That's very sweet of you.'

Mark passed her a small paper plate where he placed the gorgeous calorie bomb and then carefully laid a napkin across her knee. She felt her face flush with happiness.

She asked how he was getting along, and he seemed to understand she was referring to life after losing his wife the year before.

He lifted a shoulder and glanced over at her. 'Good days and bad. You live with someone for twenty years and your day is filled with their day. It's a bit lonely.'

'Ah, yes, I understand. My ex-husband is in Mexico. For the longest time, I let his drama consume my days just because I needed something to occupy me. You know? It was easier to talk about his problems than to fill my day up with something new.'

'Maybe we should both do something new,' Mark said, glancing at her again and looking away. 'Marfa has the Music on the Square concert starting up this weekend. Would you like to go? I could pick you up Saturday around five and we could have dinner first?'

'That would be wonderful.'

She absently put her hand up to her neck to rub the pendant of St Valentine, the patron saint of love. Just that morning, she had opened the bottom drawer of her jewelry box and pulled out the necklace, placing it around her neck in preparation for her meeting with Mark. She had prayed, and here she was, prayer granted in short order. *All I had to do was to believe*, she thought.

The conversation eventually wound its way around to the election and to the supposed reason Marta had called Mark for the meeting.

'Josie asked that I offer you an apology from her.'

Mark pulled back and looked at Marta as if she'd grown a second head. 'Chief Gray is apologizing to *me*?'

'For getting angry about your request for officers at the polling places.' Marta felt a twinge of guilt at the lie, but it was for Josie's benefit. No sense allowing angry feelings that served no purpose. 'She's just frustrated. We're understaffed. I think she worries about Otto retiring. I don't know what we'll do when that day comes.'

Mark nodded, looking both surprised and pleased at the gesture. 'It's fine. I don't have the people I need either. Everyone criticizes everything we do to try to make the voting safe and secure. People have no idea what safeguards we have in place, and then they take to social media and tell everyone how rigged the whole system is. It's infuriating.'

Marta nodded, unsure how to tactfully phrase her next question. 'Are you worried that there might actually be some issues with the voting system this year?'

'That's the problem. I just don't know. Everyone is so paranoid about vote tampering, about double and triple voting with absentee ballots, dead people casting votes, and on and on. But the majority of it is one side trying to stick it to the other side. Just out-and-out lies trying to generate negative publicity. Then when there is legitimate corruption, the secretary of state's office is running around investigating complete rubbish while the real issues are buried in the slush pile.'

'And you're afraid there is a real issue this year in Arroyo County?'

Mark crumpled up the paper bag and carried their trash over to the barrel. Marta watched him walk back to the bench, his brow furrowed in deep thought. She tried to imagine her

ex-husband worrying over the results of an election; it almost
made her laugh.

When Mark sat down on the bench, he turned to face her.
'I am indeed worried. There are probably more rules in place
for voting than any other activity in the United States. We
have reams of rules and guidelines and policies and procedures.
One of the most basic rules is that anyone who is an elected
official can't go anywhere near anything to do with polling.
But this supposed commission that Senator Striker is on doesn't
seem to fit anywhere. And the secretary of state is so overrun
with calls right now that I can't get a response. What really
worries me is that his own office staff are avoiding my calls.
If he had nothing to hide, they'd have responded weeks ago
with a statement.'

'I can't imagine far West Texas is high on the secretary of
state's priority list for examining voter fraud,' she said.

'Exactly. And meanwhile, we've got an election around the
corner that's ripe for scandal. The worst thing that could
happen is to have the wrongdoing validated *after* the election.
A recount is a nightmare. I do not want that on my watch.'

'What do you plan to do about it?' Marta asked.

'I have a plan. But it involves you.'

Arroyo County stretched from parched desert to flowing
grasslands, boasting some of the most diverse plant and animal
life in the state. The grasslands in the northern part of the
county received mountain runoff and water from underground
springs. The locals called the wet area the mudflats due to a
depression in the desert that filled with rain during the
monsoons. Sauly Magson lived along the Rio Grande on
the other side of the mudflats, in an area thick with carrizo
cane grass, cottonwood trees, willows and sandy river
beaches. While Josie loved the desert, she thought Sauly's
riverside retreat was the prettiest spot in the county.

His home was a three-story converted grain elevator currently
painted a deep charcoal-blue, the color of the West Texas sky
during a summer thunderstorm. Over a dozen windows of
various shapes had been installed in what appeared to be a
random manner over the four sides of the structure. But once

inside his home, a visitor discovered that each window framed a particular view that Sauly appreciated. Josie pulled her SUV to a stop next to his old beater pickup truck and knocked on his front door. After several minutes with no answer, she walked down to the river where she found Sauly in cutoff jean shorts sitting cross-legged on his dock, staring out into the water. His bright yellow kayak was tied up to the side of the dock and seemed out of place, too cheerful for the sad slope of his shoulders.

Sauly's bare back was the color of cinnamon in the evening sunlight. His gray hair hung in a rough ponytail down his back, and a threadbare bandana was tied around his neck. Josie said his name softly and asked if she could talk with him. Without turning, he patted the place next to him on the dock. She took her boots and socks off and rolled her uniform pants up to sit next to him and dangle her feet in the running water below them.

'I'm so sorry about Jezebel. And I'm sorry to be here bothering you, but you know I want to make things right. I want to find out the truth for you.'

Sauly nodded and took a moment to speak. 'You aren't bothering me. I'm glad for the company, if truth be told.'

'Did the sheriff come talk to you last night?'

'Yes. He told me where they found her. You know she loved the outdoors, but she was never one for hiking. She was a water rat like me.'

'You don't think she would have been out walking on Pinto Canyon Road?'

'No. She would not have.'

'Do you have any ideas about why she might have been there?'

He turned to face Josie for the first time. 'Her car was at her house. Seems obvious someone took her there.'

'I've been to her house. There wasn't anything out of place. Do you think someone could have picked her up for some reason – maybe they took a drive, got out to take a walk, and she slipped and fell? Maybe the person panicked and left? That's one theory.'

'Stop it. You know that doesn't make sense.'

Josie didn't believe that theory either, but she wanted to get Sauly's initial thinking. 'Why do you say it doesn't make sense?'

'You know her purse is in the kitchen?'

Josie nodded.

'She never left without that purse and her phone. She wouldn't have gotten in a car to go all the way over to Pinto Canyon without her purse. I can't even imagine what she'd be doing over that way.'

'Do you have ideas about what happened?'

He faced the water again. 'Somebody drove to her home, picked her up and killed her. Then threw her over the edge of that mountain as if she were garbage.'

'Do you have any idea who might have done that to her?'

'That girl would not have hurt anybody. If she sees a spider in the house, she'll push it into a cup and take it outside so she doesn't have to hurt it. That's the kind of person she is, and these people who don't even know her are saying terrible things. Saying she was abusing those dogs of hers. She called me several times, crying about the lies they were saying.'

'You said that someone drove to her house and picked her up. We didn't see any sign of a struggle, which makes us wonder if she went with someone willingly and got into some kind of trouble after she left the house. Can you imagine her leaving with someone who might have wanted to hurt her?'

Sauly stared out at the water for a long time and said nothing.

'I'm so sorry to ask you these terrible questions so soon after Jezebel's death. I hope you understand I'm only doing it because I have to. I'm sure you know the first twenty-four hours after a—'

Sauly nodded and cut her off. 'I understand. It's just hard to talk about.'

'Would you like to stop for a while? Maybe go get a drink and clear your head?'

'No, you keep going. I'm fine.'

'OK, then. The people who were giving her a hard time – do you know if Jezebel knew any of them personally? Any of the people saying the hateful things?'

Sauly rubbed both his hands over his face and then looked at Josie as if he were struggling with something he didn't want to say.

'If you're worried to tell me something that you aren't sure is true, go ahead and tell me. Then it's my job to track down the facts. I've found that if someone has a worry about something, there's almost always some truth buried in their worries. That's what police work is about, putting together all the little pieces until we have the bigger story.'

He shook his head, his eyes bright with the worries he had probably been carrying about his daughter for quite some time.

'Ever since Jezebel got involved with that highfalutin senator, things weren't the same with us. She changed. She wasn't doing right, Josie. I love my kid with all my heart, and I supported her a hundred percent. You know, when that happened with the lady dying on the river, that wasn't her fault. She did it because she believed in people. She believed that man was telling the truth about his wife. I think that senator got her when she was down, when she was vulnerable, and he manipulated her good nature.'

'You mean she was struggling over the woman's death still, and Senator Striker took advantage of her?'

'I do believe that. But she started making bad decisions. It's why she ended up in the bottom of that canyon, and it is breaking my heart.'

Josie was quiet for some time, taking in Sauly's words. She hadn't expected him to know much about Mike Striker and his dealings with Jezebel.

'Do you know much about the business dealings that they had together?'

'I know the dogs were just one thing. There was more than that.'

'What do you mean?'

'She quit telling me things like she used to. And if it was breeding dogs, then why wouldn't she tell me everything? I'd question her about meetings, and she'd avoid me. She'd leave town for a few days and then spin some story about visiting an old friend in Florida. Jezebel didn't have old friends. That's just not who she was. When she left somewhere, she left it for good. It pains me to say this, but I didn't believe the stories she was telling me.'

'Did you know about any large sums of money she had received?'

Sauly leaned away from Josie and looked at her as if she were crazy. 'Not a chance. She was living at her brother's place because she was broke. She was even going to move in with me for a while, but her brother got the job in Germany. That's when he asked her to watch his place.'

'Any chance the two of them were working together?'

'No. Jamey is her half-brother. He's an engineer for a German car maker. He's not much of a businessman, or a people person. His brain's all wrapped up in numbers and figures.'

Josie nodded, weighing how much she should share with Sauly. She decided to keep the bank account quiet and wrapped up her meeting. Sauly stood while Josie put her socks and boots back on, and then he walked her out to her car.

'I know you're trying to get someone to adopt her dogs,' he said. 'The sheriff told me to stay off her property until the investigation was closed, but I'd like to at least look after them until someone takes them.'

'I hated to ask you, but that would be great. I talked to Roy earlier today about you feeding and watering, and we agreed that would be fine. We need you to stay out of her house for now, until the investigation is over, but taking care of the dogs would be a big help.'

Mike Striker had not been happy about the move to Texas. His wife had been downright pissed. To slow down his third march to divorce court, he'd bought them an oil-boom home west of Artemis in an area called The Canyons. He'd spent money that had not been part of his five-year plan. But damned if he didn't love the house now. He'd gone from the raw insanity of Manhattan to a gated community in the desert with a two-tiered swimming pool that faced the most magnificent sunsets he had ever seen. Five sprawling homes had been artfully placed around a scenic loop that offered glimpses of the other homes but also provided enough privacy to stand naked on the stone deck surrounding the swimming pool if you were so inclined. His wife hated seeing his naked ass and had just yelled out of the kitchen window the night before, 'Put your pants on! You look like a savage.' With a cigar in one hand and a cocktail in another, gazing out across the rugged mountains surrounding their home, he thoroughly enjoyed the warmth of the sun on his bare ass. The feeling was success. Money might not have bought him love, but it had absolutely bought him happiness.

But now, sitting on his patio with a cocktail in hand and his pants securely buttoned, he felt his world teetering on calamity. He thrived on problems and orchestrating outlandish solutions that could get him out of any jam imaginable, but this was starting to feel beyond him. He had called his brother for a reality check, but the ten-minute lecture had fried his patience.

'Listen to me, it's all damage control at this point,' Morey said. 'That's all business is in the end. You've dealt with worse.'

'It's not like New York City. There are no secrets in this goddamned town. You take a dump here, your neighbor knows it before the shit hits the bowl.'

'So work it to your advantage. If news travels fast, then get your message out immediately. The girl's dead. She worked for you. What do you want to say about it?'

'It's not just that the girl's dead; it's everything the girl knew, and I have now lost the ability to control any of it.'

'What's got into you? You haven't lost the ability to do anything! You have to make it happen,' Morey said. 'Look. Break this down. You said, "everything the girl knew." What did she know? Business, personal, both?'

'Business, mostly.'

'OK, then let's deal with the business first. Was the knowledge in her head or on paper?'

'That's my point. I don't know.'

'Then we assume the worst. Let's say she wrote down everything you said. Did she have an office?'

'No office. She worked from home.'

'Good. Was she organized? Did she use a kitchen table, a laptop, a computer?'

'I don't know. I never paid any attention. She was organized. And careful. I don't see her having a big paper trail, but it's hard to tell,' Mike said.

'All right, here's what I've seen since I've been here. You got a small-town police department – no money, limited staff. My guess is they haven't even made it to her house yet. Let me see what I can do.'

'Jack's staying at the motel in town. Take him with you,' Mike said.

'Leave him out of this. I told you before, I got this.'

'He's a grown man. He's here because he wants to be. Not to mention the female cop he's been hanging around with. That could be a big help.'

'Leave my son out of this,' Morey said. 'You and I created this mess; you and I will clean it up.'

Mike held his tongue. Jack had more to offer than Morey would allow. The kid was handsome, a charmer. He could be useful. Especially if he could get the cop on his side. Mike thought she was an A1 pain in the ass, but the kid seemed to like her.

'You don't know anything about this town. How are you gonna help?'

'I've had twenty-four hours in this shithole, which is plenty of time to know there are fifty loopholes we use to our advantage. The sheriff's department is located at the jail. The jail and the trauma center have been modernized. Cameras, locks and so on. But they're so backed up that the city police are investigating the murder. And the police department building is a fifty-year-old dump. The cameras are cheap, the locks are cheap, the alarm system is cheap. There are dead zones in the radio reception and fifteen- to thirty-minute response times. Single-pane windows and no deadbolts in the PD. And, the best part, they shut down for several hours each night. Once the third-shift officer goes off duty, the building is locked up until seven the next morning.'

Mike listened intently, shaking his head as his brother listed the details.

'It's doable, is what I'm saying. So let me check on the female's house tonight. If it's clear the cops took the records, then I move to Plan B.'

'All right, good. This is good. You keep me posted,' the senator said.

'I'll keep you posted. And you leave Jack the hell out of this.'

ELEVEN

Otto leaned back in the driver's seat and sighed as the air conditioning spiked cold, sending glorious shivers down his spine. For several seconds, he closed his eyes and let the air freeze-dry the sweat across his forehead, thanking God as he had countless times before for the modern convenience that made living in the desert tolerable.

He finally opened his eyes to stare through the plate-glass window of the police department, looking at the shadow of the stairwell in the back of the building. He should go back in and carry the blasted boxes of evidence back downstairs and lock them up. It was a cardinal rule of law enforcement – a rule he had insisted upon from the officers that had worked for him through his tenure as chief. 'Laziness is death to a cop. It is the inexcusable sin.'

Otto jumped and hollered at the hard rap on his window. He looked out and saw Carla Striker leaning her head back in a belly laugh.

He rolled the window down as she was already apologizing for scaring him.

Otto smiled, hoping he looked more good-natured than he felt at that moment.

'I really wasn't trying to give you a heart attack,' she said, reaching through his window to pat him on the arm. 'Rough day?'

'No, just preoccupied. Thinking about the pierogi Delores promised me for supper.'

'Ah, you're off shift. Well, that's fine, I'll catch you tomorrow,' Carla said.

'No, no. I'm not in any hurry. Does this visit rate a trip into the office or a seat here in the nice cool air conditioning?'

Carla walked around his SUV and slid into the passenger seat.

When she and Senator Striker had moved to Artemis, she had surprised people by joining Delores's home economics club. Delores had come home after the first meeting with a favorable review of her, and they had grown to be friends over the past year. 'She wears extra makeup, extra hairspray, she talks extra loud, but, you know, I really like her,' Delores had said. 'She's as down to earth as anyone I know. She's not uppity or full of herself like her husband.' As was typically the case, Otto had agreed with his wife's assessment. He liked Carla as well.

She wore a pair of slim-fitting white pants and a bright-colored summer top and sandals, and smelled of a flowery perfume that would give him a headache if she sat too long in his vehicle.

She asked about Delores and tried to small-talk, but Otto could see she had come with an agenda.

'What's on your mind?' he finally asked.

She blew air out as if getting ready for a major revelation, and he became more interested.

'This is awkward. I've always been a loyal person. Even when things were going belly-up with my last husband, I kept my mouth shut and soldiered on. But Mike Striker is too much. He has pushed me too far. He has crossed the line on too many different levels.'

Otto had heard preambles like Carla's before. She was gathering courage. He thought it all stemmed from grade school where no one liked a rat.

'It's just hard to know where to begin,' she continued.

'Is this related to his job or something more personal?'

'It's both, although I guess all you care about is his job.'

'You believe your husband has broken a law as it relates to his work as a senator?'

'I do.'

'Why don't you start by telling me what's bothering you. You don't have to go in any chronological order. This isn't a police report. You're just talking to a friend here.'

Carla nodded. 'All right, then. What has bothered me from the very beginning is the dogs. I have been a solid member and monetary supporter of PETA for thirty years, and I think

Mike's obsession with this track located in the middle of a desert is cruel and absurd. Last night we got into a huge fight over it. It's not about the dogs; it's about the money for him. That's what he keeps telling me. But I said, that's even worse! It *should* be about the dogs. If he had any kind of conscience, it *would* be about the animals and not his freaking bank account.'

'I've talked to the commissioners, and he's found a loophole in the gaming industry guidelines. As far as we can tell, there isn't anything we can do about the racetrack. He'll need the approval of the zoning board and several other community groups, but that's what this run for mayor is all about. I think we're all clear on that by now.'

'What we can do about it is not let him build the damn thing to begin with.'

'And how will you do that?' Otto asked.

'Have you heard rumors about the election?'

'In regard to . . .?'

'Cheating,' she said, her tone hard. 'In regard to my husband fixing the election.'

Otto nodded, glad to finally be getting to the meat of the conversation. 'I've heard that, yes.'

'I'm here to tell you that I've seen and heard enough over the past two weeks to confirm any doubts I may have had. He and his piece-of-shit brother have figured out a way to hack into the QuickTab voting machines. I can't give you specifics, but they have no doubt Mike will win this election.'

'The senator and his brother? They have the experience to hack into a voting machine?'

Carla cocked her head and grinned at Otto. 'I bet you don't know that Arroyo County is the only county in the state to have purchased this QuickTab system. Ninety percent of the counties in the state went with another system.'

Otto frowned. 'I can't believe Mark Jackson would stand for that.'

'Our voting commissioner?' She laughed. 'That man doesn't have a clue. We're a small county with limited money, and Mark Jackson's bottom line is money. You really can't blame the poor bastard. QuickTab was low bid. People assume just because it's a voting machine that it has checks and balances in place, and that whatever certification it has stamped on the side of each machine means something. Bullshit.'

'Surely Mark looked into these machines before choosing them,' Otto said.

'I'm sure he did, but he was sold a line of bullshit. Want to hear how I know that?' she asked.

'I do.'

'Mike's brother, Morey, was part of the sales team that sold the machines to Arroyo County.'

'What?'

She laughed at Otto's wide-eyed expression. 'Mark Jackson and his committee didn't know that when they bought the machines. I'm sure one of the other salesmen made the deal so he never heard the name Striker.' Carla rolled her eyes. 'He manipulated that voting committee from two thousand miles away. They were convinced they were getting the deal of a lifetime.'

'You're saying that our county bought voting machines that are already rigged in your husband's favor?'

'I'm saying they bought a voting system that Morey has figured out how to rig. I can't get into that part of it because they're too cagey when they talk. I just know that's their plan.'

'Carla, what you're saying is a serious accusation, but if you don't have any proof of wrongdoing, there's nothing the police can do about this. I'll share this with the state voting commission, but they may not take the word of a disgruntled wife. Not to mention the number of complaints they're getting right now about vote tampering and rigging. I'm sure they're swamped.'

Carla crossed her legs and turned in her seat to better face Otto. 'What if I told you that my cocky husband, who thinks he's so smart he can hack an election, isn't smart enough to figure out that his own Facebook app tracks his every movement? I have proof that he's been to every polling place in the county. Every single one. That ought to at least be enough to get the commission to inspect the machines.'

'I'm listening.'

Carla grinned. 'Mike doesn't have his own Facebook

account. He uses mine to occasionally log in and see pictures of his grandkids. He has the app on his phone, but he uses my login. So, a couple of months ago, I read an article about how Facebook tracks everything we do, and I was checking my settings to see if that's really true. Sure enough, there's a feature that tracks everywhere that we go when we have our phones in the car with us, which is all the time, of course. Do you have Facebook on your phone?'

'I do. Delores set it up so I could see pictures of our grandkids.'

'Right,' she nodded. 'Typical man. And do you have your own login?'

'I have no idea.' Otto felt ridiculous. This seemed like something he should know.

'Then there is most likely a list of locations, dates and even times of everywhere you've been on your phone right now that Delores has access to.'

Otto raised his eyebrows.

'Let me show you.' She pulled a laptop out of her bag and opened Facebook. She talked as she tapped and scrolled. 'You go into your settings and privacy shortcuts. It's in your location history. You can do this on your phone, too; this is just easier to see.' She passed the laptop over to Otto, and he saw that there was indeed a map of Texas that showed red icons on the various cities that she or Mike had traveled to, along with a list of dates and exact times.

Carla told Otto to click on one of the red dots and the map zoomed into a specific location and stated that someone had been at that location from two fifty-two p.m. to three forty-nine p.m. 'You want to see where Mike was back on April fifteenth?' She chose that date and a new map and list appeared. 'I can show you the dates and times when he visited every single one of the polling sites in the county.'

'But if it's on your phone and his, how could you prove who visited these sites?'

'Because I deleted Facebook off my phone. It's only on Mike's phone, and he has location accuracy turned on so his maps work better. So when I pull up my Facebook account, the only phone that it's attached to it is Mike's.'

Otto nodded. 'I'm impressed.'

'Oh, there's more.' She pulled up a date from the previous week and passed the laptop back over to Otto. 'Click on the entry that says, "Place in Marfa," with the time from nine forty-five p.m. through eleven twenty-one p.m.'

Otto did and saw that the map zoomed in on a downtown street in Marfa. He stared at the map for a moment and asked if it was the Greenfield Estates subdivision.

She gave Otto a wide smile. 'Why, yes, that is the Greenfield Estates subdivision, and guess who lives there? The twenty-four-year-old campaign manager that Mike hired six months ago. Would you like to see the photographs I took that confirm that little tidbit? I didn't need to hire a private detective. I have Facebook and the internet. I have a series of photographs and travel logs to the homes of two different females who my husband has been sleeping with for several months. This is Missy Sherwood's home. It was honestly a piece of cake. I parked a block away, walked around the side of the house and peaked in windows until I found the bedroom where I snapped photos of Mike having sex. The girl didn't even shut her blinds. And Mike was too stupid to think beyond the length of his—' She rolled her eyes. 'He can plot a business takeover like a master and is a complete disaster in his personal life, screwing up everything he touches, including me.'

Otto watched her fake smile turn to what he assumed was a mixture of sadness and anger.

'The image of that man's white whale of an ass sticking up in the air is seared into my memory for a lifetime.'

'I'm sorry, Carla.'

She made a dismissive sound. 'It's what I get. My gut told me he was a snake. I should have known.'

'Are you OK if I ask you a few questions?'

'Absolutely. It's why I'm here.'

'What about Jack, Mike's son? Is he involved in this?'

Carla twisted her mouth into a doubtful frown. 'I don't think so. At least, I hope not. Jack's a good kid. He doesn't have the win-at-all-cost mentality that the brothers have. Mike and Morey grew up competing with each other on every level, from sports to girls, until they finally decided to join forces. That's when things went real bad.' Carla stared at Otto for a moment. 'As far as Jack goes, I never liked his mom, but she did a good job raising him to at least have a conscience. Honestly, though, Jack is part of the business, so who knows? Maybe they've groomed him for the good-cop role.'

Otto wondered if Josie had followed through on her date with Jack. He'd have to get Marta to do some digging. He certainly wanted her to find a good man, but the emphasis was on *good*.

'Let's talk a little more about the voting machines,' Otto said. 'We've heard that Mike's been showing up on the days the company is installing the machines to inspect them.'

She shook her head. 'No, not the day of. He waits a day or two. He doesn't want to be confronted by any poll workers who are there to watch the installation. He gets the installer from QuickTab to go back with him a day or two later to inspect. He tells people he's serving on a congressional commission on voting oversight.'

Otto jabbed a finger in her direction. 'Yes! That's exactly what Mark Jackson told us.'

'Good for him. Did Jackson believe the story?'

'No. He's made calls, but he can't confirm or deny anything at this point. We've got an officer working on it, but we're overrun, with the sheriff's department being down several officers. Are you saying he's not really serving on any voting oversight committee?'

'I really don't know. I'll do some digging and get back to you on that one. Knowing Mike, he found a way to break the law and come out looking like a bigwig serving on some committee. That's how he operates.'

Carla shut her laptop and pulled a stack of papers out of her bag. 'You'll find copies of the maps, locations, dates and times, along with a typewritten explanation of what I just told you. I've listed the date that I first discovered the location tracking and the date that I removed it from my phone, and even my login and password for the Facebook app so that the voting commission can check for themselves. Mike doesn't have any idea about any of this, but he'll have those records erased in a heartbeat when he finds out. You need to act fast.'

'And what will happen when he finds out you've gone behind his back and exposed him?'

She offered up her big fake smile again. 'Then I'll expose his big white ass in Missy Sherwood's bedroom all over the internet, and then I'll follow up with the same photo at Ava Bransteader's house. For that one, I think I'll use the heading "Striker Strikes Again."'

TWELVE

Since his years in Vietnam during the war, Sauly had learned to keep a low profile. He had made his money working dozens of different jobs throughout the years, maintaining his freedom, working as his own boss with his own set of values to guide him. Jezebel came to him with a head full of nonsense about what it meant to be an American. Her mother had painted the US as not just the land of opportunity, but the land of opulence and easy money – a place where any dream, however crazy, could materialize with the right connections. But while her head was filled with nonsense, her heart knew better. When her mother sent her to live with Sauly as a teenager, with orders to 'get a job and a big house in California,' Jezebel had high hopes but also a mature realism that had surprised him. It hadn't taken her long to understand that the life her mother expected for her was not going to happen living with her father. Surprisingly, she had taken to Sauly's way of life and seemed genuinely happy. Until she met Mike Striker.

Sauly drove down Jezebel's lane and passed her house, feeling the sharp pain of loss like a blade through the heart. He did not stop until he was on the other side of the kennel – away from the house and the memories of Jezebel and her brother Jamey in the house together, the three of them eating dinner on the side patio, a bottle of wine and a boisterous conversation on some topic one of the kids would throw out for debate. He pushed the memory from his head, still unable to make the phone call to Jamey to tell him about his sister. He promised himself that he would call in the morning.

As he approached the kennel, the dogs' barking grew frantic, maniacal even, as they realized someone had come to care for them. Sauly listened as they jumped against their chain-link gates, the noise echoing off the cinder blocks and concrete. When he pushed the door open and turned on the overhead fluorescent lights, the noise increased to the point that he had to cover his ears with his palms. He walked around the room to each cage, crooning for them to quiet, promising dinner and fresh water.

An hour later, he had the dogs fed and watered, and was making the rounds again, cleaning out their cages. By nine o'clock, they were cared for and lying down quietly, convinced for the moment that all was right in their worlds again.

Sauly knew that Jezebel was up early in the mornings with the dogs, going through the feeding routine all over again, so he had planned to stay the night and take care of the morning feeding again before heading home. He hoped to get the dogs on a schedule, thinking it would help him move through his own horrible days if he had responsibilities.

He took the sleeping bag off the back seat of his truck and rolled it out on to the pine needles under a small grove of pinyon pine located fifty feet behind the kennel. He lay down on top of the tattered old military bag and looked up through the needles to catch pinpricks of light from the stars above him. The moon was nowhere to be seen, off completing its rotation around the earth somewhere else that night.

Sauly took a long slow breath to let the spicy scent of the pinyon deep into his lungs. He had many favorite smells in nature, but the pinyon was among his top three. Fresh, dried or burning, it gave off a scent like no other pine. He focused on his breathing, forcing the angry thoughts and images into a black well at the base of his brain. Sauly had never allowed anger to enter his sleep world. He considered sleep as a time to mend the damage the body and soul experienced throughout the day. It was a practice he'd developed during his time in Vietnam, and it had continued with him throughout his life. He knew that he would live to be over a hundred years old, and the thought of stretching out those days without Jezebel in the world with him was making his focused meditation impossible that night. Anger lit up his thoughts, shining down into the well and exposing sixty years of toxic thoughts that he was not prepared to face.

He opened his eyes and caught a flash of light in his

peripheral vision. He picked his head up and turned it so that he wouldn't make a sound. Remaining flat in the pine needles, he caught the light again and saw the arc of a flashlight sweeping across the ground. He heard the light crunch of gravel as the person crossed over the driveway and moved toward the kennel. The light stopped, shone around the yard and then headed toward the kennel again. The door opened, and the dogs began barking again, although, with their bellies full, the sound was half-hearted. Sauly could see the light move around the building through the windows placed on each wall. After less than a minute, the person left the building and headed toward the road at a faster pace. The dogs, apparently worn out from the chaos of the last few days, were quiet again almost immediately, and several minutes later, Sauly heard the start of an engine down the road.

As Sauly was cleaning out the dog cages, Josie was sitting in a booth at the Legion with Jack Striker. He'd called out of the blue and said he'd stopped by the Legion earlier that day for lunch, and Carol had agreed with him that Josie would absolutely love a hamburger and a beer for dinner that night. Carol had been correct. Josie had gone home depressed after her meeting with Sauly. She had been ready to walk back to Dell's to bum a beer when she'd gotten the call from Jack. Dell had been giving her crap about getting out into the world and making a few friends for years, so he hadn't minded when she called and reneged on the beer.

Jack had picked her up in his truck, wearing a plaid shirt and jeans, smelling freshly showered. During the entire time she'd dated Nick, their relationship had consisted of long weekends spent locked inside her house, trying to make up for lost time, with the weeks occasionally stretching into months of not seeing each other. The weekends had been frantic and filled with guilt as they both clung to careers over commitment. As Josie walked into the Legion that night with Jack, feeling his hand on the small of her back, she realized how much she had missed a night out on the town, even if the town only held 2,500 people, and the date consisted of bottled beer at the Legion.

Carol brought them each a beer and suggested hamburgers and fries, explaining that the burgers came from a local ranch where they processed their own meat. Jack gave her a thumbs-up, and she winked. They watched her walk away, admiring her prosthesis tattoos.

'I like her,' he said. 'Straight up, no bullshit.'

'That's Carol,' she said. 'You have friends tucked away in cities all over the globe?'

He shrugged. 'I guess. Probably more acquaintances than friends. I haven't stuck around long enough in any one place to make too many lasting friends. A drawback to the job, I guess.'

'Do you really think it's a drawback?'

He grinned and pointed at her. 'I bet you're a good cop.'

'I have a fairly accurate bullshit meter.'

'It wasn't complete BS. I love the travel. Seeing the world, trying out new places, seeing how other people live. But I'd like to share it with someone. Life's always more fun when you have somebody to share it with. Trouble is, there aren't too many women who are interested in hopping around the globe looking at rocks.'

As they finished their hamburgers, Jack ordered another round and asked Josie if Artemis was her forever home. She laughed at the term and said she didn't really think about life that way.

'I love the desert. I love West Texas. But I can't see myself being anywhere forever.'

Jack nodded, eyeing her carefully. 'You know how when someone gives you directions to their house, and you picture the trip in your mind? You imagine yourself heading down the road, turning left at the gas station and then driving past the library and turning right at the traffic light and so on. I used to try to think about my future that way, but it never took long for my map to end. I'd try to imagine myself five years from now, even a year out, and I couldn't see it.'

'Why do you think that is?'

He shrugged. 'Maybe the same reason you can't see yourself living in the same place forever. Some people grow up and move into the family home and never leave. Perfectly happy to live out life on the same plot of land their grandparents settled a hundred years before.'

'There's no plot on the East Coast your family's owned for generations?'

'Nah. We're all wanderers. That's why you shouldn't worry too much about Uncle Mike. He'll get the itch to move on in a few years.'

'And we'll get stuck with a dog track and animal rights protestors marching up and down Main Street.' Josie watched her phone vibrate against the table and saw it was Otto's number. He wasn't one to call off-duty without a good reason, so she picked up on the first ring. 'What's up?'

There was a pause on the line, and she wondered if he'd placed the call accidentally, but she heard a noise, heard him sniff and try to clear his throat, and her body filled with dread. She stood from the booth and walked outside into the night.

'Otto, what's going on? Is Delores OK?'

'Oh, God, Josie. It's bad.'

Josie leaned her back against the cinderblock building and braced herself.

'It's Marta. She's been shot.'

'What? Where are you?' she said, instantly disbelieving.

Otto took a ragged breath, and Josie started toward the parking lot before realizing she didn't have her car.

'I'm at the old fire house, behind the school. I just got here.'

'How bad is it?'

'She's dead, Josie. We're too late.'

'No, Otto.' She clenched her eyes shut to keep the tears back. 'What happened?'

'We don't know. She's on the floor in the basement. I'm with her now. I saw Marta's car and Philips's sheriff's car so I stopped in to check on them.' Otto broke down into sobs.

'I'm at the Legion. I'll be there in five minutes.' Josie had reached the table where Jack had stood from the seat as he watched her rush across the room. He dropped a couple of twenties on the table to cover dinner. He didn't speak, just nodded and pointed toward the door, understanding something terrible had happened.

Jack started his truck, and she could feel him staring at her.

She looked out of the window, focusing her anger like a hot ember to keep from falling apart. She would have to tell Marta's daughter, Teresa, a sophomore in college.

'Do you know where the high school is?' she asked.

'Sure.'

'Head that way.'

Jack pulled out, and Josie finally said, 'Marta Cruz, one of the other two officers in our department, was murdered tonight.'

'Josie, I'm so sorry. Do you have any details?'

'Otto just arrived. I don't know anything yet.'

Jack increased his speed down River Road, headed toward town while Josie called Sheriff Roy Martinez who had just heard the news from his deputy, Scott Philips, and was headed that way. Next, she called Ramos, her state police contact, who said he was already on the way. She wanted to be sure the key people were there from the various police agencies, the people she trusted most.

When she hung up, Jack said, 'I need to tell you something.'

She looked over at him, having almost forgotten about his presence.

'I had a meeting scheduled with Officer Cruz earlier today, but it was canceled. I just thought you should know that upfront.'

Josie felt her face grow hot. 'Why would you have had a meeting with Marta?'

'I was at the gas station yesterday and ran into her.'

'So you know Marta? You knew her well enough to just run into her at the gas station and set up a meeting?' Josie asked, feeling an unreasonable surge of anger that this man she'd just met had somehow inserted himself into a murder investigation.

'Hey, I'm just telling you what happened. I've been with you all evening. Don't start talking to me like I've done something wrong here.'

She raised a hand. 'I get it. I'm sorry. What happened at the gas station?'

'I was inside paying for gas and a few things, and she came up to me, asked if I was Mike's nephew. I said yes, and we talked a few minutes about the dog track. Just small talk.'

Josie noticed he'd slowed his driving speed as he was talking, and she pointed ahead of them. 'You need to hurry.'

He nodded and sped up. He looked nervous, a bead of sweat breaking out across his forehead. 'Anyway, she asked if I knew anything about the voting machines my uncle had been investigating for the voting commission. I said I knew he was on some oversight committee. He'd told me about the commission. I knew he was worried about the fiasco with the presidential race. This was his attempt to help put measures in place to make sure the machines were tamper-proof.'

Josie watched him talk and wondered suddenly if she'd made a terrible mistake.

'So Officer Cruz asked if I would meet her at the fire house this evening to show her what I knew about the machines.'

'What time were you supposed to meet her?'

'At seven. I told her I didn't know much, but that I'd be glad to meet her. Honestly, I thought it was odd that she'd ask me. I wondered why she hadn't asked my uncle. And then I figured she probably had, and he'd been an ass and told her no.'

Josie looked away from him, seeing the high school up ahead. She would have to go explain to the other officers that the man who had just dropped her off had a meeting scheduled with Marta at the fire house, at the time of her murder, but he had canceled and then taken Josie to dinner instead. It did not look good.

'Why did you cancel the meeting?' she asked.

'I didn't cancel it. I talked to Mike earlier today. I mentioned I had a meeting scheduled with a cop, with Officer Cruz, and he started giving me shit about it. He told me he was going to cancel the meeting. I said I would call her, but he said, no, he would do it. He said if she wanted to ask him questions, she should go to him directly. So that was the end of it.'

'Did he schedule a meeting with her?'

'I have no idea. I didn't talk to him after we spoke earlier today. He said he would cancel the meeting.'

'Why didn't you mention this to me earlier this evening?'

'Why would I? It was my uncle being his usual self. And, honestly, I understood. He didn't want me stepping into the middle of his campaign. I didn't really know anything or have anything I could offer to help. That's not why I'm here. Why get mixed up in something that wasn't any of my business? That's how I saw it.'

'So you never talked with Marta again after you talked to her at the gas station?'

'No.'

'Did anyone see you at the gas station with Marta? Did anyone see you talking to her?'

'What the hell? Why would you ask me that? You don't believe me?'

'Jack, this woman was shot at around the same time, in the same building, where you were scheduled to meet with her. You think these questions aren't going to come up?'

'I have no idea who saw me there. It was yesterday. I didn't pay any attention. Outside of you, I probably only know half a dozen people in town, so no one stands out.'

He pulled on to the access road that wrapped around behind the school to the fire house. A sheriff's deputy was putting up yellow tape across the parking-lot entrance and cordoning off the area. 'You can stop here,' she said.

'Josie, I'm sorry about your officer. Just let me know, OK? Let me know how things go?'

She nodded and got out of the truck, not trusting herself to respond.

The Artemis Community Building was still referred to by the residents in town as the old fire house. It had been used as a storm shelter for several decades and was one of the few city buildings with a basement. The ground floor had been used as a fire house, with the basement outfitted as a shelter with shelves lined with temporary provisions. Two years prior, the city received matching state funds to build a new fire house with an attached training facility, much needed in their rural area of the state. But bureaucracy had made transitioning to a community building a fight played out in the newspaper at least once a month. Defining what constitutes a community building had turned into a political debate that no one seemed capable of winning.

The thirty-by-forty-foot white pole barn had two large bays
for fire trucks, and one empty bay that had been used for
meetings, trainings and the area where the volunteer firemen
congregated while on duty. The folding tables and chairs that
the fire chief had used for meetings had remained in the
building and were occasionally used by groups who could
finagle the building from the county commissioners to use for
an event. This year would be the first year the building had
been outfitted as a polling place.

Two deputy cars were in the parking lot that lay to the
west of the building along with Otto's SUV. Marta's car was
parked directly in front of the building outside one of the
bay doors, along with the Ford F150 that belonged to
Texas Ranger Juan Ramos. Josie saw that a box of latex
gloves and another of plastic booties were sitting on the
concrete pad. She slipped the booties on and gloved up,
mentally realizing how hyper-alert she felt. She realized her
ability to process the scene would be handicapped, but she
would do everything in her power to hold it together for
Marta's sake.

Josie stepped underneath the yellow tape that had been
applied across the open garage bay and headed for the door
at the back of the room that led to the basement. She spotted
Ramos walking up from the basement in his Texas Rangers
cowboy hat. He waited for Josie to reach him.

'Josie, I'm so sorry to be here right now. This is a terrible
tragedy.' He pointed toward the parking lot. 'Philips radioed
to let me know you were here. Otto's downstairs. He's a mess.
I just want you to be prepared. It's not a good scene.'

She nodded once. 'Cause of death?'

'Gunshot. One to the heart. One to the head.'

Josie bit back an involuntary urge to cry out. 'Is Cowan on
the way?'

'He is.' Ramos glanced at his watch. 'He's maybe ten
minutes out. You sure you want to go through with this? No
one would blame you for not going down there.'

'You can't be serious,' she said, narrowing her eyes before
he raised his hands in surrender.

'That's fine. We'll scan the scene and then get you and

Otto out of there. I may need help getting him out. I already tried once.'

She followed Ramos down the concrete steps, barely lit by a forty-watt single bulb hanging from the ceiling. She said nothing yet about the meetings Marta had scheduled with Jack and Mike Striker, but Josie couldn't imagine why Marta would be in the basement. The voting machines were located upstairs.

The stairs were enclosed by concrete walls that opened into a room less than half the size of the room above. Josie saw Otto sitting on a folding chair in the corner of the room, bent over with his head in his hands. The sight of him clearly devastated almost brought her to her knees, and then she saw Marta lying on her back in a pool of her own blood, with a hole in the center of her head. Josie turned and pressed one hand to her mouth and the other to her gut, fighting to keep from vomiting on to the crime scene floor.

Ramos left her alone to compose herself, taking deep breaths, steeling herself to face a woman she cared deeply about, a woman with whom she'd joked hours before when she had walked into the office to collect her paycheck that afternoon, now lying dead on the floor.

Josie went to Otto first and kneeled down, placing a hand on his back.

'You doing OK?' She stopped talking when he lifted his head from his hands, his face red and swollen from tears.

'What kind of wretched animal tracks a woman to the basement of a building and shoots her in the head and in the heart? I want to be a part of sending this person to the death chamber. Just let me be.' Otto locked his eyes on Josie until she nodded and stood.

When she turned, she found Ramos watching them. 'I just talked to one of the best crime scene techs in the state. He's on his way. I need to have this room cleared out for him.' Ramos tilted his head back toward the stairs. 'Let me show you what we have.'

Josie followed him back to the stairwell, and they faced the room as if just entering. He pointed from right to left around the perimeter of the room. 'You can see the shelves are mostly full of boxes and tubs and canned goods. From what I've seen, most of the boxes are decades old. There's a box of rusty cans of green beans that expired over ten years ago. Cobwebs are thick.' He pointed to one of his deputies who turned and nodded at Josie. 'He's making his way around the room with the tape, marking off where the cobwebs remain intact, where the dust on the floor hasn't been disturbed.' He pointed to the area where they were standing, and the area where Otto was sitting. 'This area to the right of the stairs wasn't touched. There's a very small area that was disturbed.' He pointed to the floor, where Josie could see a line of tape clearly outlining an area that stretched about fifteen feet into the room. She could see an area roughly eight feet around Marta's body where footprints intermingled.

'At first glance, does it look like there was a scuffle between Marta and this other person?'

'Right now, all I've confirmed is two very clear sets of footprints in the dust. Either someone didn't care about getting caught or they were so caught up in the emotion of the moment that they didn't bother trying to clean up the area.'

'Or they were in a rush to avoid being caught. This took place during daylight hours,' she said.

Ramos nodded. 'You asked about first glance. It doesn't look like she was down here long. It looks as though she came down and walked a few feet into the room, almost like she was walking into the room and allowing space for someone else to have a conversation.'

'I can't imagine why she would have come down here. The last I heard, nothing has moved forward with the community building. It's still tied up in political blustering. So why come to this building and then down to a storm shelter that no one has stepped in for months?' Josie didn't wait for an answer. 'Are there cameras outside?' she asked.

'No, we've checked,' Ramos said.

'What about the high school?'

'They don't reach here,' Otto said. Josie and Ramos turned to face him. 'Some kids from the high school vandalized the building a few months ago. We had film footage from the high school that showed them walking out the back set of doors and heading this way, but the camera didn't reach beyond the last row of cars in their lot.'

Ramos nodded. 'OK. Let's head out. We don't need anything that could taint this investigation. From here on, you report directly to me. You aren't on the case, but obviously we'll keep you posted. We'll keep communication open. But you can't openly investigate. We're clear on that?'

Josie nodded agreement. As Otto followed Ramos up the steps, she turned back to face Marta, forcing herself to take in the body, her face, the uniform shirt saturated in blood. Josie knew it would be the last time she would be allowed on to the crime scene, and it pained her to leave her friend of fifteen years lying on the floor.

Ramos stood next to Otto with his arms crossed, his frown intensified by the lines cut deep into his forehead. 'Are you aware of any case Marta was working that would have brought her to this building?'

'I am,' Josie said.

Ramos pulled a small notepad and pen out of his shirt pocket.

'Mark Jackson came to the PD a while back requesting officers at all of the polling places in town. I lost my temper and basically told him it wasn't doable. Being the peace-maker, Marta talked to him after I left, and he told her that Senator Striker has been examining the new voting machines after they're installed. He shows up and tells people he's on some congressional oversight committee on voter fraud.'

Ramos stared hard at Josie. 'I get the oversight, but surely there's something to prohibit an elected official from touching those machines.'

'We thought the same. Marta was checking into it . . .' Josie caught the look from both Ramos and Otto that said, *And look what happened to her.*

'I discovered something else on my way here. I was at the Legion when Otto called – with Jack Striker, Mike Striker's nephew. I didn't have my duty car, so he drove me over. On the way here, he said he was supposed to have had a meeting with Marta this evening at seven, but his uncle canceled it.'

'Striker has family living here? I thought his family was from out east?' Ramos said.

'They are. His nephew came into town to help with the dog track. He's a geologist. He was brought in to survey the land.'

'You're dating him?' Ramos asked.

Her first inclination was to tell him it was none of his damned business. 'Just friends. I met him while he was doing some survey work out at Bobby Maiden's place.'

Ramos said nothing for a moment, just stared at Josie.

'Why would Striker's nephew have had a meeting with Marta?' Otto asked.

Josie explained Jack's story about running into Marta at the gas station, and how she had wanted to ask him questions about the voting machines at the polling places.

'Bullshit. Why wouldn't she have just gone to Striker?' Ramos said.

'That's why Jack claimed his uncle was angry. Jack claimed he didn't get into it with his uncle. He said he assumed Marta had asked to meet with the senator, and figured his uncle was being an ass and turned her down.'

'Why did Jack say the senator canceled the meeting?' Otto asked.

'Jack said he told his uncle about the meeting and the senator was pissed, wanted the meeting canceled. Jack said he would cancel the meeting, but his uncle told him no, that he would do it.'

'His uncle wouldn't allow him to cancel his own meeting?' Ramos said.

'Do you know the senator?' Josie said. 'He's a control nut. And Jack claims he didn't think much about it. He figured his uncle's campaign wasn't any of his business.'

'So he let his uncle cancel his meeting with Marta, and then he took the chief of police out for a drink at the Legion? You don't think that sounds a little bit hinky?'

Josie shrugged, forcing her face to remain passive. 'It's easy enough to check. File a warrant for phone records. We'll find out exactly who called who. We can check the timeline with the stories we get from the senator.'

Ramos nodded, but his expression was hard. 'There is no "we." I'll take over from here. This has been professional courtesy.'

Josie pulled back. 'What's with the tone? You asked me a question, and I answered it.'

'There's no tone. I just want to be clear where we stand. I understand you're going to want to be involved. I would, too, if one of my officers had been shot.'

'Not just shot, *murdered*,' said Otto.

Ramos ignored him. 'So I just want to be clear that after today our organization takes over the investigation.'

Otto turned and walked away. Josie wasn't sure if they were being overly sensitive or if Ramos was being an ass, but her phone was buzzing, and she saw it was Sauly calling. She excused herself and took the call.

'Josie. Somebody was just here.' Sauly half whispered the words, and she wondered if psychedelics were involved. She was angry and exhausted and not prepared to deal with Sauly.

'Where are you?'

'I'm at Jezebel's.'

The hair stood up on her arms. 'Who was there?'

'I don't know. I was sleeping outside, so I could take care of the dogs again in the morning. I saw someone with a light.'

Josie shut her eyes. She didn't have the patience to pull the information out of him piece by piece. 'Just tell me exactly what you saw as it happened.'

Sauly slowly spun out the details of watching the light swing across the yard, move to the kennel and then back out to the road where a pickup truck with its lights off pulled away.

'Was this person inside Jezebel's house?'

'I don't know. I noticed the light after I was lying down and couldn't sleep. My truck was parked behind the kennel, so whoever it was probably didn't know I was here.'

'Did you see the person at all? Get any details like height, size, whether it was a male or female?'

'No. All I really saw was the flashlight beam swinging back and forth.'

'OK, we'll be out shortly to take a look. Have you been inside the house?'

'No. You told me not to. I could go check things out now.'

'No, don't do that. If someone was in there, we want to check for fingerprints, check for signs of entry. We don't want your fingerprints getting mixed in.'

THIRTEEN

J osie needed a vehicle before she could drive to Jezebel's. Otto offered to take Josie back to the PD to pick up a pool car to drive home that night. She told Otto she would get one of the deputies to take her, but he declined, saying he would drop her off and then head to Sauly's. Josie was worried about him. He looked ready to drop from exhaustion, but she knew that he wasn't ready to leave. It felt as though they were giving up on Marta.

They said little on the drive to the police department. It felt to Josie that there was so much to be said that saying anything felt trivial. Nothing they could say on their drive into town would solve anything, so why speak?

Otto dropped her off and pulled away to get a head start at Sauly's. Josie entered through the front door with the intent to run upstairs to grab the keys to the old Jeep four-by-four that they used as an occasional off-road pool car. Her current worry was that the Jeep wouldn't start.

She shut the door behind her, but before she could turn on the lights, she noticed a strip of light coming from the back of the building and realized the back door was standing ajar. Her initial reaction was instant fury that the dispatcher hadn't locked the door, but then she remembered that Lou Hagerty, their day dispatcher, had worked seconds that day. With no third-shift dispatcher available, they had to lock the building down at ten thirty each night. Lou would never have left the building unsecured.

Josie pulled her weapon and stood silent, listening for movement, allowing her eyes to adjust to the dark. She knew the building like her own home: how many steps it took to reach the back door, where she needed to swerve to keep from hitting the intake desk that stuck out into the pathway to the back of the office. Rolling her steps, she walked without sound to the back of the office, clearing the room. The outside alleyway light illuminated the back door. As she approached, she noticed flakes of gold metal glinting in the light from the street and realized someone had drilled out the deadbolt. She kicked the doorway open further and stepped into the alley where she shone her flashlight up toward the camera across the alley that caught the back entrance to the PD. The camera had been shot out. All she could hope was that the shooter had walked up to the camera before shooting.

Josie called Otto and told him the office had been broken into. He ordered her to stay put until he arrived back. Back inside, the dispatcher's area appeared untouched, and the evidence-room door, which looked like a storage closet door, was still locked. Having cleared the downstairs, she flipped the second-story lights on. Hearing nothing, she made her way up the stairs and cleared the small rooms and storage areas before doing the same in their office. Once the lights were on, she stood in the center of the room, scanning for a sign that would tell her what the intruders had been after. Papers on the floor around the three desks made it clear someone had been in the office, but it wasn't the disaster she had been anticipating.

Otto called out for her, and she yelled down that the building was clear. Winded and red-faced, he walked into the office, looked at his desk and stumbled over to a chair at the conference table. He slumped into the chair and moaned.

Josie rushed to him, worrying he was having a heart attack. 'Should I call a medic?' she asked.

'No, it's not that. It's worse. I made a terrible mistake.' He motioned to his desk. 'Earlier, when I left this afternoon, I was tired and my knees hurt. I'd already carried one box of evidence down.'

Josie took a step back, already dreading where he was headed.

'There were two more evidence boxes that I left on my desk. They're gone.'

'What case?'

'Jezebel Black.'

'Otto, seriously? You should have had Lou carry them. That

evidence is now worthless. It's tampered with. Inadmissible in court.'

'I know that. I'm sorry.'

She saw the misery on his face, and she turned and walked away before she said what he already knew. If Jezebel Black's case was tied to Marta's murder, the investigation could have just been severely compromised. It was inexcusable.

When she turned back, Otto was bent over in the chair with his head in his hands. 'I'm too old for this, Josie. I can't do the job anymore. I'm tired. I'm slow. My judgment is clouded. You should fire me now and get it over with.'

'Stop. You're tired and made a terrible decision. It happens to everyone at some point.'

'But it can't happen during a murder investigation. It can't happen when you're investigating a fellow officer's murder.'

'It shouldn't happen, but it did. So we deal with it.' Josie took a pad of paper to the table and sat beside him, but he remained bent over, staring at the floor. 'Otto, I don't mean to sound uncaring, but I can't afford to have you lose it right now. Things are falling apart. Marta is gone. I cannot be the only officer in this department. I need you on top form. You get that, right?'

He sat up, looked at her with bleary eyes and nodded.

'While this is fresh in your memory, I need you to list everything you can think of that was in each of those evidence boxes. You're sure it was just two boxes?'

'I'm positive. Her laptop and the other box are in the evidence room. There were three boxes.'

'Had you gone through each box?' she asked.

Otto nodded.

'Then you itemize everything on this pad of paper in as much detail as possible.'

Josie left Otto to his task and walked downstairs to call Ramos to tell him what had happened.

FOURTEEN

After two hours' sleep, Josie woke at four a.m. and took off for Corpus Christi. She'd had to repeatedly redirect her thoughts throughout the drive to shove Ramos out of her head. She understood protocol required him to remove Otto and her from the investigation into Marta's murder, but while making it abundantly clear that he didn't want them working it, he'd also cut them out when they almost certainly had valuable information about her last day that they'd not explored. Ramos had done what she felt was a cursory interview with her about the cases Marta had been working, and then when Josie had said she wanted to be the person to inform Marta's daughter in Corpus, and Marta's ex-husband in Mexico, Ramos had readily agreed and basically sent her on her way.

It bothered her because Ramos was one of the most thorough investigators she knew. It made her wonder if he already had information that pointed toward a known suspect, or, worse yet, if he had learned that Josie was dating a possible suspect and was going to approach the investigation with the PD shut out. Either way, he had escorted both her and Otto off the property once the crime scene tech had arrived. And then she'd had to make the call that the police department had been robbed of evidence in a case that could be linked to Marta's murder. Ramos lectured her as though she were a rookie cop incapable of running her own department. Her face had burned red with humiliation. Packing her bag that morning was one of the darkest moments in memory. Her friend and coworker had been murdered on Josie's watch, and she had basically been relegated to desk duty.

The meeting with Teresa was as heartbreaking as Josie could have imagined. She had made the eight-hour trip to Texas A&M in Corpus Christi and stopped first to talk to the campus police. One of their officers had helped Josie track down a counselor on campus who sat beside Teresa while Josie made the death notification. Josie provided the few details that she had, but Teresa was in such a state of shock that she was barely able to ask questions. Josie knew part of the reason Teresa had traveled so far to go to school was to avoid the difficult relationship she had with her mother. Now she faced the horror that she would never find the peace that both mother and daughter had wanted but couldn't figure out how to achieve.

As the school-aged daughter of a small-town cop, Teresa had known her actions were under constant scrutiny. To some of the town's adults, there was nothing more satisfying than catching a cop's kid doing something, *anything*, that could pass for bad behavior. Marta had preached this message until Teresa went from feeling unfairly judged to deciding that if her mother was going to treat her like a wild child, then she was going to get the benefits of the parties associated with it. By her freshman year of high school, Teresa drank, smoked and cussed with the best of them. At sixteen, she had used her babysitting money to bail her twenty-one-year-old drug-dealer boyfriend from jail. Marta had screamed and cried and told Teresa how she had brought shame to their family. In response, Teresa had run away, hitchhiking her way into Mexico to stay with her alcoholic father.

Between the bitter divorce years earlier and the judgment Teresa felt from her mother, her high school years had been rough. Josie wondered if the recent work toward repairing their relationship would end up being a comfort for Teresa or would make the realization that she had lost any further chance at reconciliation even harder to accept. When Josie left Teresa's apartment, her two roommates and the counselor had been with her. It was a good start, but Josie knew from experience that the night-time hours were the roughest, when the guilt and shame of the daylight hours forced their way to the surface with no one to help rationalize away the bad deeds.

Almost as rough as the night-time hours was the eight-hour solo drive home. The first two hours of the trip, from Corpus Christ to San Antonio, were a break from the West

Texas desert; she passed sprawling herds of grass-fed beef, and farms growing cotton and corn and peanuts. But the three-hundred-mile stretch of Interstate 10 provided hours to think about Marta, to spin theories on who would want such a good-hearted, unassuming woman dead. Josie imagined vengeance killings from criminals recently released, her unstable ex-husband, a man she had dated for a short time several years ago who had turned into a stalker for a few weeks, but with each new idea, her reasoning always returned to the person who seemed to gain the most from Marta's death: Mike Striker. And that thought inevitably led her to Jack Striker.

As she hit the halfway mark on the drive home, Josie received word from dispatcher Lou Hagerty that one of Ramos's team had retrieved all of Marta's case files. The tough-talking Lou was in tears as she described the state troopers hauling out Marta's possessions in boxes.

'You don't even want to walk into your office,' Lou had said. 'You know how neat Marta always kept her desk. It's a mess now. Papers and folders scattered across her desk where they dug through files. I'll get it cleaned up before Otto comes in. He's not doing well. He's angry one minute and close to tears the next. Then they grilled me on the break-in. They made it sound like it was my fault they got in. A bunch of bullshit. Questioning *us* like we're the crooks.'

'What are you talking about?' Josie asked.

'How I locked the building up the night of the break-in. If we have standard protocol for locking up each night. Which, of course, I told them we do. Then I had to show them our written procedures for locking up evidence. They went down in our evidence locker and were looking around. It just pissed me off. I said we always lock up our evidence. The guy says, "Obviously, you don't since two boxes were stolen." I wanted to throat-punch him.'

'You know how this works,' Josie said. 'They aren't going to treat us any different. Just get a tough skin, be professional and answer everything as honestly as you can. Even if it looks bad. Better to be truthful than have to explain a lie later on.'

'Who would have done this?' she asked.

'I don't know, Lou. Obviously, Jezebel was mixed up in something more complicated than raising greyhounds.'

Josie spent most of her drive on the phone, following up on details. She called Ramos twice to check in, and finally left a voice message for him to be sure and check Marta's case notes for any reference to voter machine tampering. If she had actually stumbled upon proof of tampering, then Striker might have been desperate enough to kill her, to save him not only from losing the race but from then losing his chance to build the dog track. Money and power were the two obvious motivators for murder, and Striker was looking at both. She suspected Jezebel Black had been a part of that scheme as well.

At eight o'clock, Josie pulled into a gas station and received a third call from Jack. He'd left messages asking her to pick up, to let him know something. She stared at his name on her phone and, against her better judgment, answered.

'Hey, sorry I haven't called,' she said. 'It's just been busy.'

'No, I get it. You don't need to apologize. I'm sorry for hounding you, but I just need to hear your voice. To know you don't think I'm caught up in some terrible plot against your officer.'

'Why would you say that?'

'Because a state trooper came to the motel earlier this evening and grilled me for almost an hour. He's obsessed with the fact that I didn't meet with your officer but took you out to dinner instead. I don't get why that's such an issue. It's a small town. You're one of the few people I know. We went out for a bite to eat. And somehow that connects me to a woman's murder?'

'Who interviewed you?'

'A Texas Ranger. Had a cowboy hat on.'

'Juan Ramos?'

'That's it.'

'You do understand that he thinks you used me as an alibi? That you set things up so your uncle or someone associated with the mayor's race or with the dog track would have access to Marta, while you made it look to the police like the meeting was canceled.'

'What are you even talking about? That is crazy!'

'It's crazy to you. But from a police officer's viewpoint, from someone who doesn't know you, it makes pretty good sense. You set up a meeting to get Marta to meet you at a remote location with no cameras.'

He cut her off. 'I didn't set up the meeting! She saw me at a gas station and asked if I would meet her. None of this was my idea.'

'Hang on. Unless new information has come up, there's no proof that Marta set the meeting up and not you.' He started to interrupt, but Josie cut him off. 'Just hear me out. Once you had it organized, your uncle conveniently removed you from the meeting and you then arranged to meet me for an airtight alibi. I'm not saying that's what I think happened. I'm trying to help you understand why the police are interviewing you.'

'My God, Josie, it doesn't make sense at all.'

'Here's one of the issues the police are struggling with. There is nothing that connects you to setting that meeting up with Marta. You say she arranged it at the gas station. And there is nothing that connects you to canceling the meeting. You say your uncle did that. There is nothing that actually connects you to Marta, and yet you are supposedly the reason she was at the fire house, by herself, at that time of night, when she was murdered.'

'That's why it doesn't make sense to see me as a suspect! If I wasn't connected but I was guilty, then why would I have even told you this? I told you about the meeting to be transparent, to help!'

Josie paused, giving Jack time to think through the facts that she had dwelled on all the way across Interstate 10. 'So the only person actually connected to Marta through phone records is who?'

'My uncle.'

'Which basically makes you—'

'His alibi. Shit.'

'I'm sure the way Ramos sees it, Mike wanted to talk to Marta about what she knew about the machines, but he didn't want any record of meeting with her. So he has you concocting this big story about meeting with her and canceling it. It gets Mike off the hook in case Marta had something in her calendar about meeting with him at the fire house. So, yes, you are basically your uncle's alibi.'

'You can't believe any of that is true. You know my uncle and you know me. This is all crazy. We're not murderers.'

Josie started to tell him that those were the same words that every murderer said when accused by the police.

'It would be much easier to disbelieve that theory if there was some other reason Marta would have been at the firehouse.'

'How do you know she didn't show up to look at the machines on her own? Maybe Mike canceled the meeting, and she decided to go on to the fire house anyway. To check out the machines on her own.'

'I don't know. It doesn't make sense to me. I could go stare at a voting machine, but I'd have no idea what I was looking at. And definitely no idea how to find out if it had been tampered with.'

'Just let me come by tomorrow after work to talk in person. I need to see you. I need you to see me, to stop thinking about me like a criminal in your investigation.'

Josie arrived home at just after one in the morning, ready to drop into bed in time for a seven o'clock alarm. Stripping her clothes off as she walked down the hallway, she stopped short when she reached her bedroom, the hairs on her arms rising. Her hairdryer lay in a pile on her neatly made bed. She slipped her shirt back on and lifted her foot up to retrieve the sidearm out of her ankle holster.

She entered the bedroom and quickly walked around the perimeter, through the bathroom, and then swept the rest of the house until she was satisfied she was alone in her home. She checked the digital monitoring pad beside her front door to make sure there had been no entrance or exit attempts since she left that morning. The system was clean. There was no need to check the video file. The camera had malfunctioned six months prior; she'd meant to replace it but had been lulled into a false sense of security. The alarm system

on her windows and doors was state-of-the-art – at least,
five years ago it had been – and the police department had
been running along with no major issues, so she had let her
guard down.

She walked back into her bedroom and leaned against the
wall, staring at the hairdryer. Josie was not a fanatic when it
came to a clean house. If she missed a week with the vacuum
or a dust rag, she'd get it the next. But there were certain
routines she followed without fail, more out of habit and
efficiency than anything else. One of them was her shower
routine. After she showered, she dried off and twisted her
hair up, dressed, applied moisturizer and mascara, brushed
her teeth and blow-dried her hair. This all took place in her
bathroom. A basket that she stored under the sink held all of
her hair supplies. She pulled it out each morning, dried her
hair, stuffed the hairdryer, brush and hair product back in the
basket and replaced it under the sink. Every time she took a
shower, she followed the same routine. Other than to pack
her hairdryer for a trip, she could never remember a time
when she'd taken it out of the bathroom and placed it on the
bed. There was no need. It made no sense.

Someone had come into her home; she was sure of it.
Someone was messing with her, but for what purpose? She
considered packing a bag and booking a room at Manny's
Motel, but it seemed absurd. Not to mention, Jack was staying
there. She was having a panic attack over a missing dog collar
and an out-of-place hairdryer, which on some level felt even
more sinister than if someone had broken into her home and
trashed it.

Josie went to the control panel for the security system and
reset the fingerprint reader to use her thumbprint. As she went
through the steps, she wondered again about Nick and his
jacket, which someone had left on her front door. He was the
only other person she could think of with the knowledge and
skill to break into her security system without detection, but
she couldn't imagine him being a part of this psychological
harassment. One of the traits she had most appreciated about
him was his straightforward approach to life. If he had a
question, he asked it. If he wanted to talk to her, he'd pick

the phone up or drop by. But if it wasn't Nick, who stole his jacket and why leave it with her?

After a fitful night's sleep, Josie met Otto at the sheriff's department for an eight a.m. debriefing with Ramos. After thirty minutes of listening to him hint at information while offering nothing, she and Otto walked out together, frustrated at the lack of progress.

They stood next to her car in the parking lot. 'You're still intent on making the trip to Mexico today?' he asked.

'I am. You remember Marta's friend, Sergio Pando? He's meeting me. I won't be driving around town alone.'

'It's still not safe.'

Josie was anxious to get on the road, but she saw the worry in Otto's eyes. 'You have time for a cup of coffee before I take off?' she said.

'Hot Tamale?'

'I'll meet you there.'

Josie parked her car in front of the police department and was ready to follow Otto across the street to the diner when Mayor Simon O'Kane stepped out of the city office and called her name. He was dressed in his daily mayoral attire: fitted pants and a button-down shirt, the collar loose, no tie. O'Kane was born in Northern Ireland and grew up in the 1980s during the Troubles, when car bombings and hate crimes were part of the daily fare. Josie enjoyed his European view of West Texas, and his hipsterish sense of style, minus the highbrow attitude. She could tell by the tilt of his head and the sympathetic frown that he was coming to offer condolences. He put his hand out and she took it, and then leaned in for a long, heartfelt hug. O'Kane was a good man, and she believed they both wished there was the necessary physical attraction between them, but as much as they'd tried, it just wasn't there.

'Josie, I am so sorry about Marta. I had intended to come see you yesterday, but things in the office fell apart.'

'Thank you. I appreciate that.'

He pulled back but kept her at arm's length. 'How's the investigation? I talked with Ranger Ramos this morning, but he didn't offer much in terms of details.'

'I've just left a meeting with him. He's playing this very much by the book. I doubt he's shared any more with Otto and me than he did you.'

'What's your gut telling you? Was it local? Do you think it had anything to do with this crazy mayoral race?'

'I hate to admit this, but I don't know yet. Marta had concerns about the race, but murder?' Josie felt her face flush as she said the word, still finding it hard to believe.

'Do you need security?'

'For me? Because of Marta?' She looked at him in surprise, realizing he was serious. 'No. I'm fine. We need officers investigating, not babysitting.'

He glanced away and looked uncomfortable with her answer. 'Yes, right. I suppose I wondered for myself as well. Obviously, I don't need a security detail, but I can't help wondering how heated this mayor's race is going to get? Surely, I'm not in danger from whoever shot Marta, am I?'

Josie felt a twinge of guilt that she'd not considered the question herself. 'No, I've not heard anything that makes me think you're in danger. The rumors are around Senator Striker keeping himself out of trouble.'

O'Kane changed topics and asked Josie to keep him informed of the progress on both Marta's and Jezebel's cases and headed back to his office.

Inside the Hot Tamale and seated at the booth by the plate-glass window, Lucy brought Josie and Otto cups of steaming hot coffee and teared up as she told them how sorry she was about Marta's death. Both Josie and Otto had eaten breakfast, but she paid no attention. She promised a breakfast like no other, and Josie settled into the fact that she would not be leaving for Mexico any time soon.

'It's kind of you to make this trip, but no one would expect you to drive across the border to make this notification. They haven't been married for years,' Otto said.

'Don't think so highly of me. It's not a sympathy call. I'm going for information. You know Marta still loved Javier; even after her family forbade her from seeing him, she still made the trip several times a year to bail him out. She gave him money when he needed it. When his alcoholic antics became too erratic, she'd go spend a day or two to help him sober up.'

Otto shook his head. 'I didn't realize that. She was supporting him?'

'Helping out when things got bad. Which was frequently.'

'I wouldn't call that helping out. Don't the AA people call that "enabling"?'

'I think she saw past the alcohol to what he could have been. His father was a curandero; supposedly, Javier had the same ability, but the alcohol kept him from using it.'

'A witch doctor?' Otto asked.

'You have such a way with words. He was in touch with the spirit world. They heal with herbs and potions.'

'You want to hunt down a witch doctor to tell him his ex-wife was murdered. You don't always use good sense. I am sure that Sergio would tell this man what happened to Marta.'

'I just want to touch base. I know Marta made a recent trip. Maybe Javier knew something that was going on in her life that was causing her problems. Marta kept to herself. I don't want to assume all this is about the mayor's race and miss something unrelated.'

Otto nodded and grew quiet for a while. 'What do you think her family will do about the funeral?'

'I'm sure her parents will want her buried in Mexico City. She once mentioned a family cemetery where her whole family has plots already arranged for them.'

Lucy came to the table with a tray filled with plates of traditional Mexican breakfast foods.

'Chilaquiles with avocados and refried beans.' Lucy twirled her finger around over the plate of deep-fried tortillas that had been soaked in a red sauce, and finished with dollops of cream, cheese and sliced onions, with a fried egg on top. 'Soggy for Otto. Crunchy for Josie.'

She placed cups of sweet creamy café con leche in front of them and then plates of French toast with bowls of warm syrup to the side for dessert.

'Lucy, you are a saint,' Otto said.

She placed her hand on her heart and teared up again as she walked away.

After trying all the dishes, Otto sat back to rest a moment and sip his coffee. 'You have a feel for where this is headed?' Otto asked.

'I feel confident that Jezebel's murder is connected to Mike Striker. But Marta? I just can't figure it, unless she had found something damning that Mike needed to cover up.'

'If Marta had learned something about the senator, I think she would have called you before meeting with him on her own.' Otto pointed at Josie as if he'd just remembered something. 'Also, here's something that occurred to me this morning. In that meeting with Ramos, he said he's got a source with the Rangers checking into the MDFT thing.'

'Mobile device forensic tools.'

'Yes, to break into phones. But he said it could take months to actually access her phone.'

'That would be my guess. She had an iPhone, and she had the passcode set. Ramos said they've already checked with her daughter and mother to see if they might have known her passcode, but no luck.'

'That's the thing that's bugging me,' he said. 'Do you remember sitting around the staff Christmas dinner at our house last year, and there was a conversation about getting old? About trying to remember all the passwords we have?'

Josie shrugged. 'Vaguely.'

'I remember it well. I remember Marta making a comment about her daughter creating some Google document so Marta could save all her passwords and her daughter could help her find them when she lost them. I remember this specifically because I thought it was a great idea. I even told my daughter about it. Mina said she'd do the same thing for Delores and me. Of course, it never happened, and I still can't remember how to log in to half the TV and internet garbage we have.'

Josie nodded. 'I do remember that now. I remember being glad that it sounded like Marta and her daughter were talking again. I'll call Teresa about the password.'

'Good. I have something else for you, too. I wasn't ready

to share this with Ramos yet. You remember I said I talked to Carla Striker, the senator's wife?'

'Yeah, what was that about?' she said.

Otto leaned back in his seat and grinned. 'You will enjoy this one.' Otto shared the information about Carla tracking her husband's moves using Facebook. How she not only had dates and times of Striker meeting with two different mistresses, but also the dates and times that he had visited every polling place in Arroyo County.

'Show me how this works,' she said, finding it hard to believe that it was that easy to track someone.

'Open up your Facebook account.'

'I don't have one.'

Otto rolled his eyes and opened his phone.

'You have Facebook?' she asked, grinning.

'Don't be a smart ass. Delores put it on my phone so I could see pictures of Mina and the grandkids.' He poked around his phone, stopping to sop up some syrup with his French toast. 'Look at this.' He passed his phone to Josie. 'Carla showed me this, and I haven't turned it off yet because I wanted to see how accurate it is. It's dead on. You can see when I left the house this morning, what time we arrived at the sheriff's department for the meeting. You can see the day that Marta died, and what time I arrived at the old fire house.'

Josie scrolled through several weeks of data, shaking her head. 'We don't need the government to watch people. We have Facebook. How did Carla get the information off Striker's phone?'

'They share the same Facebook account, just like a lot of couples. Carla turned the location tracker off her phone. Mike doesn't even know it's on his phone. When she pulls up the app and looks for location, she sees everywhere he goes, every day.'

'Shit. Every police department in America ought to use this,' she said, laughing. 'We come unglued about the NSA gathering information, but we let a private company, which makes a profit off us, follow our every move. It's a crazy world.'

'While you were in Corpus yesterday, I followed up on this. I got the schedule from Mark Jackson on when each machine was installed in each polling place. It's all taken place over the past two weeks, getting them ready for the election. Striker didn't visit the location when they were installed. He waited a day or two each time and then visited.'

'What's the purpose of that?'

'I think he wants the poll workers long gone. No doubt, they would have questioned how an elected official could be involved in a voting oversight committee. Think where the polling stations are: schools, churches, community centers. So, he goes back to a school two days after the machines are installed and says he's there as part of the federal oversight commission and needs to check where each machine is installed and so on. He talks to a busy school secretary with a puking kid and an angry parent in her office, with the principal needing school records and child welfare on the phone. She says, "Sure, the machines are in the gym on the stage. Go on back.""

Josie nodded along with the scenario. 'And the priest at the church welcomes him inside, saying, "Sure thing, Senator Striker, I'll show you where everything is located. Take your time.""

'I talked to Jim Baker who runs the daycare center. I asked him if Striker had come in to examine the machines. He said yeah, the senator had come in the week before to check the machines out. He walked around the daycare and told them all what a great job they were doing. The senator said his office had some grant money he could get sent their way. I asked Jim if he thought that was acceptable practice, and here's what he said. "He's a senator. What do I know? I figure he knows what he's doing more than I do. And if he wants to give our kids money for new playground equipment, then I'm all for it.""

'Striker knows what he's doing all right,' she said.

'The positive is that Carla gave me a printout with dates and times where Mike has indeed visited every single polling place in the county,' said Otto.

'Why is she sharing this with you? She's not worried this

may come back to bite her? That her husband is going to find out and head straight for divorce court?'

'She's counting on it. But she wants to be the one filing. She also showed me how she tracked his movements to two different females' homes. Then she took pictures of Mike, in the act, with the two females. I think she's counting on the bank accounts reverting to her if he's in jail.'

'I don't know if it works that way.'

Otto ate the final bite of French toast and shoved the plate away from him. 'The money isn't her motivation. She wants to see Mike get what he deserves.'

'Good for her. I'm happy to help.' Josie sipped at her coffee and finally said what she'd been avoiding. 'What about Jack? He's Carla's nephew. Did she say if he's involved in all this?'

'The gist of it was that Jack's mom raised him well. Carla doesn't like Jack's mom, but she conceded that Mike's first wife did a good job raising her son. He has a conscience. However, she also said that he's still a Striker, so who knows.'

'Damn it. I blame you for this,' Josie said.

'Blame me for what?'

'You and Dell, always on me to get out into the world, date, meet people. Look what happens when I do. It turns to shit.'

'You have to meet the right kind of people, Josie.'

'And how do I do that in a town this size?'

'Maybe you should try online dating,' he said.

Josie stood. 'That's it. I gotta get on the road.'

Otto grinned and patted the table. 'All right. I'll leave you be. Sit back down a second. Next steps. While you're in Mexico today, what's our focus here?'

She sat down. 'Continue to concentrate on the connection between the two murders. Mike Striker.'

'I think he's a snake as much as you do, but I'm not totally sold on that connection.'

'He was Jezebel's boss, and then Marta was supposed to meet with him the day she died?'

'He was Jezebel's boss, but that was in terms of raising greyhounds, not necessarily the election.'

'Jezebel didn't make a quarter of a million dollars raising greyhounds.'

'True enough.'

'Striker wants to win the election to get that track built and make his fortune.'

'It's a bit of a leap to say that just because Striker wants to make money on pari-mutuel betting that Jezebel made a pot of money just by associating with him.'

'When you searched her house, did you see anything to indicate she was working with someone else to make that kind of money?'

'Just the flyers showing land for sale in Florida,' Otto said. 'But that looked more like she was going to spend money than make it.'

'See what you can find in terms of her savings account and the Florida land. And see if you can get an interview with Mike Striker, talk to him about Jezebel's business connections. Maybe you'll have better luck.'

'Got it.'

'One more thing. I keep thinking about the scrap of paper I found in Jezebel's pocket. That paper had Kip Esposito's name and number on it. Can you call him, and check in with Mark Jackson again on what he's hearing on the election?'

Josie stood again, but Otto reached out a hand to stop her. 'Listen, we need to talk about the missing evidence. What I did was—'

'Was a mistake,' she said. 'Don't plan on using this as some excuse to step out on me. I can't lose both my officers.' She patted Otto on the back. 'I'll text you later and let you know how things go tonight with Javier.'

FIFTEEN

Otto paid for their breakfast, both of them having long forgotten whose turn it was to buy. Sometimes he took a turn or two, sometimes she did, but neither of them worried the other would take advantage. Even though he wasn't capable of telling her, he was certain she knew how much he appreciated her as a friend and as a boss. He had a great deal of pride in the work that their small three-person department did, and it was hard to imagine moving forward without Marta.

Outside the restaurant, Otto tipped his head back to the blue sky and sighed as a warm breeze passed over his face. He closed his eyes and had the surreal feeling that he was standing in the village in which he grew up in Poland. A balmy breeze passed over him, carrying the scent of grazing red cows and green pastures on hillsides that stretched into mountains up into the clouds. What a life he'd had growing up: simple and serene. He thought about his daughter and her marriage drama, and grandkids struggling with all manner of troubles at school, and he wondered if his childhood was as uncomplicated as he remembered it. Their life had revolved around the small village, where everyone knew everyone else's every move; he and Delores couldn't wait to move away, but now they shared stories about their idyllic youth.

Otto opened his eyes and saw the grocer across the street standing in the window staring over at him. Otto waved, and the grocer waved back and then wandered away to his duties, apparently satisfied that the cop across the street wasn't losing his mind. Otto didn't think he was losing his mind, but the melancholy he'd been feeling of late was growing. He missed his parents, dead now going on ten years, and he knew that a trip back to his hometown wouldn't solve anything; it would

most certainly disappoint. He imagined that Poland was experiencing the same troubles as the US, but it was nice to think
there were still a few places in the world where grassy meadows
and kind neighbors were the norm.

He decided to extend his reverie and walk down to the
hardware store where Mark Jackson worked. The store was
part of a small chain that stretched across the west, charging
exorbitant prices so people could 'do it yourself' and spend
as much on the required tools to do an odd job as they would
have if they'd hired a professional.

The bell jangled on the door as Otto entered. Seeing no
employees or other customers, he wandered through the
aisles until he finally found Mark through a set of swinging
doors in the back of the store, staring down at a roll of screen
and a screen-door frame lying on a long table. He looked up
at Otto, glassy-eyed, as if he'd been standing and staring
for a very long time.

'Everything all right?' Otto asked.

Mark ran both hands over his face as if trying to wake
himself up. 'I'm sorry. What can I help you with?'

'Maybe you ought to sit down a minute,' Otto said.

Mark looked uneasy, as if knowing he should be working
rather than sitting on the job, but then sat down in the folding
metal chair next to him. 'I'm sorry. I haven't been myself
lately.'

'No worries. I was hoping to talk a minute. I can come back
another time if you'd rather.'

'It's fine. I'm fine. Just tired, that's all.'

'I was hoping to touch base with you about the election.'

Mark said nothing.

'I believe Marta had told you that we'd be taking up positions
at the polling places. Obviously, everything has changed. I'm
just wondering what your thoughts are in light of Marta's
death. I know you had concerns about the election before. I'm
wondering what you're thinking now.'

Otto watched in shock as Mark said nothing but allowed
tears to stream down his face. His arms hung limp at his sides,
as if the act of raising them to wipe away the tears took a
strength far greater than what he could muster. Otto stood and

found a bathroom; he brought back a pile of paper towels and laid them in front of Mark.

Perplexed, he sat across from Mark and asked, 'Were you close to Marta?'

Mark choked back a sob and covered his face with one of the paper towels, crying silently into it for some time as Otto looked away in embarrassment.

After several minutes, Mark apologized again, speaking softly. 'After my wife died, I thought I would remain single for the rest of my life. I couldn't imagine ever feeling joy again. And then Marta and I connected, and it was like someone turned the light back on. Not only was I happy but I was excited about life. I was excited to see Marta. Seeing her on the street, coming out of the police department and getting into her car? She made me feel something again.' Mark pushed his fingers into the corners of his eyes, clearly frustrated with his show of emotion. 'We weren't necessarily close, but I liked her a great deal. We had made arrangements to go out for dinner. We had plans to go to the music festival in Marfa this weekend.'

'I'm glad to hear she was looking forward to a date with you. Marta was a good person. She deserved happiness but spent too much time worrying about her family and everyone else. She'd not told me about this weekend, but I had noticed she seemed happier of late.'

Mark nodded, staring down at his hands lying in his lap.

'I'm so sorry to ask you questions right now,' Otto said.

'No, please, anything I can do.'

'Do you know how she was involved in the corruption end of the election? I know she talked to you about election tampering, and I know she was looking into Senator Striker. We're just trying to understand what she could have found that could have led to her death.' Otto put his hands up when Mark looked up at him in surprise. 'We're just investigating it as one of several possibilities. Her death could be totally unrelated to the election.'

'I feel so terrible about it. Responsible even. She had asked me, "If you believe there is corruption in this election, then how do you plan to prove it before the election?" And I had told her, "That's where you come in." We were working on a way for her, or the police, to be able to download the software from one of the machines. We were just talking about it, but we'd not figured out a way to make it happen. We assumed she would need a warrant for such a thing, but I don't know where she was in the process.'

'Why didn't you tell us this before?' Otto asked.

'I assumed Chief Gray knew she was looking into it.'

'Could Marta have gone to the fire house thinking she was going to download software?'

'I don't know. It's all I can think about. That I encouraged her to do something that caused her death. I picture her lying on the floor in that basement, and I can't help thinking that it's all my fault.'

Thoroughly depressed, Otto walked back to the office and up the stairs, wincing at the pain in his knees with each step. He sat at his desk and stared at the list of evidence he had itemized from the two stolen boxes. Sheriff Martinez had investigated the burglary and had spared him the humiliation of a lecture on proper police protocol, but Ramos had cut him no slack. When Ramos found out about the break-in, he had come by the department to dress Otto down in person. Otto took the beating because everything the man said was true. It had indeed been irresponsible and unforgivable, given the stakes of the investigation. But when Ramos stomped off, Otto had clocked out early and sat in his police car where he unpinned his badge and held it in his hand for a very long time. It wasn't until a chance text from Delores showed up on his phone, asking him to stop for laundry detergent on his way home that night, that he finally pulled away.

Otto picked up the manila folder with the list of missing evidence and shoved it in his bottom desk drawer and noticed the sticky note that read, *Dugout*.

Otto found Dugout at the ball field coaching a T-ball team. A scattering of five- and six-year-olds were taking their turns walking up to the base and swinging a plastic bat at a ball perched on what looked like a large golf tee. Otto watched Dugout stop the pitcher and adjust a little boy's hat so he could see out from underneath the rim of his plastic ballcap. Dugout finally noticed Otto standing on the sideline and ambled over, smiling and waving. He'd always reminded Otto of Mr Haney on *Green Acres*: a goofy conman who owned half a dozen crooked businesses, with none of them profitable enough to pay his bills. Dugout could have worked half as hard in life if he'd just gotten one legitimate job through the years.

'How's it going, Officer Podowski? I bet you came to volunteer your time as a batting coach.'

'Ah, no, my coaching days are long over. Those little kids would run circles around me.'

'They run circles around each other!' Dugout pointed to the team bench and both men sat. 'What can I do for you?'

'I'm here about a Facebook group you're a member of.'

Dugout looked surprised. 'Oh, yeah? Which one?'

'It's called Citizens Against Animal Cruelty.'

'Oh, yeah. That's a good one. They want to put an end to this stupid racetrack. No way you support that dog track, right?'

'What's your complaint with the racetrack?'

'You can't be serious. I mean, what's not to complain about? When has betting ever helped anyone? Not to mention, we're going to put a track in and make those poor beautiful dogs run around it in this crazy heat?' Dugout had been keeping an eye on his batters but turned to study Otto for a moment, then pointed at his head. 'See! Look at that sweat on your head. And it's only the end of April! Imagine those poor dogs running that track when it's a hundred and ten degrees outside. It's criminal.'

'What's your complaint about Jezebel Black?'

'Who?' Dugout looked confused.

'The woman you called an animal killer on her Facebook page.'

Dugout swatted his hand through the air. 'We're just making a point. That's all. Trying to get people to wake up. To think about how bad this is for our town before we elect the man that's going to build it.'

'Jezebel was a breeder. She wasn't racing the dogs. Why talk so bad about her?'

'They're all out to make a profit off those poor dogs. They deserve a better life, is all. I mean, it's terrible what happened to her, but still. She brought all this on herself working with a guy like Striker.'

'What's that supposed to mean?'

'I'm just saying, she made her bed so now she's got to lie in it.'

'So you think someone spray-painting "animal hater" all over the side of her house was the right thing to do? Stealing her dogs, probably terrorizing those dogs in the process – that was OK? Making her fear for her life because she was trying to earn some money in an honest way, by raising dogs? Then someone kills her and dumps her body off the side of a canyon to rot. And you think she brought that on herself?'

Dugout looked worried, afraid he'd said the wrong thing to the wrong person. 'Now, listen, I didn't have anything to do with that kennel getting vandalized. And especially nothing to do with her being killed. I just don't want that racetrack. People not standing up for what's right is what's wrong with the world right now. It's why we have criminals in office.'

'And you just happen to be the one who knows for certain what's right for everyone else?' Otto said.

'I know for certain that dog track is a bad idea. I can tell you that.'

'You know anything about Ms Black's dogs that were stolen? I've been hearing rumors that it was someone from your group, the Citizens Against Animal Cruelty, that took the dogs.'

Dugout turned to study Otto. 'How come you're here giving me all this crap? I didn't do anything wrong. Getting on somebody's Facebook page isn't a crime.'

'True enough. But vandalizing her house and stealing her dogs is. Committing murder is.'

'What the hell? We just want the racetrack to go away. I just post, not all this other stuff you're talking about.'

Otto noticed Dugout's words trailed off and he averted his eyes as he mentioned the 'other stuff.'

'What would help clear your name is if you'd provide me a list of the people who are in your Facebook group.' Dugout started to protest, and Otto put a hand up to stop him. 'I know they have usernames, but I'm also sure that you know some of those people from around town. You get me a list of the usernames and their identities, and we'll be squared away.'

Dugout looked at Otto as if he'd been conned, but he agreed to make the list.

Otto stood and put a hand on Dugout's shoulder. 'I'll be seeing you.'

Along the 1,200-mile border between Texas and Mexico are twenty-eight international bridges and border crossings. Just thirty minutes from Artemis, and on the other side of Presidio, lies the Presidio–Ojinaga International Bridge, a two-lane, with the plans to expand it to four lanes having been stalled for years. She had discovered one constant during her time living on the border: progress was slow.

Josie had seen very little change in the Mexico Travel Advisory from the US Department of State over the past decade. US citizens were still asked to reconsider travel to Chihuahua, the Mexican state bordering West Texas. Crimes and kidnapping, with most brought on by the drug cartels, were still listed as significant, even during daylight hours. Serving as a police officer in an area often controlled by warring drug cartels was a dangerous business. Over the past year, the state police commander in Ojinaga had been gunned down and his truck set afire, and the man who had been running for mayor was still missing after disappearing six months prior.

Sergio Pando was Josie's closest police connection and friend living in Mexico. Still living in Ojinaga, Sergio was a single father whose wife had been killed in a car-bomb explosion when their daughter was a baby. Her death had nearly destroyed him. He had said if he'd not had his daughter to raise, he didn't think he would have made it through the first year without his wife. He had leaned heavily on Marta that year. She would cross the border with Teresa, her own small daughter at the time, and watch the girls each weekend while Sergio went to work.

Sergio and Marta had grown up together playing in the river in the tiny town of Barrio Montoya in Mexico, with thirteen kids between their two families. Sergio had confessed to Josie years ago that he had grown up imagining that he and Marta would marry one day and raise their own family together. In high school, both their fathers had taken jobs in Ojinaga at a new factory in town, and that's when Marta had met Javier.

Sergio said Javier had been a brooding young man, angry that his family had placed the title of curandero on him when he wanted nothing to do with medicine or helping others. He wanted a life of street cars and adventure, and instead felt weighed down with the needs of women who couldn't bear children, old men needing warts removed, colicky children, women with wandering husbands – an endless request for cures that he cared nothing about. But there was no mistaking his gift. Javier had a connection to the spirit world that he'd fought his entire life. This conflict had given him mythical status in the region, with people coming from hundreds of miles away to be blessed by the man they called *el santo reacio* – the reluctant saint.

When Josie called Sergio to tell him about Marta's death, he had already been contacted by her mother. After receiving the call from Marta's sobbing mother, Sergio had driven to Mexico City to offer his condolences. She said she blamed her daughter's death on Javier. He had wasted a gift of sight, taunting the saints who then punished him through those he loved. Josie had listened to Sergio talk on and on about their families and the anger they all felt toward Javier, and yet when she'd explained to Sergio that she was coming to Ojinaga to talk with Javier, Sergio had insisted on coming.

'It's not safe,' he'd said. 'You know the reality. It's a small town. Any American poking around looking for someone stands out. Within an hour, everyone would know that Marta's boss, an American police officer that no one trusts, was walking the streets. You'd never find Javier. You'd be lucky to find one open door anywhere in the village.'

Sergio instructed Josie to dress in jeans and a T-shirt with her hair in a ballcap. 'Wear nothing that would draw attention. If anyone asks, I'll introduce you as an old friend from California.'

He had taken the day off and met Josie at the International Bridge where she left her car for the day. They had driven to a taqueria in Ojinaga, where they sat outside, and Sergio caught Josie up with his family news, and finally with the gossip surrounding Marta's death. While Marta's mother blamed Javier, some of her family and most of the locals in Ojinaga blamed US law enforcement and border corruption for Marta's death. As paranoid as northerners were about Mexico, the same held true in reverse. Sergio said the general feeling was that Marta had been targeted as a Mexican law enforcement officer and murdered by corrupt Immigration and Customs Enforcement agents.

As they finished their lunch, Josie asked Sergio about his position in the National Guard, just enacted in 2019 by President López Obrador. The goal had been a reduction in crime and violence.

Sergio drained half his beer and slapped it on the bar top, his face red with anger. 'The National Guard has assumed all federal policing functions. All the people see is a new version of the same old corrupt machine. And who can dispute it? In 2020, we saw the second-highest homicide rate in Mexico.'

Josie listened on as Sergio described a system rife with corruption, in a country desperate for both law and order. He talked on about the countless good cops he worked with, desperate to clean up their country in a world that trusted no one. She finally signaled the waiter and paid their check, knowing that Sergio could have sat talking for hours.

* * *

Sergio made the ten-minute drive to Javier's home. He lived in the same squalid conditions as the last time she had met him. The house was located along a row of interconnected one- and two-story boxlike homes with a tangled mess of power lines drooping on to the rooftops. The brightly colored houses looked even brighter against the dusty, gray, treeless streets, void of any landscaping. Javier's place was located atop a bright-blue building with a large advertisement painted in yellow and red across the front that read: *Agua Chili!*

Sergio parked his car in front of the house and scanned the area for trouble. Seeing no one else on the street, Josie checked the sidearm he had provided her and slipped it back into her ankle holster. She opened the door to Javier's building and stood for several seconds to allow her eyes to adjust to the dark stairwell. At the top of the stairs, she knocked several times but heard no noise from inside. The door across the hallway opened, and a woman in her seventies, wearing a tattered bathrobe, stuck her head into the hallway, speaking rapid Spanish.

In Josie's own halted version of the language, she asked where she could find *el santo reacio.* The woman pointed down the stairs and to the right, repeating the phrase *perro malo.* She became more animated the longer Josie questioned her. She was fairly certain the word *perro* translated to dog, so she assumed the woman had misunderstood Josie's inquiries. Back in the car, Sergio laughed when he heard Josie's translation, saying the woman had most likely understood Josie perfectly.

'Perro Malo is a neighborhood bar just down the street. In English, it means bad dog. It's a rough crowd but it's early. How about an afternoon beer?'

'Absolutely.'

The bar was located in a brown-colored stucco building two blocks from Javier's home. Josie didn't see any dog signs on the outside of the building, but the saloon-style swinging doors designated the building as a bar to anyone outside the neighborhood who might be curious.

The dim interior was crowded with colorful hanging banners and garlands and streamers. A large mirror covered with shelves and hundreds of bottles gave the illusion of a well-stocked bar, although Josie thought most of the bottles appeared empty.

Sergio led them to a couple of empty stools at the end of the bar, where he ordered them both a Modelo. The bartender nodded at Sergio and slid a bowl of peanuts down the bar toward them.

Josie sipped her beer and watched Sergio scan the bar, nodding to a group of four old men dressed in traditional Mexican frontier outfits with snap-front shirts, vests and cowboy hats. The men sat leisurely around a table full of empties. Sergio lifted a finger to Josie, signaling for her to stay where she was at the bar as he wandered over for a chat. Josie noticed another table behind the old men with three younger men leaning in toward each other, talking quietly as they kept their eyes on Sergio. One of the old men turned and scowled at the table of younger men before turning back to Sergio. At that point, one of the younger men noticed Josie sitting at the end of the bar. He consulted the group before standing to face her as the others looked on.

Josie took a long draw on her beer with one hand and slipped her other hand down to make contact with the foot that was propped on the rung of the bar stool. She located the butt of her handgun and moved the leg of her jeans out of the way for easy access.

The man approached her with the intentional lazy bravado of a thug looking to intimidate. Josie didn't take her eyes off him and watched his smirk fade to anger. She was supposed to be deferring, turning away from him in fear, but she refused to give him that satisfaction.

'Americano?' he said, grinning, with his head tipped back in a cocky pose. 'We see you in a second. Lady don't belong in this bar.'

Maintaining her eye contact, Josie said nothing.

'You no talk? Don't be afraid.' He reached his hand out as if to stroke her thigh and she knocked it away with her beer bottle.

He grinned wider and turned back to the other two men who were laughing at him.

One of the other men stood from the table and approached, yelling out, 'Mamacita! Descarado.'

Josie watched as Sergio's hand came down hard on the first man's shoulder. Sergio hollered something friendly, laughing as the man turned in surprise. Josie couldn't keep up with the Spanish but watched as Sergio spun his finger in the air and motioned toward the man's table, apparently buying the three assholes a round of drinks.

Once the two men finally wandered back to their table and the testosterone settled, Sergio sat back down at the bar and sighed. 'Such a game. Watch your attitude. Whatever information you want is not worth guns being pulled.'

She nodded. 'You think anyone could still identify me from the Medrano Cartel situation years ago?'

'There are some of the family that still hate you and all that you stand for; I have no doubt about that. But those boys just saw a new female and couldn't resist making fools of themselves.' Sergio sighed. 'I'm glad my daughter is in Mexico City, away from these kinds of men. You know, arrest rates for women are up four hundred percent. Narco related. Young pretty girls from poverty. They are the targets now, not just the boys.' He put a finger up to the bartender for another round.

'Did you mention Javier to the men you were talking to?' she asked.

'No. I just got a good look around the bar,' Sergio said. 'I didn't see him because he was in the can. So drunk he can't make it back to the bar.'

Josie turned to see Javier stumble into a booth where a young man sat frowning at the drunk across the table.

'You're sure that's him?' Josie said.

'The man stole Marta from me. You think I wouldn't recognize him?'

'And the other guy?'

Sergio shrugged. 'Someone looking for answers from a drunk. Same as us.'

Josie felt the truth in his words and watched as Javier

shouted something unintelligible to the bartender, who ignored him.

'I know Marta was still giving him money and bailing him out of trouble. I wonder how much he still relied on her,' Josie said.

Sergio took in a sharp breath and looked away for a moment to stifle his emotions. 'I will never understand what she saw in that wretch of a man. He'll be passed out in a gutter until someone pities him enough to drag him home and sober him up.'

Sergio ordered them another round as the table of three stumbled out of the door. The bartender had quit serving Javier after he had fallen asleep on the table in the booth. The young man sitting across the table from him had poked at him, called out his name and finally given up and left him.

With only the old men and Sergio and Josie in the bar, the bartender finally wandered down to chat with the two of them. Sergio introduced Josie as his married cousin from Los Angeles, and the bartender paid her little attention.

'I heard about your friend, the lady cop, across the border,' the bartender said. He propped himself up with an elbow on the bar and cracked a peanut open one-handed and popped the nut into his mouth. He nodded his head toward Javier. 'Your lady friend was the only one who could talk to that fool. He'll be dead by week's end.'

'Any word on what happened to her?'

Josie heard the word *el chisme*, which she knew to be gossip in Spanish, but the men drifted off into their native tongue and soon seemed to forget Josie was sitting at the bar with them. Thirty minutes later, after several other customers arrived, the bartender wandered off and Sergio filled Josie in on the *chisme*.

The bartender claimed that Marta had come to Mexico to visit Javier about a week ago. She'd brought him food and, according to the neighbor lady that Josie had met, had got into a yelling match with him in his house. However, Sergio reminded Josie that with walls not much thicker than paper, everything can sound like a fight, especially between an ex-husband and wife. The woman, a frequent customer at the Bad Dog, had been telling people that Marta had left Javier's place and was found murdered two days later. The woman's take on it had been that it was better to have stayed with a drunk curandero than faced the corrupt Americans on the other side of the border. The bartender had shrugged, as if he didn't have much of an argument against the old woman's logic.

An hour later, Javier woke from his nap and made his way to the bathroom and back up to the bar, where Sergio moved to sit on one side of him, and Josie sat on the other. Javier glanced at Sergio and shook his head as if he couldn't believe his bad luck.

He paid no attention to Josie but stared down at the bar and asked Sergio to spot him a beer.

'Tell me about Marta. What have you heard?' Sergio said.

'What's to hear? She's gone. She left me. I told her leaving me would do us no good. Neither of us. But she never would listen. Everyone else wants to pay money to listen to me. Come for hundreds of miles to hear what I say. But the one person that matters to me? She doesn't listen. And look what happens to her.'

'Did she have enemies? People who were after her in Artemis?' Sergio asked.

'I need a beer.'

'You don't need anything. You need a bed and some hot soup. You're skinny as a rail.'

'Leave me be,' Javier said. He glanced over at Josie, most likely looking for someone else to buy him a beer.

Josie caught the desperation in the yellow-tinged eyes but could still see the rakish good looks Marta had been drawn to. Thick dark hair hung low over his eyes. He was the kind of rough man that attracted women on a mission to help. Josie had never wanted that mission and was not attracted to him. She had little patience for his type, finding him frustrating and weak. She typically had the urge to beat the shit out of men like Javier rather than mother them.

'When Marta came to see you last week, did she mention anyone who was angry with her? Or did she mention any cases that she'd been working on?' Josie asked.

Javier shook his head no and asked Sergio for a beer again.

Sergio leaned around Javier to look at Josie. Sergio looked disgusted by the encounter and hooked his thumb toward the door, ready to leave.

'Javier,' Josie said. He looked at her, obviously surprised that the woman sitting next to him knew his name. 'I'm Chief Josie Gray. I worked with Marta as a police officer.'

Josie felt a tap on her back. She straightened and saw that Sergio was trying to get her attention, signaling for her to stop. He'd made her agree not to mention law enforcement in their conversations, but she couldn't come all this way for nothing more than a nod from a drunk.

'I met you several years ago when Teresa ran away. I came to your apartment. Do you remember?'

Javier appeared to be holding his body up by leaning against his forearms on the bar. His head was turned toward her, his yellow eyes bloodshot and filling with tears. She could see the recognition in his expression.

'I tried calling, but she won't answer.' Javier's words were slurred and soft but intelligible.

'I visited her yesterday. She has friends at school. It would help her a great deal if you could visit. Do you have a passport?'

He shook his head.

'Keep calling. Don't give up. She needs you right now.'

'She needs her mother right now. Not me.'

'Well, you're all she has, so it's time to sober up and take care of your daughter.'

'Why are you here?'

'I need to know what you and Marta talked about this week.'

'It's none of your business what we talked about.' Javier turned toward her in anger, his breath reeking of a body decaying from the inside out.

'Help me find out who did this to her. What was she worried about? Did she talk about any cases she was working?'

Javier ran his hands through his oily hair, hanging his head down almost to the bar top. 'I don't know. I don't know what we talked about.'

Josie shouted his name in anger and felt Sergio at her back. The bartender had walked down to see what her issue was.

'Let's go. Now,' Sergio said.

Josie passed Javier her business card, and Sergio reached down and picked it up, angrily pointing toward the door.

Back in Sergio's car, he pulled away from the bar, his face red with anger. 'You've heard the term "femicide"? That's a real term here. It's not some journalistic thrill word used to excite people. Last I read, ten women, each day, are murdered in Mexico. It's a shameful number that destroys me as a father to a teenage girl. It's a number I don't play with. I warned you before we went into the bar what I expected.'

'I'm sorry, Sergio. You're right.'

'You are a female in a foreign country. You are a cop in a foreign country. There are people here who do not value those things and would kill you for either of them. You don't believe me? I can give you names of women killed because they crossed some imaginary line in the sand.'

'I get it. I am truly sorry. I let my anger over what happened to Marta cloud my judgment.'

Sergio was quiet for quite some time. He wasn't a man to show his anger, and she felt bad for provoking him. But she was also angry at a system that had shut her out of an investigation that mattered more than all others, angry at a country that allowed machismo to trump human life and dignity, angry that her friend's daughter was dealing with her mother's death on her own because her dad's head was stuck in a bottle.

Stopped at a red light, Sergio brushed imaginary dirt off his arms. 'What did Marta ever see in that filthy man?' The tone of his voice made it clear he was struggling with his own anger.

'He needed her. Marta wanted to cure him. She thought she could help him.'

Sergio laughed bitterly. 'I needed her, too. And I actually wanted her help!' He pulled his car into the parking lot for the International Bridge. Once he had stopped the car, he leaned back in his seat, obviously over his anger, and asked, 'Speaking of love, what's the latest with you and your kidnapping friend? Nick was his name?'

Josie nodded, glad Sergio had brought the topic up. She had wanted to tell him about her suspicions that someone had twice entered her house. With Marta's unexpected death, Josie was trying to hide her fears that her own personal incidents might be related to Marta's murder. She didn't want to sound alarmist, especially given Ramos's reaction to her having dinner with Jack Striker. She couldn't tell Ramos and didn't want to bother Otto with her troubles, so who else was there with an objective eye?

'Nick and I quit seeing each other several months ago.'

'Two law enforcement types rarely work in my opinion. Two big egos in one relationship is never good.' Smiling, he glanced over at her and misunderstood her serious expression. 'I'm sorry. You're upset. I shouldn't joke.'

'It's not that. I'm not upset. But something odd has happened. And with Marta's death, it makes me . . .' Josie stopped. 'I don't know. I hate to bring it up. I'll sound paranoid.'

'How long have I known you? More than ten years? I can describe you in many ways. Stubborn and opinionated, yes. Paranoid, no. Tell me what's going on.'

'It sounds ridiculous to say it, but I think someone is messing with me. Someone who knows my habits. My dog died a few months back. I kept his leash in my kitchen pantry when he was alive, and it remained there after he died. It just reminded me of him. When I went to take a walk the other night, I noticed the leash is gone. I know you're thinking I could have lost it or moved it, but that's what I mean about knowing me. The dog's leash was always in the same place, and I've not moved it in months. I have had no need to move it because my dog is gone.'

Sergio was nodding. 'I understand.'

'Also, I came home from work the other day and found my hairdryer lying on the bed.' Josie laughed aloud. 'I know that sounds crazy. It's why I haven't mentioned it to anyone. But I never take my hairdryer into the bedroom. It stays in the bathroom, and I put it under the cabinet after I use it each day. I know those two things sound crazy, but I'm telling you, someone came into my house and stole the leash, and they left the hairdryer on the bed for me to see.'

'You're telling me this after I mentioned your old boyfriend. You think Nick is harassing you?'

'I don't. It would be totally unlike him. But his leather coat was also left on my front porch a couple of weeks ago. No note, no explanation.'

'Did you call him?'

'I did. I called twice, but he hasn't called back. That's typical if he's working in the field. He's not the jealous type. He's not a stalker. But he's one of the few people who know my habits. He knows about my dog dying, and he knows I like things put away. I like a neat house.'

'You have security cameras?'

'No.'

'Josie! You're a cop! A female living alone. Come on.'

Sergio lectured her on taking safety precautions and following up with Nick.

'Get the state police involved. Get cameras up immediately. Change your alarm codes.' Sergio paused to consider Josie for a moment. 'You realize this is all the more reason you should have been more careful today. Your actions were hot-headed and foolish. I understand your anger over everything that has happened, but you cannot let it affect your judgment.'

'I get it,' she said. 'And I appreciate your concern. I needed this nudge to take it more seriously.'

Sergio had taken the incidents far more seriously than she had expected. On the drive back to Artemis, Josie called Nick again and left a message, asking him to call her, saying that it was important. The longer she considered the number of people who would know her habits, the fewer people she had to choose from. Nick was in a high-stakes, stressful profession. Maybe the stresses were getting to him. Worse yet, maybe someone had gotten to Nick.

SIXTEEN

J osie spent the next morning contacting people from a list of agencies and individuals she had identified as having an interest in buying greyhounds. Whoever stole Jezebel's dogs wasn't going to keep them without attracting attention, and the greyhound community was small enough that word would get out if the dogs were being shopped around. Josie started with several local dog breeders, all of whom said they'd been hoping to hear something on the missing dogs and would call if anything came up. The greyhound associations she reached out to accepted her contact information but hadn't heard of anyone trying to sell them.

Josie talked to a greyhound breeder in Houston who stated that she was recognized by the American Kennel Club, and that she only bred companion dogs rather than racers. She explained that selling a dog like Jezebel's red brindle without papers might fetch five hundred to a thousand dollars. The same dog with the official pedigree, registered and micro-chipped, would be worth upwards of four thousand dollars. Josie called Otto to see if he'd found any registrations on the dogs in Jezebel's paperwork, but he had not. Otto said he would go back out to the kennel to see if Jezebel kept anything official tucked away in a closet where she kept the dogs' supplies.

The breeder from Houston also suggested Josie contact local livestock auction houses, where the dogs might be sold with less attention paid to their provenance. Josie started with the auction house she was most familiar with and finally found her lead.

Dell Seapus, Josie's neighbor, made a monthly trip to the Everly Auction Barn whether he needed animals or not, just to sit in the stands and watch the show. Josie hopped a ride every few months because along with the trip to Alpine came the supper at Everly's Steakhouse, her favorite place for a ribeye. Josie called the auction barn and talked to a ranch hand who said they had received two greyhounds the week before that were slated for auction over the weekend. He didn't have access to the paperwork, but he promised to have the secretary gather the information and have it ready by six when she came back in to work a split shift. Josie called Dell and asked if he was up for a drive to Everly's if she bought dinner; as expected, he readily accepted the offer.

At noon, Josie and Otto drove to the jail for a meeting with Ramos and Sheriff Roy Martinez to discuss progress on Marta's investigation. Seated around the conference table, Ramos started right in.

'We've pulled the digital video from the access road to the high school, as well as the parking lots. The video cuts off about twenty feet outside of the back parking lot of the high school, so we don't have footage of the road as it wraps back around to the fire house. We've checked for any out-of-place cars, any cars that traveled the access road or parking lots after hours the week before Marta was shot. Nothing out of the ordinary. We did identify Marta's car. We've time-stamped her – but it appears whoever else met her at the fire house drove in from the back way. As you know, there is a dirt road that leads back to the fire house, but no cameras.'

'Any luck with vehicle prints on the dirt road?' Otto asked.

'Philips got a clear tread where a vehicle left the dirt road and drove on to the paved parking lot. Just a basic car tread. No prints matched the Lodge Edition truck prints they got off Chinati Road.'

Ramos also explained that the crime scene tech had used video technology to examine the layers of dirt and dust on the concrete floor, examining how it had shifted with the movement of the two confirmed people. The technician was able to examine the shifting particles of dust to choreograph the steps of the two people from the time they came down the steps, through Marta's shooting and the killer's exit. Ramos said they believed Marta was the first person down the stairs, and that a male suspect followed her down, walked several steps toward her, turned away from Marta and then back again, shot her, walked to her body, where he dropped to his knees, maybe felt for a pulse, and then stood, backed away, turned and exited back up the steps. The only thing the person did to clean up the area was to grab the two bullet casings off the floor. The crime scene tech hoped to pull a partial print out of the dust.

'We're looking for clothing fibers that might have collected in the dust. Something that could help us identify the person as local or—' Ramos stopped abruptly.

'Or East Coast?' Josie said.

Ramos cleared his throat. 'Exactly.'

'Are there ties to Mike Striker or members of his family?' she asked.

'I'm not prepared to get into those specifics at this time.'

'We appreciate you sharing what you have this morning. But this isn't a news briefing. Why hold back at this point? We acknowledge that Marta was a coworker and a friend, but give us some credit. We're also cops with a hell of a lot of years' experience between us. We're also working another murder investigation that could be connected.' Josie took a breath, forcing herself to reign in her anger. 'Two women were murdered in our town.'

'I told you from the beginning, these briefings would be general to keep you updated. You know it's not appropriate—'

Otto cut him off. 'What's not appropriate is that we have two females who were murdered within days of each other. Mike Striker is a person of interest in both investigations. We need to move beyond some bullshit protocol and share what information we have.'

Ramos stood and picked up his files in one swift motion. 'These briefings are a professional courtesy. I'm not going to sit through a critique this morning, I have work to do.' He slammed the conference door behind him.

'I apologize,' Otto said, his face still red with anger.

'Bullshit,' Josie said. 'You asked a fair question. This isn't like Ramos.' She looked at Martinez. 'You know what's up with him?'

'I heard he's got pressure from the governor's office to clear this up before the election next week,' the sheriff said. 'They need Striker's win. Thirty-one seats in the senate with five predicted to swing left. The governor isn't happy about Striker's run for mayor. They needed him to keep his senate seat Republican. The Republicans can't afford any bad press. The female running in his place isn't doing well in the polls.'

'Why does it always come down to politics?' she said.

'Don't underestimate this. The Democrats haven't controlled the senate since 1996. This would be a monumental upset. I hear Striker's cut the governor in on the racetrack to keep him off his back. He's wanting state money to support the build.'

'Help me understand a possible connection to Marta's death,' she asked.

'I'm just saying there are a lot of big egos pushing for Striker to win this election and get the racetrack built. He has the state support he needs. It's the city of Artemis that's his hold-up. If he doesn't get elected and get the commissioners to support the track, he could lose a multi-million-dollar deal,' the sheriff said. 'And also lose the support of the governor and the Republican party. That's a lot to lose. Some powerful motivation.'

'Striker's wife has printed GPS tracking data that puts Striker at every polling machine in the county since they set the new machines up. He showed up a day or two after they were installed, saying he's on some federal voting oversight committee. Jackson and Marta were convinced Striker had tampered with the machines,' Otto said.

'You checked his whereabouts the day of Marta's death?' Martinez asked.

'We did. His Facebook app showed that he was at home from noon the day of Marta's death, through seven o'clock the next morning. But if he met with Marta, he could have left his cellphone at home. He may not know about the Facebook tracking, but he might have been paranoid enough to realize the potential for some other GPS tracking on his phone.'

'There's also the possibility that Striker is behind Marta's death, but not the man that pulled the trigger,' Josie said.

Martinez frowned. 'I don't know. Striker is an egotistical

ass, but hiring a gunman to kill a cop? Do you see him hanging out with hired killers?'

'He's no saint,' she said. 'I heard there was a realtor who arranged the sale of Bobby Maiden's property for Striker. Bobby's telling people a guy named John Smith came to his trailer and forced him to sell his family home. We've not been able to track Smith down, but I heard he may be from out of state.'

'Have you told Ramos any of this?' the sheriff asked.

'He walked out before I had the chance,' Otto said. 'I also finally got an interview with Striker yesterday while Josie was in Mexico. I had hoped to dig into Jezebel's business relations with him, but he was pretty cagey. He kept turning his answers back to the greyhounds, saying she was helping him develop the breeding side of the racetrack. Then he took a phone call and cut the interview short.'

'Marta was supposed to have met with Striker's nephew, with questions about the machines, the night she was killed,' Josie said. 'And I can't get Ramos to give me information on any of this. He knows me as a cop. He knows I can keep my emotions out of this investigation. The whole thing just feels off to me.'

'How hard is Ramos getting squeezed? The media is referring to Marta's death as an officer shooting under suspicious circumstances,' Otto said.

'Pissed me off,' she said. 'I've been checking online. There's not been one mention of her death in the *Chronicle*.'

The sheriff whistled softly. 'And you think all of this goes back to election tampering. Let's get someone from the company who sold us those machines to come down and check the software. Could Mark oversee that as the voting commissioner, especially with it being so close to the election?'

Josie laughed at the absurdity of their situation. 'It gets worse. Mark told Otto that Arroyo County is one of the few counties in the state that purchased these machines. Guess where they came from?'

The sheriff shrugged.

'The East Coast. From a company owned by Mike Striker's brother.'

'That can't be true,' the sheriff said.

'He wasn't the front man on the sale of the machines, but we confirmed he works for the company in some capacity.'

'Mark Jackson and Marta were just piecing all this together,' Otto said.

The sheriff turned to Josie. 'And Striker's nephew, the land expert from Manhattan, was supposed to have met with Marta at the old fire house, but Uncle Mike got pissed and canceled the meeting.'

'And Marta was killed later that same evening, while I sat in a bar with the nephew,' Josie said. Her face flushed as she said the words.

'Had she talked to you about her concerns?' he asked.

'Not after she started working with Mark Jackson. We were on different shifts and we hadn't connected. Ramos claims he couldn't find any notes in Marta's records on the voting machines,' Josie said.

'Does that sound right?' the sheriff said.

'Marta was notorious for not writing things down. I've given her hell over that for years, preaching about the paper trail. So, no, that doesn't surprise me,' she said.

'Let me talk to Ramos to make sure he's clear on the election tampering. I'll see if he'll give me anything,' the sheriff said. 'You also mentioned a possible connection between Jezebel Black's death and Marta. What's the latest on her investigation?'

'I talked to a state investigator earlier today,' Otto said. 'Just above where Jezebel's body was found in the canyon, they identified fresh tire tracks where someone had pulled off on the side of the road. They confirmed the tread came from a Ford Lodge Edition. I guess that edition has a special set of off-road tires that were made specifically for desert conditions. It's an expensive vehicle.'

'Rolley Hines has the Lodge Edition. I bet he spent a hundred grand on that truck,' Martinez said.

'It's good news, but those tires are also used by quite a few ranchers in the area. If nothing else, it confirms that whoever dumped her body has money,' Otto said.

'I may have found the two greyhounds that were stolen just

before Jezebel was killed,' Josie said. 'A livestock auction barn in Alpine. I'll drive over after work tonight and check it out.'

'Someone took the greyhounds to auction them off?' he said.

'It looks like it. It's a little easier to remain anonymous through the auction barn, but they should have records.'

Through the years, some of Josie's best police work had taken place in her car. On or off the clock didn't matter – just driving down the road with the radio off and the windows down. There was something about the combination of fresh air and wind and the wide-open territory spreading out beyond that allowed her thoughts to expand and make connections.

She had received another voicemail from Jack, asking to stop by her house later that evening. Rolling down the road now, thinking back to the few times they had spent together, she thought about their easy interaction and the intensity of the physical attraction. Even given the terrible circumstances, she wanted so much to enjoy this new chance at romance, but like so many other times in her past, her job was in jeopardy of killing another relationship. She'd never been married, would most likely never have kids – and for what?

She wondered what it would take to get her out of Artemis. She loved the desert. West Texas felt more like home than her own hometown in Indiana. But she acknowledged that some of that came from her dysfunctional childhood. It wasn't the place as much as the people. If she had the right person in her life, couldn't she find happiness anywhere? She watched the cream-colored desert roll out beyond her car and imagined packing a suitcase, throwing it into Jack's pickup truck and following him out of town. Why not move to the East Coast? Why not move to the Congo? She was a good cop, but she could be a good cop somewhere else. Maybe she had talents that went beyond carrying a gun and puzzling through the habits and thought processes of criminals.

Jack had the free spirit, the wanderlust, that she had always been envious of. She imagined that inner desire to move would complicate a person's life, but she also imagined that it would add a layer of excitement that she craved more with each year's passing.

She thought back to the conversation they were having at the Legion before the terrible phone call from Otto, when he said life was better when shared with someone. And she remembered him saying that he'd stopped by at lunch and talked to Carol about having dinner with Josie, how Carol had agreed with him that Josie would like a burger for lunch. She frowned at the memory, knowing something wasn't right. Then she realized it was the timing. He had stopped by the Legion at noon that day. Would he have invited Josie to dinner at six if he knew he had a meeting with Marta at seven? She needed to find out when his uncle had called him and told him the meeting with Marta was off. She hoped that phone call came in before noon.

After work, Josie changed into jeans and boots and fired up her old Jeep. The Jeep was part of a fleet of retired military vehicles that the city had used as police cars for her first ten years on the job. They carried the necessary four-wheel drive for their remote area, but, most important, they were low bid. When the department received the grant money for their new SUVs, Josie had purchased her old Jeep for five hundred dollars. The Jeep's suspension was useless, and the heat and air had long since died, but it would make for a nice ride to the auction barn with Dell.

Alpine was located on a high plateau that typically provided a pleasant respite from Artemis when the summer temperatures got too much. Average highs throughout the year ranged from sixty to ninety degrees, and average lows between thirty and sixty-five, making for a more tolerable desert climate. And as a small college town, there was an arts vibe with live theater and music, poetry readings, along with feed stores and food trucks. It was one of Josie's favorite towns in West Texas.

The auction barn was set up much like a dirt-floor movie theater, with plastic folding seats that led down to a small arena where the animals were led in for auction. A scale screen showed each animal's weight, and the auctioneer stood behind a podium. Everly's used two spotters in the arena to watch for bidders and then relay the bid to the auctioneer. The process was fast-paced and involved thousands of dollars for some animals. Knowing his budget before the auction, Josie had bid on a few cows for Dell through the years, just to experience the excitement of placing the bid. She'd understood immediately the thrill of winning and the risk of paying too much.

The auction barn operated a weekly sale every Saturday morning, and occasional sales of other animals were held throughout the week as needed. Josie had never been in the barn without the noise of animals and the excitement of money to be spent and made. Dell led her down the stairs and into the small arena, then out the back to the stalls that contained animals coming up for auction over the next week. The smell of dirt and straw and manure was strong but not unpleasant. It was obvious that Everly took care of the animals and ran a clean operation. She and Dell walked up and down the rows of stalls and saw two pinto horses and a dozen goats, but no dogs.

Cal Everly talked Texan in such an exaggerated way that Josie assumed he'd come from out of state and was overcompensating, but Dell claimed the man had grown up a rancher's son in El Paso. The *y'alls* and *ma'ams* and the way he overstressed the first syllable in every word were a bit much for Josie's taste, but Dell found him amusing.

Dell had turned being a loner into an avocation. Friends were a pain in the ass, so how Dell could hang out with a man who turned every comment into a full-on commentary was beyond her. They found Cal in his office, located in one of the animal stalls at the end of the livestock pens. Cal was sitting in a metal chair at a desk that appeared to have been nailed together out of a couple of old wooden pallets. For a man so full of bluster, and who had more money in the bank than Josie could accumulate in her lifetime, he appeared to live a very simple life.

Dell introduced Josie and they small-talked about the auction barn, allowing Cal to get his blustering out of the way.

'The cattle we AUC-tion are the FI-nest SPEC-imens you will find in *allll* of West TEXas. I can assure you of that, ma'am.'

Josie caught the touch of a smile on Dell's face as he kicked at the dust with his boots.

After several minutes, Dell finally broke in. 'Josie's hoping you can show her the dogs that got brought in for auction. We didn't notice them in the pens.'

'Those dogs weren't about to stay put in these pens. They're in that smaller auction arena across the way. You ought to come up for one of those auctions on Wednesdays. Small animals. Chickens, minks, dogs, snakes, you name it. Auctioned off a dozen chinchilla last week. Damn rodents brought two HUNdred DOLLars a head.'

Cal had walked out of the barn with his words trailing behind him. Josie and Dell followed, assuming they were headed for the smaller arena.

They walked toward a fully enclosed metal pole barn located fifty feet across a dirt courtyard. The ranch had the feel of a compound, with buildings laid out in what appeared to be a random arrangement, built as new needs arose. A brick ranch house lay at an angle off to the right of the arena. Another half-dozen smaller sheds were scattered about.

Inside, the smaller arena had the look and smell of a veterinarian's office, with a tiled entryway and hallways and offices with closed doors. Cal led them down a hallway toward the noise of animals in cages, and once inside the swinging door, Josie immediately recognized Bella in one of the cages. The sight of Jezebel's prize dog brought a lump to her throat. What a sad sight.

Once Josie visually confirmed the two dogs had belonged to Jezebel, Cal told a receptionist to pull the dogs from the auction lineup and then said his goodbyes, leaving Dell and Josie standing in front of the receptionist's desk while she retrieved the records.

The receptionist was in her fifties, dressed in khakis and a button-down shirt, and appeared to be very efficient at her job. She ran a copy of what she called the 'intake' paperwork and handed it to Josie.

'Every once in a while, we'll get someone who doesn't want to list their name on the paperwork. That always makes me suspicious. That's what happened with the dogs. A man came in with the two dogs on leashes and said he wanted to auction them off. When I gave him the paperwork, he handed it back and said he doesn't give his name in writing.' The woman rolled her eyes. 'I explained that the auction barn policy is that we won't take any animals without a full name, current address and a photo ID. He stood there, staring at me for a while – thinking I would change my mind, I guess. He finally pulled his ID out and gave me the paperwork. I'm glad to see the police are checking this one out. I wouldn't be surprised to find out those dogs are stolen. It happens occasionally.'

The woman spoke with Cal over the phone, and he agreed to hang on to the dogs until the police could confirm their rightful owner. Josie thought the name on the paperwork sounded familiar but couldn't place it. She texted the name to Otto.

At the auction barn. Guy that brought the dogs in was Randal Beamis. Heard of him?

That's Dugout. Let me deal with him tomorrow.

Good enough. I'll put the paperwork on your desk.

SEVENTEEN

C arla Striker stood in front of her kitchen sink, looking out on to the back deck, watching her husband standing at the edge of the pool with his cocktail. He was staring out across the desert valley into a magnificent orange sunset, looking content with his successes. He was supposed to be grilling steaks for his brother Morey and nephew Jack, but the grill was smoking. Carla knew that the outer appearance of her husband was no indication of the thoughts he was harboring on the inside.

She banged on the kitchen window, and when he turned to look back at her, she pointed toward the grill and watched him hustle over to flip the meat. Mike was wearing golf shorts and shirt, having spent the afternoon on a golf course trying to hatch some new deal with a combination of men looking to make their fortune. When she and Mike first started dating, she had loved going to the endless parade of events and fundraisers with him, socializing and talking about current events and the difficult issues communities and businesses were facing. It had been at least a year into their marriage before she realized her engaging husband was a showman. The smiles and laughter he rolled out in a crowd turned to silence as soon as they got into the car to drive home. In the beginning, she had thought his silences were because he was angry with her, but she soon realized that her life-of-the-party husband was an introvert. Politicking and glad-handing were necessary to making deals, his true love in life. As the marriage progressed, it dawned on her that he had chosen her as a partner because she was good in a crowd.

Carla watched Mike shut the grill and look up, his face breaking into a wide smile. Morey and Jack approached him, patting backs and laughing, already ribbing each other about something. She envied their easy camaraderie. In ten years of marriage, she had never understood why she and Mike couldn't have that same sense of ease with each other.

Morey followed Mike to the bar cart, and when Carla saw Jack heading for the house, she returned to her cutting board. Jack was the only one of the two men with manners enough to come inside and say hello.

'Hey, Aunt Carla.'

She smiled as he kissed her on the cheek.

'What can I do to help?'

'You are a sweetheart. You can pour both of us a glass of white. It's in the fridge. You don't drink that nasty bourbon your uncle and dad drink, do you?'

'I don't. The smell of it makes my stomach turn.'

As she sliced tomatoes, she noticed him opening drawers to find the corkscrew, and it made her happy that he felt at ease in her home. She wondered how he would respond when he learned of her going public with Mike's affairs. She liked to think her nephew would be supportive of her and angry with his uncle, but blood ran deep. She'd learned that lesson when her first husband's family dropped her like a hot potato the day he walked out.

'Tell me about the transition from Congo to Texas,' she said.

'I have transitioned nicely to far less rain and way fewer people.'

'You don't miss all the excitement of a big city?'

'I wouldn't call it excitement. It was more nonstop drama. Everything was a crisis. Or a celebration. It was exhausting. I like the slower pace here – at least for now.' He glanced over at her and grinned. 'Although I've found that people run pretty hot and cold here.'

'As in they can be very friendly or very hateful?'

'Exactly.'

'Welcome to my life. I've never understood why people think if you are married to someone, you become that person yourself. Same for you. You are Mike Striker's nephew. Mike is either loved or hated. That means you will either be loved or hated.'

'Because of the racetrack?'

She laughed, but it sounded sad and weary, even to her own ears. 'Because your uncle has that effect on people.' Jack nodded but didn't comment, so Carla pointed at the bowls of salads and platter of bread on the counter. 'I'm sure the steak is about done. Why don't you carry all this outside and I'll get the potatoes out of the oven.'

Dinner was nice. The conversation was light and full of childhood stories of the brothers competing, at sports, with girls, in business – in every situation imaginable. Who could chop a tree down the fastest with an ax, who could run to the mailbox the fastest carrying a barbell with one-hundred-pound weights, who could get the lowest grade on their algebra test and not get grounded by their dad, and on and on.

Carla sat at the end of the table, closest to the kitchen so she could clear the table and refill drinks, while keeping an eye on the conversation in front of her. Jack sat to her right, next to his dad, and Mike sat across from them. She watched the interaction between the brothers with amusement, but she could see in Jack's expression that he was experiencing the same sense of unease, especially as the bourbon flowed and their voices grew louder. The conversation eventually turned to their many business ventures and grew more heated as details were thrown around and decisions debated.

Given her plan to file for divorce once the election was over, she had taken an increasing interest in Mike's business dealings, but as she had shown no interest in the past, Mike paid no attention. Carla sat at the table with her cell phone, appearing to scroll through her social media accounts, occasionally showing Mike a photo during a lull in the conversation to demonstrate her ambivalence. However, any detail that sounded important in terms of the election or her impending appointment with her attorney, she recorded.

The conversation finally drifted to the election and the polls, which showed Mike winning by ten percent.

'You can't rely on these local pollsters,' Morey said.

'You can't rely on the national pollsters either, but we still use them,' Mike said.

'You got any muscle working the polls?' Morey asked.

Mike laughed when he saw Jack's eyebrows raise. 'It's a

term, kid. Meaning people passing flyers, saying what a first-rate guy I am. Your aunt's passing out homemade cookies – isn't that right, sweetheart?' he said, tapping the back of her phone.

She looked up from her phone and glared before returning to it.

'Honey, I just got a fresh bottle of Woodford Reserve. It's in my den. Would you go fetch that and some fresh ice for the bucket?'

She saw Jack shake his head and grin at his uncle's choice of words. Carla had been shuttled out of rooms so the men could talk so many times through the years that the request came as no shock. But she was prepared this time. Still glancing at her phone, she flipped to an app she had ready, selected record, then stood and laid her phone on the bar cart where she was sure the conversation could still be picked up. Jack offered to help, but she declined. Carla took her time inside the house, filling the ice bucket, cracking open the seal on the new bottle of bourbon. From the back of the kitchen, she could see out of the French doors to where the three men were having a heated discussion. Jack was clearly angry, with both hands on the arms of his chair as if he was about to push himself up and away from the conversation. Once the heat in their gestures appeared to die down, Carla hustled back out with the bottle and ice and set them on the table.

'Fetched and delivered,' she said.

The three men looked up at her as if they had no idea what she was talking about.

Two hours later, with Morey and Jack gone and Mike snoring in his recliner in the den, Carla took her cell phone outside and walked down the path behind the house that led to the neighborhood loop. At nine o'clock, the streetlights below lit up the paved road but left the area on the hillside in shadows. She'd made this walk before. Standing about a third of the way down the rock-strewn path, she could look back up at her house and see directly into Mike's den where his recliner faced a bank of windows. She could see the chair outstretched and a body lying prone. She was certain that a half-empty tumbler of bourbon was perched on the end table next to him.

Carla opened her phone and pressed play. She listened to the swish of the sliding French door being closed and Jack said, 'When did you get here? In Artemis?'

'What's that supposed to mean?'

Carla turned the volume up and held it closer to her ear, her eyes fixed on the recliner inside the house. She thought it was Jack's dad that asked what he meant, but the brothers sounded a great deal alike.

'What I mean is, at dinner you made a comment about how it had been good to meet Janine, Uncle Mike's campaign manager. I talked with her, too, several days ago, right before she headed to the airport to fly to Louisiana for a week for some fundraising event. If you met her, you've been in town several days longer than you told me. And I'm wondering why that is. Why you got here early. And why you both lied to me.'

'First of all, it's none of your business why I got here early.'

She listened as ice cubes hit the glasses and the bourbon flowed. Both Mike and Morey were slurring words.

'But it is my business,' Jack said, his tone clearly frustrated. 'We've been through this a hundred times. You aren't just my dad and uncle. You are my business partners. So when you make bad decisions, it affects me, too. I'm just wondering what kind of bad decisions the two of you were making behind my back.'

Morey and Mike both started speaking at once, and Carla couldn't make out their words.

She finally heard, 'Shut your damn mouth,' and the talking stopped for a moment.

'Jack's right. He's a business partner. If you can't separate that he's your son from the business, then one of you needs to step down.'

'Screw you, Mike. If you didn't put us into situations where we have to break the law, we wouldn't even be talking about this.'

'Break what law?' Jack said.

'Shut the—' Morey started to say.

Mike cut him off. 'Your dad broke into the police station in town. Turns out he knows how to pick a lock.'

'You son of a bitch. You couldn't wait to tell him,' Morey said.

'What the hell are you talking about?' Jack said. 'This is a joke, right?'

Carla felt nauseous. How could they all be so arrogant and so stupid?

'You just love the idea of Jack thinking his old man's a piece of shit, don't you? I come here to bail your ass out of trouble, and this is the thanks I get?' Morey said.

'Come on, you dumb ass. Jack spent ten years in the Congo. He's seen more shit than you and I put together.'

'Hey!' Jack yelled. There was a moment of silence before Jack started talking again, his voice lowered. 'Are you saying that the break-in at the police department, the one that was on the news this week, was you? You stole evidence in a murder investigation?'

'Damn you, Mike. You had no right.'

'I don't care about his right to talk, Dad. I care about you messing around in a murder investigation. And just as important, why was it necessary?'

Mike laughed, and Carla felt her face burn red in anger. She stared up at the recliner, through the brightly lit windows of their beautiful home and couldn't believe this was her life.

'It's not what you think. We had nothing to do with that woman's death,' Morey said. 'But your uncle was in business with her, and there are certain records we don't want in the wrong hands. This was no more than gathering up those business records before the local cops got hold of them and didn't know what they were looking at.'

After a moment of silence on the recording, she heard Jack's voice again, his tone incredulous. 'You broke into a police station?'

'You have no idea what your old man can do,' Mike said.

'If you don't shut the hell up, I will get up out of this chair and beat the living shit out of you.'

'Does anyone else know this?' Jack said.

'No one. And you be careful talking to that girlfriend cop of yours. That's why you didn't need to know any of this.' Morey's voice grew so quiet that Carla could barely hear it on the recording. 'You have crossed the line this time. You ignored the one thing I asked of you. If you say one more thing to Jack about Jezebel Black, we both walk on you immediately. Do not push me on this.'

Carla heard the swish of the French doors and realized she had mistaken the stillness around the table as resolution, when it had been pure threat, brother against brother.

EIGHTEEN

With a dozen tasks to accomplish, Josie started work at the police department an hour early. She started with a phone call to Davey Johnson, the head of the parks department in Arroyo County. She explained that she was trying to track down all those who had keys to the old fire house.

'That'd be a tough one to come up with, Chief. I just loan out keys as needed. I don't really keep a written list.'

'Who gave Marta keys to the community building?'

'That was me. But she's had keys for quite a while. And let me just say how sorry I am about what happened to her. It's just terrible. Such a nice lady.'

'Thanks, Davey, I appreciate it.'

'Do you think you know who did it? It's all people are talking about.'

'That's what this phone call is about. We're trying to track down who had access, other than Marta, the night she was killed. What about getting me a list of who you've given keys to over the past six months?'

'Look, I hate to admit this, but there's so many people with keys. We've talked about changing the locks, but it's just one more expense. I loan out the keys and people just make copies so they can get back in after they give me the original back. I get reports of people using this place all the time. But honestly, I figure it's supposed to be a community building, so what does it matter? At least, people are using it. It's not like it's got items people want to steal. It's pretty much an empty building with some old military meals and jars of peanut butter in the basement.'

'You didn't give Marta keys to the building the day of her murder?'

'No.'

'Did you give anyone else the keys?'

'No.'

'Had you ever given Senator Striker keys to the building in the past?'

He paused, surprised at the mention of the senator. 'Yes, but keep in mind that I've given plenty of people those same keys.'

'You're saying people who are running in the election have access to the buildings where the voting machines are located?' she said.

'Now, come on. He's a state senator! If you can't trust him, I don't know who you can trust!'

Josie spent the rest of her morning working on the Jezebel Black investigation. She laid out her notes on the conference table. She flipped back to her own conversation with Sauly, and Otto's information after he interviewed Sauly. Sauly had been sleeping outside when he saw a flashlight and watched someone walk back to the kennel. The person had entered the kennel, shone the flashlight around and left. Then Sauly heard them walk down the road, where they got into a truck and drove away with the headlights remaining off. When Otto checked the house, the doors were still locked. Sauly assured Otto that he hadn't entered Jezebel's house, and he hadn't noticed the intruder trying to break in, but he also couldn't assure Otto that the person hadn't already broken into the house and looked around.

She looked at the initial time Sauly had called her and flipped through her notes for when the digital camera at the police department had been shot out that same night. There was a forty-seven-minute difference in time. It would have been plenty time for someone to have checked Jezebel's house for whatever paperwork they were searching for and then driven to the police department to finish the job. Maybe they were looking for something specific. Given the price of a full-blooded dog with papers, maybe someone was looking for the certification on her dogs, although breaking into the police station seemed a risky venture for a twenty-thousand-dollar profit – and that was assuming the thief would then be able to return to her home and steal the dogs. Josie didn't think the dogs were the draw.

Josie heard Otto's slow tread up the stairway and watched him enter, smoothing over the white flyaway hair that fluffed around his mostly balding head. He put a paper bag on her desk and sat down at his own. She pulled out two glazed donuts and thanked him, realizing she'd skipped breakfast.

'The most important meal of the day, Josie.'

She poured them both coffee from the pot at the back of the office and filled him in on what she'd been working on.

'Sauly was certain the vehicle that drove away from his daughter's home was a pickup. And the vehicle driven by the person who disposed of Jezebel's body on Pinto Canyon Road was a truck.'

'And ninety percent of the residents of Arroyo County either have a truck or have one at their disposal,' Otto said.

'If the prowler at Jezebel's house is the same person who broke into the PD, they were most likely looking for paperwork, and it was most likely tied to the business she was involved in. Did you find out anything more on the Florida business?'

Otto brought a stack of paperwork over to the table and sat down next to Josie. 'The flyers she had in her notebook traced back to two land development companies in Florida. One of them is involved in two different lawsuits over land scams. From what I read on the lawsuits, they basically send out these flyers to people from out of state. They seem to target retirement-aged people. People looking to invest their money. The company sends doctored paperwork, photos of the land that's been partially developed – although the land hasn't actually been developed at all. It's the same swampland that they've been selling in the Everglades for sixty years.'

'People are still falling for the land scam after all these years?'

'Sounds like it. I called one of the claimants listed on the lawsuit and she gave me an earful. She said she bought a quarter-acre plot of land for seventy-five thousand dollars, with the promise that she would be able to double her money in three years.'

'How much is the plot of land actually worth?' Josie asked.

'Nothing. It is literal swampland.'

'How would the bank allow that? Surely, they required an appraisal.'

'They aren't selling to people like you and me. They're selling to people with money already in the bank, people who want to use it as an investment. They waive the appraisal. Or, more often, the seller uses their own finance company. That's what happened to the lady I talked to. She said her husband had died and she had money she knew she needed to invest. When this company approached her about investing in real estate, she thought it was a smart move. She'd grown up hearing that real-estate values always go up. It's the one sure investment. She said they offered to take care of all the financing for her and she thought it was a great deal.'

'What kind of recourse does a person have?'

'This lady said she's been fighting it for two years, but she claims she's getting screwed by an attorney now. She says the company claims the paperwork is all legal. It's not their fault she didn't get it appraised. They claim that's what their appraiser said the land *would be* worth. The key phrase there is "would be."'

'How does Jezebel play into this?' Josie asked.

'I haven't gotten that far. The receptionists I talked to from both companies had never heard of Jezebel. My next step is checking her bank statements to see if she had any financial interactions with either of them. Meanwhile, Philips from the sheriff's office is going to meet me out at Dugout's place in twenty minutes to make an arrest over Jezebel's stolen dogs. If he was the person who drove the truck to Jezebel's house the night it was vandalized, that could change the investigation.'

Josie waited until Otto was out of the office to make the call she had been avoiding.

'Ramos.' He picked up on the first ring.

'This is Josie. I know you don't want to talk about Marta's case with me, but I need one detail cleared up for my own peace of mind. And if it isn't cleared up, it's a detail you should be made aware of.'

Ramos sighed. 'Listen, you and Otto have this all wrong.

You two seem to think I'm shutting you out because I doubt your abilities, or I think you can't handle working the case since Marta was a coworker. That has nothing to do with it. I want the bastard that killed a fellow police officer to hang from a noose.'

Josie leaned her head against the large picture window that faced the courthouse across the street. She watched people walking along, minding their own business, probably thinking about grocery lists and dentist appointments. She wondered if any of them had the weight of murder on their minds.

Ramos talked on. 'I have been through enough trials to know that a good attorney will use anything in his power to destroy an investigation. I do not want to see Marta's murderer walk free because I mishandled something. And if the attorney can prove bias on the part of the investigating or arresting officers, then that could destroy us at trial. You get that, right?'

'I do get that. I apologize.'

He paused, as if surprised at her response.

'I have the exact same worries. It would destroy me if I thought I did something to harm the investigation. We'd just heard the governor was putting pressure on you, and we worried it might impact things.'

'He *is* putting pressure on me! But it's sure as hell not going to affect how I approach this investigation.'

'Putting pressure on you because of the election?' she asked.

'Yes. I have explained every way I know how that telling someone to rush a murder investigation does nothing.' Ramos made a noise as if disgusted. 'Ask me your question. If I can answer it, I will.'

'I need to clear up the timing with Jack Striker the day of the murder.'

'The senator's nephew?'

'Yes.'

'Go ahead.'

'He made the comment at dinner the night Marta was killed that he had stopped by the Legion for lunch that day and talked to Carol. He said that he and Carol discussed whether I would like to have dinner with him that evening at the

Legion. I called Carol and confirmed this. She pulled up his credit card transaction and he checked out at twelve thirty-seven p.m. Carol said it was while he was standing at the cash register that they discussed us having dinner that evening. What I want to confirm is when he talked to his uncle on the phone about canceling the meeting with Carla.'

'Explain why that matters,' Ramos said.

'He picked me up at my house at six p.m. We didn't even get back into town until six thirty. He wouldn't have scheduled dinner with me at six, knowing that he had a meeting with Marta at seven.'

'I follow,' Ramos said. 'If Mike Striker canceled the meeting before lunch that day, it would mean Jack's evening was freed up and it would make sense he asked you out.'

'But if the phone call between Jack and his uncle took place after lunch, it means that he scheduled dinner with me already knowing that the meeting with Marta was never going to happen. I would guess at that point he would have been using dinner with me as a decoy.'

'That's good. The problem is, I have no reason to get a warrant for Mike Striker's phone records. A judge is not going to issue that on a sitting senator unless there's a damn good reason.'

'No, but you have Marta's records. You can at least see what time Marta received a call from Striker. If it was before noon, there's no need to ask for the records. It makes Jack's story make sense.'

'I do have Marta's phone records. You have Mike Striker's number?'

'Call Otto. He can get it easily from Striker's wife, Carla. I think Otto has other information he needs to share with you about Carla as well.'

'I've heard she's not happy in Artemis,' Ramos said.

'She's also not happy with her husband. She'll be a good source if it comes down to needing information.'

Josie left work that evening carrying a box she'd had delivered to the PD instead of her home address. When she got home, she opened it up and watched a video on installation, and then set up cameras at both doors. But she'd also learned a few things from Nick about security. Shooting out a digital camera installed on someone's doorstep was a simple act. The cameras on the two entrance doors to her home were blanks. The recording cameras were installed from tree branches in the front and back yard, as well as both sides of her house. They were quality cameras, allowing her to zoom in with excellent clarity.

She had just put the ladder back in her garage when she noticed dust down the road and then heard the approaching pick up. Jack pulled into her driveway, but he didn't get out. She walked to his open driver's side window.

'Hi,' she said. 'Want to come in for a visit?'

'I wasn't sure I was welcome. I just had a talk with the state cop investigating your officer's death.'

'Of course you're welcome. Come on inside.'

Josie led the way into her house, not at all sure if what she'd said was true. She'd not received a follow-up call from Ramos, so she was looking forward to hearing Jack's side.

Josie got them both a beer, and they walked on through the kitchen to sit on her back deck. They each sat in a chair facing toward Dell's house and the mountains beyond. Jack was clearly preoccupied and uncomfortable with the visit.

'On my travels, I've been in some precarious situations. I faced the Congolese National Police when they accused our company of stealing cobalt from the government. But a murder investigation is a pretty scary thing. And this isn't about my company. It's about me. And the part that has the police most concerned about me is that I asked you out to dinner. One of the cops called me earlier and was quizzing me on my timeline that day. What time I talked to Mike, my uncle, when you and I got to the Legion to eat dinner. I'm starting to feel like they think I'm a murderer and I can't for the life of me figure out what I did. And I thought maybe that idea is coming from you. So here I am. If you think I had something to do with Marta's murder, then ask me anything. Let's clear the air right now. I will be one hundred percent honest with you. And I will help you verify everything I say to the best of my ability.'

Her initial reaction was to say, *Of course I don't think you're involved*, but the stakes were too high.

'I appreciate you offering,' she said. 'While I want to assure you that I don't believe you killed Marta or were part of her murder, I'm also part of the investigation. I know why the police are asking you these questions. The timeline in any investigation is always critical.'

He cut her off. 'Ask me. Let's get this over with.'

'Describe your day, the day of Marta's murder. When you talked to your uncle about canceling the meeting and so on.'

'I started that day at the build site taking soil samples. I was out there until about eleven in the morning when Mike stopped by. He had some questions on perc test results that had been mailed to his office.'

'Perc test?'

'The racetrack is so far out of town that it won't be part of the town sewage treatment. We were discussing waste treatment feasibility. It was then that I mentioned I had a meeting that evening with Officer Cruz. That's when he got pissed and told me that I shouldn't meet with her.'

'I thought you were talking to your uncle on the phone?'

He gave her a confused look. 'I never said I talked to him on the phone.'

'I guess I made that assumption. So, again, there aren't any phone records to support your story,' Josie said.

'This is such bullshit! I didn't go around that day thinking to myself that I should have this conversation on the phone so I can prove my story to some cop who thinks I committed murder!'

'Hang on. I get how this kind of questioning feels unfair. You feel like you are being accused of something you didn't do.'

Even sitting in the lawn chair, Jack's body was rigid with anger. 'I don't just feel that way. That's exactly what's happening.'

'I'm not disagreeing with you. But try to see this from a different perspective. There is a woman who was murdered. Someone shot her, a bullet through her forehead and a bullet through her heart. She has a daughter in college who is devastated. The person who shot her is walking around Artemis a free man. If the police knew who the killer was, they would arrest him immediately. Since they don't know who did it, the only way to track down the killer is to ask questions. We have to piece together a picture of what happened that day – maybe what happened that week, or even further back. Sometimes dozens of people are questioned. It's not that the police believe all of those people are suspects, but those people all help put together the full story about what happened.'

Josie stopped talking and looked at Jack who was staring out at the cattle grazing in the field. He didn't turn to look at her, but said, 'I'm sorry. I realize how selfish I probably sound.'

'You don't sound selfish at all. It's why cops tend to hang out with other cops. It's hard to remain friends with someone after you grilled them about a crime they had nothing to do with.'

'This probably sounds petty to you, but I don't know if my ego can move beyond the woman I imagine sharing a bed with asking me to provide an alibi for murder. It's an odd situation.'

'It's an odd life. I wouldn't recommend it.' They sat for a moment, staring out into the setting sun until Josie couldn't stand the awkward silence. 'Let's stop this for now. For both our sakes.' She stood and waited as he did the same. He looked surprised that she was standing above him, looking down.

'I guess this is my escort off the property.'

'I'm giving you a way out. I don't want this to be any worse for you than it already has been. Once this investigation is solved, I hope we can start over.'

He stood. 'And we have a mayoral election and a racetrack standing in the way as well. There's a lot of water that has to travel under that bridge.'

Josie leaned up and kissed him on the cheek. 'Challenge accepted.'

Josie stood in the driveway and watched the dust from Jack's truck settle back on to the gravel road. She replayed their conversation, trying to search out inconsistencies in his explanations but finding none. She considered herself a good judge of character. She thought Jack was a good guy from a family with some shady businesses. But Jack was also part of that family business. Did that make him guilty by association – or just guilty? And, more importantly, guilty of what?

Back inside the house, Josie was too unsettled to waste a night in front of the TV or with a book. She wandered aimlessly from room to room, looking for something to do, until she found herself in the kitchen, staring at the hook where Chester's dog leash used to hang. She'd already called Nick and asked him to return her calls twice. She was beginning to worry. Their relationship hadn't worked due to the distance, but they had ended as friends with no ill will toward each other. So why had his coat been left on her doorstep, and why wasn't he returning her calls?

Josie searched old text messages until she found his mother's phone number and called.

'Josie! It's so nice to hear from you!'

Nick's mother carried dual citizenship, having spent the first twenty-five years of her life in Oregon, until she met Nick's dad and moved to Mexico, where she had lived for the past forty years. Hellen was a progressive woman for the rural town in Mexico where she and Nick's dad lived, but Marco had loved her entrepreneurial spirit and fully supported the car restoration business she had started thirty years before. Now, her business was known throughout North and Central America, and her independence had made their family a small fortune.

'Are you in Mexico?' Hellen asked.

'No, I'm at home. In Texas.'

The two women talked about the business and police work and the troubles along the border before Hellen asked if Josie had talked to Nick lately.

'You know, he still talks about you. He misses you. I don't know if he'll ever settle down.'

'That's actually why I was calling. I've called and left messages for him twice, but he hasn't returned my calls. It isn't like him.'

Hellen laughed. 'It's certainly like him when it comes to

his mother. I can leave ten messages and be lucky to get a return call. But he's in the field, so I get it.'

'I understand that. I'm not upset with him. I just have a police matter I need to discuss with him.'

'I do know he's embedded with one of his teams, down south in Chiapas. He's involved with a kidnapping involving the Zapatistas. It's a bad situation.'

'I understand. If you hear from him, just let him know I need to check in with him.'

'His dad has his actual work phone and can reach him in an emergency. I'll have him call if you need it.'

'No, it's fine. He has other problems to deal with. Just disregard.'

NINETEEN

Ranger Juan Ramos called Josie back the next morning at the office to give her an update regarding the phone timeline the day of Marta's death. Through Marta's phone records, they found that Mike Striker called Marta's phone at two thirty p.m., presumably to cancel.

'But,' Ramos said, 'we have other phone numbers that haven't been identified that day. He could have had a staff member call her.'

'No, Jack said his uncle wanted to call and talk to her instead of having Jack call. He wanted to make it clear to Marta that if she had issues with him, then she was to go directly to him, not to his nephew.' Josie paused. 'I asked Jack about the meeting yesterday, and he said Mike was visiting the racetrack property where Jack was working when they discussed canceling the meeting.'

'He told me the same,' said Ramos. 'Jack and his uncle talked at eleven that morning, but Striker could have waited until that afternoon to call Marta. Maybe he got busy or side-tracked and couldn't make the call.'

'Can you call Jack to confirm that? I think the follow-up is better coming from you. Tell him you may be asking for a warrant for phone records, but you'd like to get a quick response from him now.'

'Josie. I have this. I've been doing this job a long time.'

'Right.'

Josie glanced at her watch. Not even nine in the morning, and she was already frustrated. She called the sheriff's depart-ment and finally convinced his bulldog of a secretary that Josie needed a word with Martinez.

'Do you pay her extra to screen your calls?'

'I think it's her favorite part of the job. Telling people no.'

'I'm just checking in on the investigation into the PD break-in.'

'Someone had a sophisticated drilling set-up and knew what they were doing. But you can also find any of that on YouTube now, so who knows. No prints. We did have one slight break. We traced some debris on the laminate entryway off the back alley. A piece of soil caught in the tread of a boot or shoe was picked up. It was hardpacked, rectangular, so it had clearly come off a shoe. We talked to the custodian who works evenings, and she assured us the entryway had been clean that night when she left at eight.'

'I believe that. She does a great job.'

'Philips took several samples from around Jezebel Black's home and kennel. He delivered them to a woman in the geology department at University of Texas in El Paso. She said one of the samples was an exact match.'

'So the dirt on our police department floor, which had been cleaned at eight o'clock that night, matches the dirt at Jezebel Black's home.'

'Exactly. The place that someone had been prowling around an hour before the break-in at the PD.'

'I'm just pissed, you know? It's embarrassing. Do you know how many times I've requested cameras and a security system for our office? And I get denied every year. You know what they say? "Who would break into the police department? You are your own security," they say. I can't tell you how many times the commissioners have told me that. Well, there's no security past midnight when—' Josie caught herself. She had started to say, *when Marta goes off duty.*

'I have one more detail you'll like. I just discovered Mike Striker's brother is in town. We haven't been able to track him down yet, but I think he's been around for a couple of days. Guess what kind of truck he's driving?' the sheriff asked.

'A Lodge Edition Ford F150,' she said, feeling the dread settle in a bit deeper.

'You got it. I was leaving the grocery store last night and noticed it parked in the lot. I pulled in behind it and saw a rental sticker on the back of the truck. I'd have waited to see who was driving but I was headed to a meeting with my wife in the car with me. Anyway, I snapped a picture of the license plate. This morning, I traced the plate back to a rental agency at the airport in San Antonio. They told me the car was rented to a Morey Striker.'

'Well done,' she said.

'We've got a truck like the one he's rented at the location Jezebel's body was found. I'd like to get a look at his boots.'

'I'm sure he came to town because of the election. I'd sure like to know where he's been the past several days,' Josie said. 'Probably servicing the election machines Arroyo County purchased from his company.'

Josie left a message for Otto that she was headed to Jezebel Black's home. She had looked through the list of items Otto believed were stolen with the evidence boxes. He hadn't listed the registration papers for the dogs in the missing files, and they'd not found them in any of the other paperwork. Either the papers were with the stolen evidence or they had missed paperwork at Jezebel's home.

Josie drove around the yellow tape at the end of the driveway and parked in front of the house. She walked the property first, around the kennel, looking for anything amiss. She looked in on the dogs and found the cages clean and dog bowls filled with water. Sauly was on top of it.

Inside, Josie gloved up and started in the kitchen, going through each drawer and cabinet, examining each piece of paper for anything that looked even remotely connected to Mike Striker, the dogs or the land-buying scheme in Florida. She found a few sticky notes with grocery items, which she ignored, but she kept any paper with a phone number. As she made her way through the living room, she found a drawer in the coffee table that they had missed. She found a stack of cards and letters.

Josie sat down on the couch and skimmed through several handwritten letters from women who appeared to be catching Jezebel up on their lives since college. And then she found a card that had been opened and replaced in its original envelope. The front of the card was a big yellow smiley face. Inside was the note:

Jezebel,

I'm so happy for you! Put that awful year out of your head for good. You deserve this so much. So glad you have moved on – well done!!!

Love you girl,

Emma

The woman signed her first name but she had only included a return address in Houston on the envelope, not her full name. Josie called a friend of hers on the Houston Police Department and asked her to do an address look-up. Before Josie had finished going through the rest of the house, the officer had called back with a name.

'Emma Elaine Costner. She's thirty-two years old, no criminal record, not so much as a speeding ticket. Facebook tells me she's a high school chemistry teacher.' The officer provided Josie a phone number and even a copy of Emma's driver's license photo.

'This is great. I owe you one,' Josie said.

'If I ever need an address look-up for the end of the earth, I'll give you a call.'

'You got a deal.'

Josie called and was surprised when a woman answered, confirming that she was Emma Costner.

'Ms Costner, I'm Chief Josie Gray with the Artemis Police Department in West Texas. I'm calling because I understand you're a friend of Jezebel Black. Is that correct?'

'Oh, it's terrible what happened to her. Is that why you're calling? Because of her death? None of it makes any sense. Her dad called me. He thinks she was murdered! I can't even wrap my head around any of this!'

'Were you close with Jezebel?'

'Yes, we met in high school. I lived in Terlingua. We both acted in a community play together and became friends. I loved her so much. She was such a sweet person. She was so close to having everything come together for her. And now it's over.'

'Do you have time to talk to me about Jezebel? I have a lot of questions about what could have led to her death.'

'Absolutely! I'll drive to Artemis if you need me to.'

'I appreciate that. Right now, I think a phone conversation will be fine. Our biggest questions are around her current business dealings. I agree with Jezebel's dad. I think someone killed her, and I suspect it had to do with the business she was in, but the only thing I know she was doing was the greyhound breeding.'

'Oh, wow. Yeah, that was the beginning. It was crazy how things just sort of spun out of control.'

'Can you take me back to the beginning? How she moved from the trouble with the river-guide business to starting up with Mike Striker?'

Emma sighed and took a moment to respond. 'That's a big question. It's like she went from rock bottom to the best of luck to the worst of luck all in about a year.'

'If you can get me started today, we can always talk again.'

'Telling you how it started is easy. Jezebel had just moved into her brother's house out in the middle of nowhere. She was trying to pull out of the awful deal with the woman dying on the river. Her boss, Sam Greene, had fired her, telling her what a terrible person she was, and how she'd killed that woman and destroyed his business. I mean, if someone doesn't come back to your boat, and her husband tells you that she chose to walk, what are you supposed to do? You're in the middle of a river trip!'

Josie didn't want to go down that rabbit hole. 'So how did she move on from that tragedy to the senator?'

'She was driving into town one evening to get a late supper and she ran out of gas. You know how far out she lives, so she just turned around and was walking back home, and it started to rain. She said she was crying. She was having to live at her brother's house because she couldn't even afford her own place. Mentally, she was a wreck. I was really worried about her during that time. And then a car pulled up and offered her a ride. The guy had a super nice car and she's like, "No, I'm fine." He laughed and was like, "No, obviously you aren't fine. It's pouring with rain." He pulled out some ID that showed he was a senator, so she got in his car. He drove her home. He went into her house to make sure she was OK, and you can imagine the rest.'

'I don't want to assume anything during a murder investigation. I'd rather you supply the details,' Josie said.

'Well, they had sex. Which I thought was a terrible idea. I mean, the guy is married. He was wearing a ring, even that night. But jeez, she needed a little happiness in her life. Then he kept coming around. Trying to buy her property for the racetrack. You know about it?'

'I do.'

'He finally gave up trying to buy it because it was her brother's place, and he had no desire to sell. Anyway, one night Mike stopped by, they had a couple of beers, and he gave her his big master plan. If you know Jezebel, she loves a master plan. That's how her brain works.'

'I'm not sure what you mean.'

'You know how most people take jobs based on their experiences, their life skills? Not Jez. She took a job for the opposite reason. She loved to learn something new. The crazier the better. Like the river guide. She'd never commanded a boat before she applied for that job. The more I think about it, the more I think she just liked reinventing herself. And that's how she ended up breeding greyhounds.' Emma laughed. 'She was so brave. She'd do anything. Honestly, I was so happy to hear her coming out of her depression that I supported her a hundred percent for a while.'

'What happened to change that?' Josie said.

'I think this guy Mike really liked her. Or at least that was Jezebel's take on it. He thought she was great with people. Thought she was especially good at chatting men up. That whole thing made me uncomfortable.'

'What does this have to do with greyhounds?'

'Exactly! That's what I asked. She went from taking some online class on taking care of your greyhound, to all of a sudden taking off for Florida with this guy to look at land.'

Josie smiled. It was always so satisfying when a piece of the puzzle snapped into place.

'He got her into this land-buying scheme, or land-selling.

They bought land super cheap and sold it super high. I know she made money fast on it.'

'How did they get into buying property in Florida?' Josie said.

'No, that's where they went to learn the scheme. The land they were selling was around the racetrack in Texas. But they were selling it to some bigwigs in Florida. But I don't think she felt good about it. She'd try to rationalize it, but she knew they were ripping people off. And that's not who she is . . . not who she was as a person.'

'And you blame Senator Striker for this?'

'Well, him and his brother. The three of them got all buddy-buddy.'

'You didn't like them?' Josie asked.

'She just turned into someone I didn't know. Obviously, there was the married thing. Plus, not a good idea to be sleeping with your business partner. And I couldn't say it to Jezebel, but I kept thinking, why is this successful senator hooking up with Jezebel, whose life is basically one disaster after another? I mean, I loved her no end, but she was a drama magnet. She didn't want the drama, but she was always in the middle of it.'

'What can you tell me about the business partnership?'

'Not a whole lot. She was pretty tight-lipped about it. What I told you is about all I know. Again, how she got caught up in that is beyond me, but I know she was flying to Florida to meet with people.'

'I really appreciate this information, Emma. I'll start following up on this today. Obviously, call me if you think of anything, but especially in terms of the land sales. We'll be searching for names, addresses, business associates. If she ripped the wrong person off, they may have tracked her down to Artemis to settle a score.'

Josie and Otto spent the afternoon sifting through the sticky notes, scraps of paper with names and/or numbers, and a day planner that Josie had brought back from Jezebel's house. At quitting time, they had a list of Florida leads, along with a note in Jezebel's day planner written the week before her

death. Marta Cruz's name was written in the margins. It was
the first tangible connection between the two women. Josie
had called Ramos and filled him in before clocking out at six.

After dinner at the Hot Tamale, Josie got her gym bag out
of the back of her car and changed into hiking shorts and
boots. Against her better judgment, she called Jack Striker
and asked if he was up for an evening hike. The temperature
was down to seventy-nine and almost felt chilly after the upper
nineties of the previous several days.

The hike with Jack was nice. Neither of them talked about
politics or police investigations. They talked about great
places to hike, as well as places to avoid, places they intended
to go before they hit forty, and a few places they agreed they
should explore together. It was a great evening, and Josie
was thankful for the diversion from work.

When she reached her house, the sun had dropped low
enough that the front porch light had come on and was
illuminating what appeared to be a package next to the door.
She assumed it was an Amazon box until she noticed the
handle and realized it was a small six-pack cooler.

Before getting out of her SUV, Josie opened the video app
on her phone to check the activity around her front porch.
All of the cameras were offline. From where she was sitting,
she looked up into the tree to her right and could see the
camera still mounted and intact. She pulled her sidearm and
exited the car, checking each of the cameras in front of the
house, as well as the back two. All cameras looked fine, so
she was hoping for a malfunction with the software.

Josie approached the cooler and weighed her options. What
were the odds that someone had left an explosive device on
her porch? A month ago, she would have been leery, but she
would have assumed there was a greater chance of finding
an iced-down steak left on her porch than a bomb. But with
Nick's coat showing up on her doorstep, and someone
possibly gaining access to her home, the cooler was a concern.

Using a broom handle from the shed, she lifted the cooler
and carried it out to the yard. She poked at the lid until it
finally lifted free, falling on to the ground. She approached
and shone her light down into the container and saw something

buried under the ice. She used gloves she'd brought from the shed to pull out a gallon-sized Ziplock bag and a sheet of copy paper with the printed words, *Fingerprint access can be used in many creative ways.*

Josie turned the bag around and found a human finger with the bottom of it wrapped in blood-soaked gauze. She screamed and dropped it back into the cooler, taking a step away and shining her flashlight out into the night. She called Ramos and left a message on his voicemail, and then called Sheriff Martinez. She explained what she had just found, as well as the other incidents.

'Why didn't you tell me all this before? With what happened to Marta, you decided this stuff didn't matter?'

'It was a missing dog leash and a hairdryer on my bed! You know how ridiculous that would have sounded?'

'Do you have any idea whose finger this might be?'

Josie took a ragged breath, trying not to let her thoughts get too dark. 'Nick's coat was left on my front door. And he is the only person who has ever had fingerprint access to my home. I can't help wondering if someone didn't do this as some sick way to get into my house.'

'You sit tight. Don't go inside until I get out there. Call Otto and tell him you'll be staying with him for a couple of days.'

'Yes, sir.'

'I'm not kidding, Josie. I'm already in my car. I'll be there in fifteen minutes.'

Josie hung up and tried Nick's cell phone. She didn't bother leaving a message, but she did call his mom and ask her to play the trump card. She asked for Nick's dad to try to reach him on the secure line.

Ten minutes later, Otto pulled down Josie's driveway with Martinez directly behind him. Philips arrived several minutes later to retrieve the finger and run it into the sheriff's department for prints while Otto cleared the house and began taking fingerprints on the exterior doors.

Martinez sat in Josie's car with her and had her explain the other incidents in detail, focusing on the timing. He had her try to imagine what someone could want from her house, and she could think of nothing. She described her relationship with Nick and speculated who else might know her habits well enough to enter.

'I don't get the security system. When I installed this a few years ago, it was top of the line. I reset the system after the hairdryer incident, so this' – she gestured out of the window toward where the cooler had been placed on her doorstep – 'this finger shouldn't even have worked.'

'Even if we tried the finger, it wouldn't provide the access. Correct?'

'Correct.'

'So maybe that's why this is happening. Could they have used it the first two times, and that's why it was left now?'

Josie shook her head at the conversation. 'This is insanity. Why would anyone do this? What's the motive? I have nothing of value. There's so little of value they had to steal a dog leash. And for what? To terrorize me? To what end?'

'Two women have been murdered in your town. We assume both are somehow linked to the election. Can you find any connection between what's happening to you, and what happened to Marta or Jezebel?'

'There's the connection between Marta and Jezebel and Mike Striker. But I'm not sure how I would fit into that at this point, other than the investigation, but my house issues started before we even knew about the dog track.'

'Who knew you were away from your house this evening?'

Josie thought for a moment and felt an instant burn in the pit of her stomach. 'I didn't tell anyone I was going hiking, other than Jack Striker.' She jumped when her cell phone vibrated against the dashboard. She picked it up and was shocked to see Nick's name on the caller ID.

'Josie, what's going on? I'm so sorry I haven't called you. I'm on a terrible case right now. A brother and sister kidnapped. I haven't even been carrying my personal phone with me.'

'Don't apologize. You're fine. I've had some strange incidents taking place and wanted to check in with you. Make sure you're safe.'

'Everything's fine. Just dealing with psychopaths.'

'Your hand? It's OK? No accidents?'

'Josie, what are you talking about?'

She explained the cooler with the finger on ice, as well as the incidents leading up to it.

'I'm so sorry I didn't respond. You know that coat you mentioned? That was hanging on your door? I know which one that is. I had it in the back of your Jeep. I wore it camping one weekend and left it in the back. If I remember right, it was in a black duffel bag.'

Josie remembered the duffel bag. It was stuffed in a box of camping gear that she'd not used since she and Nick quit seeing each other.

'Whoever is doing this has to be someone who knows your past with me. Knows about me setting up your security system, and that my fingerprint would still be in the system.'

'I don't know who that would be. Unless someone made that assumption, given our relationship.'

'I'm sending someone to set you up with a proper surveillance system with cameras you can't jam, and to reset your security system. He'll wipe out all of the previous access prints and codes.'

'You don't need to do that.'

'Josie, you can't be buying your security system off Amazon. OK?'

She grinned at the stern sound of his voice and realized how much she missed him. 'Listen to me. This is not necessary. Your team has bigger issues to deal with than my security system.'

He was quiet for a beat too long. 'I'm in the middle of a family's worst nightmare. And whether you like or not, you're as close to family as I ever got, outside of my own parents, so you've been on my mind a lot lately. I know we can't make it work, but I still love you. And I always will. You don't get to tell me no on this one.'

TWENTY

Bleary-eyed and exhausted, Josie arrived at work to find Otto already in the office. He'd left angry with her for not spending the night with Delores and him after the cooler incident. Josie had insisted the security system had done its job because there was no log entry into the house, although someone had tried several different passcodes that had been denied. One of the sheriff's deputies had looked at her video cameras and the software, and declared that someone had 'jammed' the cameras: someone had found the same frequency as her cameras and overpowered her wireless signal, causing all the cameras to fail. By the time the initial investigation had been completed, Josie was angry and tired, and had no intention of packing an overnight bag and driving to Otto's. His last words to her before he slammed his patrol car door were, 'You're too damned stubborn for your own good.'

Josie walked into the office expecting a cold shoulder or another lecture, but instead found Otto standing over two plates of softball-sized cinnamon rolls, pouring steaming cups of coffee.

'Delores just pulled these out of the oven a half-hour ago. And you know, nobody makes a cinnamon roll like she does,' he said.

'What's all this for?'

'This is my way of apologizing for being an ass. I walked in the house last night fuming over you, and she asked what I would have done had I been in your shoes.'

Josie grinned. 'Delores just cuts right to the crux of the matter.'

'That she does. But then she offered up cinnamon rolls, so all is good.' He pulled a chair out for Josie, and she sat. 'I assume you had an uneventful night after we left?'

'Just one event. Nick finally called me back last night at

about midnight. He's fine. His ten fingers are whole. If it makes you feel better, he gave me hell for not staying at your house last night, too.' Josie took a giant bite and closed her eyes as the icing melted over the warm soft bread.

Otto grinned and finished his own first bite. 'This is one of the few foods that wouldn't benefit from an extra dob of butter. The rolls are perfect as they are.'

A few bites in, with their disagreement from the night before long forgotten, Josie explained what she had learned about Mike Striker's sexual relationship with Jezebel Black.

'That man is reprehensible,' Otto said.

'I didn't get to ask you last night what you found after going through her paperwork again.'

'A few things,' he said. 'I came across two dinner receipts, both from last month. One from McDonalds and another from a restaurant called Domu. I looked at the location, and both are in Florida, down around Naples.'

Josie pulled an empty page off a large desk calendar pad, taped it on the wall and wrote *April* at the top. In the boxes for each date, she wrote in the restaurant name as well as the time Jezebel visited each one.

'Next, I went back through her credit cards that we pulled from her home desk drawer. I had only seen statements from her personal MasterCard. I was sorting through her checkbook holder where she kept library cards, gas points cards and so on, and I found a Visa card. With Mike Striker's name on it.'

'Really? You think she stole his card?'

'Or she used it for business purchases.'

'I think it's time to cash in a favor with your buddy, Carla Striker,' Josie said.

Otto arrived unannounced at Carla's house at a little after ten. He had seen an announcement in the local paper that Mike Striker was making a speech that morning at the local Lion's Club. Carla didn't have a job outside the home, so Otto was hoping to have access to Carla and their bills for at least an hour.

He parked in front of the massive home, marveling at the money the senator had amassed. He wondered if the shady business deals diminished the senator's enjoyment of his riches, if he went to bed a half-beat shy of a heart attack each night with worry.

He rang the doorbell, and a moment later Carla opened the door wearing yoga pants and a skintight T-shirt that emphasized every bump and roll. She was holding a half-empty bag of Tootsie Rolls. She smiled warmly, appearing genuinely happy to see Otto, a characteristic Otto appreciated about her.

'I was hoping you might have a few minutes to talk with me.'

'Honey, I have been watching my workout show on the TV while eating stale Tootsie Rolls. I went to the trouble of putting on this horrific outfit, and I'm not even going to break a sweat. I definitely have a minute.'

He followed her into the front sitting room, and they sat in club chairs that faced a large window with a magnificent view of the rolling, rocky desert.

'As you know, the police have been investigating Jezebel Black's death.' Otto noticed her cheerful expression shift to one of pain, but he didn't know their relationship well enough to understand the meaning bchind the look. 'We're trying to understand the businesses she was involved in, and whether any of her business contacts could have been connected with her death.'

Carla looked surprised. 'I think my husband is a complete ass, but I don't think he's a murderer.'

'No, no. I didn't explain myself very well. We just don't know very much about the businesses that she was involved in. In fact, the only person I know for sure that she was involved with was Mike. I'm hoping you may be able to shed some light on their partnership, and especially who else she was involved with.'

She frowned and looked uncomfortable with the conversation. 'I don't know, Otto. There was the racetrack, the dog breeding. I've heard Mike and Morey talk about some land scheme, but he's pretty guarded with me when it comes to business talk. Honestly, I don't think he trusts me, but I guess for good reason.' She shrugged.

Otto held out the Visa card to Carla and she took it. 'I

found this in a checkbook holder that belonged to Jezebel. It belongs to your husband. I'm hoping you'll consider giving me access to the statements for this card so we can better understand what the business entailed.'

'You already know Mike is not tech-savvy. He keeps all his credit card logins on a spreadsheet. You can have them all as far as I'm concerned.' Carla stood and disappeared down the hallway. Several minutes later, he heard the whirring of a printer and she came back with a piece of paper with websites, usernames and passwords. 'He does the bills, so I wouldn't even know where to begin to find statements, but that's all the login information. I'm guessing the Visa is on there somewhere.'

Otto thanked her, surprised at the windfall. 'Do you know anything about a business deal he was exploring with Jezebel that had to do with Florida?'

She groaned. 'I was afraid you were headed there. Do you have any idea how humiliating it is to be married to someone who is keen on having sex with every attractive female in town?'

'I've spent my entire life in a small town. I think I can imagine.'

'Were they having an affair?'

'According to a friend of Jezebel's, they were,' Otto said.

'I confronted him about the Florida trips. He swore it was strictly business. He claimed they were learning how to sell swampland in the Everglades. I was like, "Come on, I'm not an idiot." He swore that's what they were doing. He swears people are still buying that same damn swampland today. But you know Mike. He's never satisfied with the basic plan. He hasn't told me this part, but I think he and Morey tried out the Florida land deals to learn how it works. I think their goal is selling plots of land along the Rio Grande where the racetrack is being developed.'

Otto nodded.

'You know his goal isn't really to have live dogs, right? He just wanted to get into pari-mutuel betting, and the loophole with the dog track gave him the opportunity. He figures he'll make a fortune off the internet betting.'

Otto leaned back in his comfortable chair with the beautiful view of the desert, nodding as the big picture came into focus. 'Your husband is a pretty smart businessman. Do you know what part Jezebel was playing?'

'I don't know this for sure, and I don't want to disparage the dead, but I think Jezebel was his flim-flam girl. She looked good in a dress. She could schmooze a table full of men.'

'Do you know any of Mike's associates in Florida?'

'He talks to some guy with the last name Bossonavitch. I remember him because Mike will call this man on the phone and refer to him as Boss Man. It just nauseates me. I don't know how I ever ended up in a marriage to such a sleaze.'

Otto went back to the office where he filled Josie in, and they headed straight to his computer. He found Mike Striker's Visa credit card on the spreadsheet, with a comment typed in the *Notes* column: *JB business use.*

Otto found that the card had been taken out in February of the year before, with the first expenditures paid in March, and all of them taking place in Florida. He found three flights to Florida over the past month, with her last trip taken just seven days before her death. Josie plotted each of the dates on the calendar she had taped to the wall and found the dates were lining up.

They resisted the very strong urge to access the other credit cards and accounts that Carla had provided. Josie wasn't sure of the legality of the police logging into accounts that hadn't been specifically linked to an ongoing investigation. She assumed they would need a warrant for those accounts, but since Mike's legal wife had provided the Visa login, they would make good use of that one.

Next, she and Otto split up the remaining purchases listed on the statement.

Josie started with two charges that had been made to Coston Elli's in Naples. A quick internet search revealed it as the second restaurant in Florida anointed with a Michelin star. One charge had totaled $990. The other charge had totaled $1,250. She called and a manager looked through his schedule book and informed Josie that the hostess, Gabriella Gallardo, who had been working both of the nights in question, was due in the next afternoon at three o'clock.

As she was wrapping up her paperwork for the day, she received a call from Sheriff Martinez about the cooler investigation.

'We got an international print on the finger.'

'I'm guessing it wasn't from France.'

'Good guess. Mexico. Some thug from Juarez who did time in a federal prison. His whereabouts are unknown.'

'You got my message that Nick is OK?'

'I did. Which is great news, but the thug from Juarez is not. I thought your issues with the Medrano Cartel had resolved themselves after the past several years of silence.'

'I did, too. You remember Sergio Pando, former Federales?'

'Sure. He's National Guard now?'

'That's him. He said he's not heard rumors about me, but he also said femicide is still an issue in their region. Killing women because they're women.'

'I'll be honest,' he said, 'I don't know where we go with this.'

'Fax me over everything you found on the owner of the finger. Nick asked for the information and said he'd check into it. His sources are better than anything we'd have access to.'

'It's the motivation. I don't see any connection to the election or Striker, or Marta's murder. Now with the print from Mexico, it feels even less connected to anything local.' Martinez sighed. 'This is too personal, too important, for me not to put everything I have into this, but I'm at a loss.'

Josie was touched at the angst he was obviously feeling over the case.

'I know we've been approaching this as someone who knows you personally. Knows your habits with the dog, knows your hairdryer being out would throw up a red flag. Knows about Nick's fingerprint. But I'm not sure someone would have to know anything about you. What if someone saw the dog leash, assumed you had a dog and took the leash, knowing it would be something you would miss quickly? The hairdryer was just something out of place in an otherwise clean room. Nick's coat? Just something grabbed out of the back of your Jeep. Even the fingerprint. You're thinking someone was sending you a message about Nick. Maybe it was someone sending you a message about anyone getting access to your house. They were just reminding you there are lots of ways to access your security system. They've obviously hacked it.'

'What are you getting at?' she asked.

'I want you to rethink this. You've been focusing on the few people who would know those details about you. But maybe it's someone who doesn't know you personally but wants to send a clear message. That they have hacked into your life, and that you have no control over it.'

TWENTY-ONE

The town of Artemis came together for a sunrise memorial service for Marta in front of the courthouse. Mayor O'Kane started the ceremony, followed by Josie offering a tribute to Marta as both a police officer and a friend, ending with Marta's priest offering a blessing. Due to out-of-town family members, Marta's funeral wasn't scheduled until later in the week. Josie was struggling with the fact that she'd not been able to talk with Marta's family as she would have liked, fearing that she wouldn't bring comfort to the family, only more pain.

After the memorial service, she received a call from Teresa, Marta's daughter. Josie offered her condolences again, and Teresa said that she appreciated the flowers the department had sent, but that her dad blamed the police for Marta's death.

'Can I ask why he thinks that?' Josie said.

'He never wanted my mom to be a cop. He thought it was too dangerous. Then, after they got divorced, and she became one in the US, it really made him angry. Obviously, he couldn't stop her, though. They fought over it a lot.'

'Does he have a specific reason for thinking her being a police officer caused her death, or do you mean the job in general?'

'I think in general. But that's not really why I called,' Teresa said. 'A police officer met with me the day after you came to see me. Dad was on the phone with me when the officer came to my door. The officer wanted my mom's logins and passwords to her phone and computer. My dad said absolutely not. He didn't want the police having my mom's personal information. He said the police would try to pin her death on something she did wrong.'

Josie remained quiet, listening to Teresa describe her dad's feelings toward the department. And, by default, toward

Josie and Otto. She forced herself not to respond and become defensive. Teresa didn't need any additional drama in her life.

'You probably know that I told the officer that I didn't have my mom's password. But then I got your message, about how you needed her password, too. I know you want to find out what happened to my mom as much as I do. My mom cared a lot about you. And Otto, too. I want you to have the password. It sounds weird, but it's kind of a big deal to me because of my dad. But I want you to know that I trust you.'

Josie choked back tears, swallowing hard before she could speak. 'I appreciate this, Teresa. Even more than the information, I'm grateful to have your trust. It means a lot that you know we're fighting for your mom.'

Josie drove the password over to the sheriff's department, where the evidence for Marta's case was being stored. Ramos had agreed to meet Josie there. She hoped he would allow her to see the text messages since she had gained the access. He seemed to have softened toward her since he had shared that his office was being pressured by the governor's office.

Ramos carried the evidence box into the conference room and unpacked it, while Josie filled him in on her conversation with Teresa. He pulled out a plastic baggy holding a thick black phone case, and a wave of sadness ran over Josie at the familiar sight of it. Marta had been known around the office for cracking phone screens, smashing phones or losing at least one a year, so Josie had bought her one of the cases that looked like military-grade gear.

Ramos turned the phone on, and Josie handed him an index card where she had written down the password. The phone opened up immediately. He went straight to the text messages and held the phone up so Josie could read the name at the top of the screen: Javi.

'That's Marta's nickname for Javier, her ex-husband. He lives in Mexico.'

'Hang on.' Ramos put the phone on the table and rifled

through a stack of folders and papers. 'These are copies of her phone records,' he said. 'We've got the last number that came into her phone, but it was from Mexico. We've had trouble with authorities wanting to give us the identification of the person.' He slid the paperwork over to Josie. 'Let me pull up this Javier's contact number in her phone. Read me that last received call on the statement.'

Josie read the number and looked up to see Ramos nodding.

'The last call Marta received came from her ex-husband. The same person she was texting here.' He pointed a finger at Josie. 'And that last call pinged off a cell tower in Arroyo County.'

Josie felt dread welling up in the pit of her stomach. 'I've never known Javier to come to the US. He told me he couldn't even drive to Corpus Christi to see their daughter after finding out about Marta's death because he didn't have a passport. Marta has always gone to Mexico to visit him because she had the passport. I always thought it was his excuse to keep from having to make the trip. The lazy bastard.'

'Josie, this goes no further. Agreed?'

She nodded. 'Understood.'

'Not to Otto. Not to anyone. This could be a logistical nightmare. We can't even get a phone number from the Mexican authorities, and we have to convince them we need to investigate one of their citizens for murder.'

'It's a long way from being in town to shooting your ex-wife. A woman he claimed to still love. See what that text exchange was about.'

Josie watched Ramos open the phone back up and read through pages of text messages. 'My God, Josie. The last message she sent to him was the address to the fire house.'

Rage ran through her. Like so many people, she had always been willing to give him another chance; she could only hope that he'd not done this terrible thing. How many times had Javier received one last chance throughout his life, with his wife and daughter, his family and the community, and he had rejected their hope each time?

'This will destroy Marta's daughter,' Josie said.

Ramos scrolled back through the messages. 'They're arguing back and forth about him coming to see her. She's telling him no. She says she'll see him next week. They go back and forth again; she finally says she won't meet at her house, but she'll talk to him at the fire house. She gives the exact address.'

Josie shakes her head, both shocked and not at all. 'He loved her. Why would he do this?'

Ramos scrolled back through older messages. 'He mentions someone named Mark that Marta knew. Do you have any idea who that is?'

Josie closed her eyes. In that instant, it all made sense. Everyone in the community had asked the question a hundred different ways. Who could possibly want to harm such a kind, unassuming person as Marta?

'I bet he's referring to Mark Jackson. Marta had a date scheduled with him just a few days before her death. They were going to Marfa to the music festival,' she said. 'What does Javier say?'

Josie watched him scroll through what must have been dozens of texts.

'He brought the name up first. It's obvious they had already had a conversation about Mark. Marta is telling him it's none of his business. He's telling her to come home where she belongs. Back to Mexico. That part of the conversation took place several days before her murder.'

'And we have Javier's phone in our county the day of her murder.'

'Extradition will be the issue,' Ramos said.

'He's a curandero. Basically, a respected healer in the community. He's also a raging alcoholic. The reluctant saint is what they call him. But the community is blaming the corrupt American law enforcement for her death,' she said.

'I've been involved in extraditions in the past. They don't move fast. Don't expect a quick resolution,' Ramos said. 'What about your cop friend in Mexico? Isn't he part of the new National Guard?'

Josie nodded, feeling as if her thoughts were coming up through molasses. Visions of Marta and Javier in the basement at the old fire house, Marta facing the love of her life, knowing or maybe just suspecting what was coming. Josie wondered if Marta had begged him to spare her life, for their daughter's sake, or if she had been so surprised that Javier was pointing a gun at her that she couldn't even talk.

'Josie?'

'Yes,' she said, clearing her throat, pulling herself back. 'Sergio Pando. He's a close friend of Marta's. They grew up together. He knows the kind of person Javier is. He's your best bet. I can call and brief him before you make contact.'

'You're sure he won't sabotage the investigation?'

'I'm positive. He's worried about Javier and Marta for many years.'

'Let's do it. Make the call.'

Josie called Sergio and left a message saying that she had information about Javier. He called back immediately. Josie put him on speaker and introduced him to Ramos, then explained everything they had learned that morning.

'I'm sorry, Sergio. I know this is terrible to hear.'

'It's terrible because it didn't have to happen. Did you realize that I'm the one who convinced her to move to the US? As his drinking worsened through the years, turning into binges that went from days to weeks, he became more and more angry. I begged her to break off all ties with him. I thought moving to the US after the divorce would help, but it didn't. She continued to come back to Mexico to see him, to take care of his drunken ass.'

'I want him behind bars,' Josie said. 'I want him to pay for what he's done. For destroying his own daughter.'

'I'll be blunt, Josie. You are not well liked here. Not in Ojinaga,' Sergio said. 'People blame you for Marta's death. If they see you and your government trying to come into our country, to take a beloved man from his community . . . They will never give him up.'

'Will you meet with us? With Ramos and me to help us come up with a plan?'

'If others see me cooperating with you, then you lose your one . . .' He struggled to find the right word in English. 'Help? Connection?'

'I get it. You can't meet with the enemy.'

'That's the truth of it,' he said. 'I don't want to cross the border right now. I don't want it on record, me coming into Artemis. And Ramos? You could come to Ojinaga, but no one would talk to you. It would make matters worse.'

'Meet us at the watchtower tonight? After sunset – say, nine o'clock?' She looked over at Ramos who gave her a thumbs-up.

'I'll do it,' Sergio said.

Josie gave him directions to a wide bend in the Rio that was currently choked with salt cedar, where the water was only running about four inches deep. 'You won't have any trouble crossing in your four-wheel drive.'

'I won't have a Border Patrol officer arresting me as I come up out of the river?'

'I'll have that taken care of. You'll be safe.'

Josie hung up, and Ramos sighed. 'It's a start.'

She looked at him for a long moment. 'You know that I'm going to have to tell Otto. I can't keep this from him.'

Ramos stared at her and said nothing, finally skipping over her comment as if she'd not said it. 'Does this Sergio have any pull in his department?'

'I don't know anymore,' she said. 'The National Guard has only been in existence for a few years. It absorbed officers from the military, the federal and the naval police. It's hard to say. I do know he's respected in his community.'

'Then we'll meet and see what happens. I'll see you there at a little before nine.'

After filling Otto in on Javier, they spent the rest of the day working the Jezebel Black case, trying to remain occupied while knowing that the person who murdered their friend walked the streets of Mexico a free man.

Otto left the office to track down a local developer friend of his who said he knew Michael Bossonavitch and that he could give Otto an earful.

Josie worked on the timeline, tracking Jezebel's movements in Florida, and at three p.m. she called Coston Elli's and asked to speak to Gabriella Gallardo.

'This is Gabriella.' She sounded young and cheerful. Josie pictured a pretty young woman in a black dress and heels, preparing to cater to some of the wealthiest and most influential people in the state of Florida.

'Hi, Gabriella. My name is Josie Gray. I'm the chief of police in Artemis, Texas. I'm working a case that I'm hoping you might be able to offer some information about. Do you have a few minutes to talk?'

'Oh! A police case? Me?'

'Yes, I know you weren't involved, but I think you may know some of the people who were. Would you mind talking with me?'

'No, I'm sorry. I don't mind at all. You just surprised me, that's all.'

'I understand. I'm looking for any information you can give me about a group that ate at the restaurant on two different nights, exactly one week apart. One of the checks was over a thousand dollars.'

'That's actually not that uncommon here. I know that's hard to believe. Do you know what name the reservation was under?'

'Jezebel Black.'

'Oh my gosh, I loved her! She tipped me! No one tips the hostess. We're just the person who makes it all happen, but nobody gives us a second thought. She and I, though, we hit it off immediately. She came in early, and we picked out the table by the window so we could get her a good seat by the ocean. Then she actually showed me photos of the men who were coming to dinner. I loved that! I've never had that happen. She just thought of every detail. She showed me where she wanted each of them seated. She paid me a hundred dollars both nights. I was by her side the whole time.'

'Did you notice anything odd at the dinner? Any of the men who were angry or acted out of line?'

'No, not at all.' Gabriella laughed conspiratorially. 'I shouldn't say this about one of our customers, but I don't mean it in a bad way at all. You should have seen her. She worked that table. Like, she had those men eating out of her hands.'

'Do you have the photos of the men?'

'Yes, I kept them because she had the same group both of those nights. People love to get the same table. It makes them feel like regulars. We even laughed that she and I would make a great team. I'm going to put the phone down. Give me one minute.'

Josie heard a rustling of papers and drawers opening and shutting, finally an exclamation before Gabriella came back on the phone. 'I found it. I knew I had a folder. It looks like she pulled articles off the internet where there were photos of each of them. Jezebel said they were all into land development. Big shots, if you know what I mean.'

'Could you scan me a copy of all of the information that Jezebel shared with you? I'd appreciate it if you could do it now. Then if we have technology problems, you'll know.'

Josie provided the office number and a few minutes later articles featuring four men rolled through the machine. The name of each man was neatly printed at the top of each article.

The woman came back on the line, and Josie thanked her for the information she had provided.

'Gabriella, I'm sorry to have to share this with you. It sounds like you and Jezebel had formed a friendship.'

'No. You're about to tell me something terrible, aren't you?'

'Jezebel was found murdered. The coroner's findings are inconclusive. But I'm convinced she was pushed or thrown off the edge of a canyon.'

'Oh my God, that's horrible! You don't know who did it? You think one of those men did it?' Gabriella's voice became increasingly hysterical.

'We don't know yet. We're checking into her business dealings, trying to understand if she had enemies, or someone who would have gained financially from her death.'

'This is just awful.'

'If you think of anything else, please call me. Even a small detail could help us put together something that could lead to her killer.'

'I do have one more piece of paper. I'm sure it's nothing, but you can see who Jezebel thought were the most important clients. It's where she wanted them seated, with the two best clients facing her and the ocean. She wanted eye contact.'

'That's great. Please fax that, too.'

The next piece of paper that came through was a seating chart. Jezebel would have had her back to the ocean – the worst seat at the best table in the house. But her view was on the money at the table, not the beach.

'Can you tell me anything about the men?' Josie asked.

'I knew two of the men. Well, I didn't *know* them – I knew *of* them.'

'Their names?'

'Jamison Leopold. He's probably the most well-known around here. His picture is on every billboard in south Florida. He's always super tanned and has a smile so white his teeth look painted. He has this way of throwing his head back and laughing really loud so people notice him. You should see the women fawn over him. I think he's kind of creepy.'

'How so?' Josie asked.

'I mean, fake smile, fake teeth, fake laugh. Don't you think that's creepy?'

Josie grinned at the summation. 'I suppose.' She scanned the news article. 'It looks like he's a real-estate developer – residential properties. Is that right?'

'Yes, houses and land. A year or so ago, there was some big drama about him brokering the biggest land sale in Florida history.'

'Drama because it was illegal?'

'That's what people said. But I don't know. That's not really my thing.'

'And who is the other person you know?'

'Texas Tate.' She sighed. 'I know, it sounds ridiculous. I swear, the richer they get, the weirder they get.'

'Do you know why he's called Texas?'

'I guess he's from there. I'm pretty sure Jezebel knew him. He's only lived in Florida for a couple of years, but he's made millions selling real estate.'

Josie remembered a man named Dave Tate who had sold his family's ranch a few years back for a small fortune and then broke into real estate. She remembered him moving away from West Texas, but, like Gabriella, high-dollar real-estate deals weren't really her thing either.

After Gabriella's information dwindled down to nothing, Josie thanked her for her cooperation and promised to keep her informed about the investigation.

Josie's good fortune continued after she hung up with Gabriella. She called the police department in Naples, Florida, where Jamison Leopold resided and worked. When Josie pulled up the website of the Naples PD and saw the beautiful new building surrounded by palm trees, she assumed she'd get a voice mailbox and no return call. Instead, she was patched into the chief of police, who knew Jamison well.

Chief John Haughman had worked as a major crimes detective for ten years before taking on the role of chief, and he'd worked several cases on Jamison Leopold but faced a legal team where no expense was spared Haughman made it clear that Jamison was a free man only because of his incredible wealth.

'The thing with men like Jamison is that they've spent a lifetime getting away with crimes large and small. It becomes a way of living. He clearly believes he is above the law and his money allows him to do whatever he pleases. Eventually, the right prosecutor comes along, the evidence stacks up, the stars align, and the bastard gets what he deserves.'

'Would you be surprised to hear his name in connection with a murder investigation?'

'I would not. Murder is a means to an end to a man like Jamison. He started out as a developer selling lots for cash in an area deemed unfit for construction. Over the course of about two years, he made a fortune and lost it. He learned a bit about the legal system and came back with a new plan. Second time around, he made a fortune and kept it. He's moved on to bigger investors all over the country. I could see your Texas racetrack having a certain appeal to Jamison.'

'Have you heard the name Jezebel Black in any of your investigations?'

'No. And I think I'd remember that name.'

Josie explained her possible connection to the developers and the basic details of her death.

'What did she do to get upside down with this crowd?'

'She might not have done anything. She's a former river guide. Has no background in finance. At her death, she had a quarter of a million dollars in a bank account. That may not seem like much in relation to Jamison Leopold, but for Jezebel it was a fortune.'

'And she was running with a senator?'

'He's the one with power and money. Someone recently referred to her as a flim-flam girl. I think the senator was working things from Texas and sending Jezebel to wine and dine. We're wondering if she didn't try to pull something over on someone above her skillset.'

'Clear enough.'

Josie gave Haughman the names of the other men who attended the dinners. He'd not heard of any of them but promised to get back to Josie after running their names.

TWENTY-TWO

S piral steps soared fifty feet into the air, leading to a narrow walkway that circled the watchtower. The seventy-five-year-old wooden structure allowed a clear view of the desert on both sides of the Rio Grande. Josie ran in the mornings before work and hiked frequently in the desert heat, but the climb up the tower left her winded that evening. She leaned against the Plexiglas windows on the outside of the tower to catch her breath and take in the view before Sergio arrived. She looked north across the vast unpopulated Chihuahuan desert. There were no houses or signs of human habitation for miles. Nothing but the sound of the wind singing along the guy wires.

Josie used the handrail to walk slowly around the tower, remembering the wildfires that had ripped through the area a few years back, and the nights spent on the tower watching for cartel movement across the border. She looked down to the river and let her eyes follow along the access road that led to Piedra Labrada, Artemis's sister city in Mexico. Both towns remained steady at roughly twenty-five hundred people, and both towns faced many of the same problems as other border towns: immigration issues, unemployment, pockets of disabling poverty and crime, understaffed police and fire, unfunded state mandates. But alongside the difficulties was an unshakable spirit and determination that came from raising families in tough conditions. Josie had not had an easy childhood, but she knew the tough times had molded her character in positive ways. Aside from losing her dad at a young age, there was little in her life that she would change if given the chance.

She looked out over the land and the river and the desert that stretched far into both the US and Mexico, and it gave her a great sense of pride that she played a key role in keeping the people of the Territory safe. During her tenure in West

Texas, there had been times when the town's safety had felt tenuous at best. Juarez, Mexico, just down the road from Artemis, had once been considered the most dangerous city in the world. And yet that violence had remained primarily to the south.

The watchtower was used jointly by Border Patrol and local police. Law enforcement was territorial by nature, given the various agencies' overlapping boundaries. The tower had become a place to gather with no controlling agency or rules to follow. It had made sense to Josie for the chief of police to meet Sergio, the officer from Mexico, and Ramos, the Texas Ranger, in this safe place to come up with a solution that went beyond the borders.

Josie unlocked the door to the interior of the watchtower and was glad to get out of the pelting sand and the wind. Inside, it sounded like rain as the sand hit the large Plexiglas windows. Josie walked around the room, taking in the familiar weathered wood and dust smells, inspecting for signs that other officers had been using the space.

A map rack made of old pallet wood was located in the center of the room. She pulled out the wide shallow drawers to be sure the maps were intact, and in the bottom drawer she found a stack of paperwork titled *Application for Immediate Retirement: Federal Employees Retirement System.* She picked up the packet and rifled through the pages, looking for a name. She smiled and imagined the Border Patrol agent printing the papers at his desk and then bringing them to the watchtower to look out over the land that probably felt like his own. He'd likely hiked, driven, maybe even ridden a horse over hundreds of miles of this terrain at all hours of the day for years. Despite the stress and heartache that accompanied the job, it would be a tough one to give up.

Josie watched the tip of the sun slip below the horizon before she spotted Sergio's truck round the bend of the river. She shone her flashlight on him and he motioned for her to come down. She smiled, assuming he wouldn't want the climb.

They sat in Josie's police car and she gave him a rundown

on everything she knew about Marta's investigation, from
finding the body at the old fire house, to the recent news that
Marta had texted Javier the fire house address, and that his
phone had pinged off the tower.

'All those years he refused to get a passport so that he could
cross the border to see his daughter. Marta always had to be
the one to travel. And now this. It's hard to understand how
a man who was so filled with evil could be viewed with rever-
ence by so many people.'

'Do you think it came from so many people expecting things
from Javier that he didn't feel capable of living up to? Marta
said his whole life he felt like an imposter.'

'Don't give that man an excuse.' Sergio's voice rose, and
he jabbed a finger toward her. 'I heard that nonsense from
Marta for years.'

Josie's cell phone buzzed, and she saw it was a call from
Ramos.

'I can't make it tonight,' he said. 'There's been a
thirty-seven-car pile-up on the I-10 up by Balmorhea. I'm
on my way now.'

'Any fatalities?'

'Three confirmed dead. Quite a few injured.'

'You need me to head that way?' she asked.

'No, there's cars everywhere. The pictures I've seen look
like a bomb hit. Cars piled on top of one another. I'm headed
up to reroute traffic on the interstate. Better keep your phone
on, though.'

'I'll be on standby. You be safe.'

'Will do. Send my apologies to Sergio and get me a to-do
list. We'll connect tomorrow on the extradition.'

Josie hung up and saw Sergio was already on his phone,
pulling up pictures of the disaster. He put his phone down and
looked at Josie, his expression weary. 'I don't know how much
longer I can keep this up. If I could have one week without
dealing with death. Even one *day* without murder, suicide, car
crashes, beatings. It never stops and it never gets better. Why
do we do this?'

Josie had heard that same line of questioning from other
officers over the past year. Marta was gone, and Otto was

close to retirement; she had even entertained the idea of leaving law enforcement and doing something different. But then what?

'We cannot let this man walk free after what he did to Marta. We have to see this through,' she said.

Sergio sat staring out of the window at the river sparkling in the moonlight for what seemed like a very long time. He finally handed Josie a shipping envelope filled with paperwork. 'This is an extradition package. There's information on filing a provisional arrest warrant. Once you've read through this, we need to meet with authorities outside of Ojinaga.'

Josie started to open the packet and received a series of vibrations on her phone. Surprised, she opened her phone to see she'd received notification of a failed breach of entry on her home security system. Nick had sent one of his team members to reset the system and set up a way for her to monitor information remotely from her phone. He had also set up cameras that allowed her to view all angles of her house. The cameras were now disguised, so shooting out the cameras and jamming the system was no longer an option.

Sergio looked over her shoulder. 'Someone tried to use a code on the fingerprint reader.'

Josie opened up the camera app and scrolled through each of the cameras. She pulled up the side angle and saw a person running down the side of her house toward the backyard.

'Someone is at my house!'

'Move! Give me your phone and I'll monitor while you drive.'

Josie took off. 'It's eight miles from the watchtower to my house.'

Sergio continued moving from camera to camera to monitor. 'I've got him again. I see one person. He's moving up to your door. I'm assuming this is your back patio. He's looking up, as if he's searching for a camera. Oh my God. It's Javier.'

'What the hell?'

'I'm sure of it.'

Josie floored the gas, fishtailing on the gravel road. Four minutes later, she sped down Schenck Road, turning on the SUV's spotlights to light up her house.

'This is my road. We can't lose him, Sergio. Where is he currently?'

She pulled into her yard to better light up the front of the house and slammed on the brakes. They both opened their doors and exited, yelling Javier's name, guns drawn.

As they had planned on the drive, they both scanned the front of the house, and then Josie went left and Sergio right.

'I've got him!' Josie yelled. She had just turned the corner to the side of her house and found him cowering behind the air-conditioning unit. She directed her flashlight on him, the bright light blinding him. 'Throw the gun on the ground!'

Javier stood slowly and backed against the side of her house. He held a gun in one hand and pointed it toward the ground. His other hand remained in a sweatshirt pocket.

'Slowly, bend down and place the gun on the ground!'

Sergio announced his presence behind her and yelled Josie's directions in Spanish.

They watched as Javier slowly began raising his arm, pointing in Josie's direction.

'Drop the gun or I will shoot!' The gun continued to rise. She yelled, 'Stop. If you continue to raise your arm, I will shoot!'

Josie could see the terror in his eyes as his arm continued to rise, pointing toward her, and then she understood – suicide by cop. And at that moment a shot rang out.

Startled, it took a moment to realize Javier had not shot but was falling to the ground. She saw blood just beginning to seep from his shirt. She turned to look behind her, feeling the drag on her brain, that slow-motion quality the world takes on when events go terribly wrong. Sergio's gun still pointed at Javier while his eyes moved to Josie with the unwavering conviction that events had gone exactly as Sergio had wanted. Josie bent down to check vitals and found Javier dead.

After calling 911, Ramos and then Otto, Josie's next call was to Dell to let him know the shots he had heard from his home were real, and that his property was about to be overrun with lights and sirens, but that everyone was safe. She had asked Dell once a few years back if he ever regretted deeding her the property in the front of his ranch so that she could build her home. She imagined he had not planned on the intrusions he had endured due to her line of work. He had brushed it off, saying something about the excitement she'd brought to his life, but Dell was approaching eighty, and she worried that the drama would be too much one day.

As they waited for the ambulance and coroner to arrive, Josie and Sergio looked through the security video, watching Javier approach Josie's front porch with his gun drawn, yelling, banging on the front door, then looking through her living-room window when no one answered.

'Did you realize he was this unstable?' Josie asked. They watched as Javier raged on her front porch in a psychotic state.

'I knew it. Marta knew it, too. His mental health issues were compounded by the alcohol, growing worse all the time.'

It was a terrible scene, watching a man lose control of his life, knowing those last few actions were leading to his death. He stopped yelling, finally exhausted from the effort. And then he did something that surprised them both. He stumbled back against Josie's front door and took his wallet out from his front pants pocket. He fished around inside it for quite some time and finally pulled out a piece of paper that he turned around and looked at while entering numbers into Josie's security system.

She was shocked that Javier would have had something written down on paper to help him break into her house. He'd not seemed capable of being that calculating. Until that moment, she hadn't considered that he could have been the person entering her home.

She and Sergio had covered Javier's body with a sheet to await the coroner. Josie pulled the sheet back and took the wallet out of his front pocket. A folded pink sticky note stuck out of the area where paper money was kept. She opened the note and was shocked to find Marta's name written at the top. Josie recognized her own handwriting and a four-digit number underneath her name.

She handed the note to Sergio, finding it all hard to believe. 'This is a note I gave Marta several years ago. It's from when the security system was installed. She stayed here at the house and took care of my dog for a week while I was out of town. I gave her this code because she didn't want to use the fingerprint reader. I had teased her about being paranoid that the government would somehow have access to her fingerprint through my security system.'

'Javier may have had access to your home for years, then,' Sergio said.

Josie shuddered at the thought.

Ramos had left the pile-up on I-10 and made it to Josie's two hours later, at about the same time that Sergio's commander from Mexico arrived. Josie had called and explained the situation, stating that Sergio had saved her life and his own, that Javier had aimed at them both, his finger on the trigger. His commander appeared surprisingly sympathetic to Sergio, calling him a hero for saving a life. She hoped that Javier's family and community would feel the same way when word got out.

TWENTY-THREE

T he next several days were filled with paperwork and interviews with officers ranging from the DEA to the Texas Rangers to the Mexican Consulate, all with different ideas about how the paperwork and transfer of Javier's body should be handled. In Ojinaga, Sergio had become a hero of sorts. The local papers were telling the tale of Sergio tracking Javier across the Rio and into the States where he had a mental breakdown and was attempting to shoot a single female at her home. No mention of Josie or that cops were involved. This was the story that Sergio shared with Teresa as well. One day, Josie would reach out to Teresa, but not yet.

While Josie fielded questions from one set of government agencies for Javier's death, another set was finally looking into the election scandal. With less than a week before the election, officials were frantically presenting two sides: prove foul play or convince the voters all was well in Arroyo County. Jezebel Black's death was now central, with the West Texas Citizens' Action Committee taking legal action to cancel the election. Groups were debating the misinformation and disinformation surrounding the racetrack and its influence over the election, and word had spread that Senator Mike Striker had been tampering with voting machines. The problem was that there was no clear definition of tampering. Josie had never seen anything like it.

Meanwhile, Jezebel's death had turned from a curiosity to a political separator: generally, those who opposed Mike Striker believed she was murdered by racetrack scoundrels, while those who supported Mike Striker believed she was murdered by crazed animal rights supporters. Josie hadn't found the connection to murder, but she had read enough about Jamison Leopold to know she didn't want him investing in her town.

The day prior, she had called Gabriella, the hostess at Coston Elli's restaurant in Florida, with follow-up questions about the timing of Jezebel's visit to Florida. There were times during questioning that a person became interested in the investigation on a deeper level and wanted to help, either because they cared about the people involved or because of a latent desire to work in law enforcement. Occasionally, it was nothing more than morbid curiosity.

Gabriella cared about Jezebel, but having only met her on two occasions, she also admitted to growing up watching cop shows. 'I've always wanted to be a detective,' she had said. When Gabriella offered to call Jamison Leopold's secretary to ask some questions about his schedule, Josie took her up on the offer.

Gabriella explained to Jamison's secretary that she was trying to find the dates that Mr Leopold had been at the restaurant because another guest was trying to track down a developer he'd met at the restaurant, and Gabriella thought it might have been Mr Leopold. Gabriella told the secretary, *confidentially*, that she thought the man who was asking was ready to make a very large purchase, and she didn't want Mr Leopold to miss out. She discovered that he was out of town the three days surrounding Jezebel's death, but the secretary hadn't shared the details of his trip. Josie thanked Gabriella for her outstanding work and promised to keep her informed on any developments that arose from her call. Josie then called the officer she spoke to from Naples and filled him in on the information.

Later that day, the officer called Josie back.

'There've been accusations from multiple residents that he arranged fraudulent land deals around the south Florida area, selling land that isn't even for sale. We're closing in on the bastard, but the paperwork takes forever. I called him for a lark and told him we'd like him to come in and clear things up for us. He agreed. The man has a league of attorneys, all of whom would advise him against this conversation. We usually can't get anywhere near him. There's a reason he's agreed to talk to us. I'm hoping this is a desperation meeting, but that's probably naïve. *Anyway*, I'm telling you all this to invite you to the party. As a silent observer. If you're interested.'

'Absolutely. When is the meeting?'

'Tomorrow morning at ten. That was as late as I could push it. I figured you could get a red-eye flight in tonight.'

The closest airport to fly to Fort Myers was Odessa, and the last flight out was at six that evening. She left work at noon to pack a bag and make the two-hour drive to the airport. The ticket had cost her a small fortune, but with a murder on the line, she couldn't ignore the interview.

On the way home, she received a call from Jack Striker.

'How's it going?' she asked.

'I'm in the clear, right? I'm allowed to talk to you again?'

'Why weren't you allowed to talk to me?'

'I assumed you aren't allowed to have dinner with murder suspects. But it's all over the news that you caught the guy.'

'Jack. I'm sorry about—'

'Don't apologize. I get it. I'm not calling to aggravate you. I just thought you might have dinner with me. My father and uncle are obsessed with the election, the track is on hold until after the votes are counted, and this motel room is about to send me over the edge.'

'I'd love to have dinner.'

'Let's just cut out. Take a few days off and we'll go somewhere new for both of us.'

She laughed. 'That would be pretty easy for me. I have Indiana and Texas covered. Beyond that, I'm wide open.'

'Tell me how long you have, and I'll find us a place. Maybe fly to California. We could hike the Pacific Coast Highway for a day or two.'

'You won't believe this, but I'm flying to Florida tonight. Actually, in a few hours.'

'Aren't you spontaneous!'

'Not even a little. It's for work. There's an interview I need to sit in on tomorrow morning at ten. I'm flying to Fort Myers late tonight.'

'You need a travel partner?'

Josie paused, surprised at the question. 'You know this will be a terrible trip? We won't get into Fort Myers until midnight, then a drive to Naples, and then my flight out is tomorrow afternoon at four.'

'I'll rent a car, and while you're doing your thing, I'll go walk the beach. Then I'll get us back to the airport on time to fly out.'

Josie said nothing. She knew hanging out with a person of interest in two investigations was not a good idea, but on some level she just didn't care. She wanted a life. She wanted a travel companion. And she was not a frequent flyer. It would be good to have him navigating a trip that was such short notice.

Jack continued. 'I've spent worse days than sitting next to an attractive woman on a plane for a couple of hours.'

Spontaneous, she thought. 'Then let's do it. I'll swing by the motel in about an hour to pick you up.'

Josie took a quick shower, threw a T-shirt and shorts in her bag, as well as dress slacks and a blouse for the interview. Then she found a silky camisole in the bottom of her dresser and packed it as well.

Jack stepped outside as soon as she rolled up in front of the motel. He carried a small leather duffel bag and what appeared to be a take-out paper bag from the Hot Tamale.

'You have lunch today?' he asked.

'No time.'

'I had a feeling. Burrito, right? Side of lime rice. I'd offer to drive while you ate but I guess you wouldn't let me drive the cruiser.'

'I suppose Lucy told you what I like?' she said.

'She went beyond that. She actually said this is your daily order. I get what you mean by the spontaneity thing. We're going to have to work on that.'

'There are no secrets in this town.' She readily accepted the burrito that he had laid out on the paper bag.

He placed a napkin across her thigh and popped the top on a Pepsi. 'Lucy said to get you a water, but I just couldn't imagine eating a burrito with water. That's no way to live.'

'I thought that kind of thinking was peculiar to Otto. Maybe it's more of a man thing?'

'I think perhaps it's a taste thing, but I won't say that in case it's offensive.'

'That's good of you.'

'And – just to prove I've not been skulking around town snooping out your favorite haunts – I went rogue on our trip. You said you haven't traveled much, so I took a chance and planned a trip for two weekends from now. You'll just need to take Friday off. We'll leave Thursday evening and get back late Sunday. Think you can handle that?'

'Wow. That's a pretty big commitment for me,' she said, only half kidding.

'I know it is. Think of this as immersion therapy in spontaneity. You'll tell me yes today, and then you'll have two weeks to get used to the idea that you're going on a trip to somewhere you've never been that doesn't involve a tent or a sleeping bag.'

'You aren't going to tell me where we're going?' she asked.

'No.'

She nodded slowly, grinning.

'Are you feeling uneasy?' he asked.

'Very.'

'Good. That's part of the therapy. Just enjoy your burrito and try not to think about getting into a car with someone without a clear plan.'

She glanced over and saw him smiling.

While Jack was a world traveler, most of his exploring had been solo, and he clearly wanted someone to share his experiences with. Josie tried to imagine how she might be able to travel with him without losing her job in Artemis and decided to save those thoughts for late at night when she couldn't sleep.

The flight to Fort Myers was uneventful, and Jack had booked them into a motel on the ocean. At midnight on a weeknight in late April, the streets were deserted and the trip from the airport to Naples was quick. After checking in and pitching their bags on the two queen beds, they kicked their shoes off, walked outside the ground-floor sliding doors and smiled.

'The whole trip is worth this moment,' Jack said. 'There's no other sound like waves hitting the beach, especially at night.'

Josie reached out for his hand as they rounded the sandy path and the ocean suddenly lay before them. The sound of the waves opened up all around them, and the salty damp air felt like heaven after a day spent driving and flying. A clear sky and a moon that was just shy of full lit up the white caps, making them glow against the dark.

He squeezed her hand as they walked out into the water, allowing it to rush up on to their thighs. He turned and grabbed her around the waist, still smiling. 'You make me so happy, and I can't even explain why,' he said, laughing. He pulled her into his body and kissed her forehead, her cheeks. 'Maybe the new mayor would give his chief of police a sabbatical to go explore the world for six months.'

Josie kissed him, touching her tongue to the saltiness of his lips. 'You do have some pull with this supposed new mayor, don't you?'

Jack ran his hands down her back and up her shirt as a wave crashed up against them, pushing them toward the beach. 'That was a sign,' he said, grabbing her hand and pulling her toward the room.

The interview with Jamison Leopold was surprising in a number of ways. Josie realized how little experience she had with interviewing suspects with great wealth. There were certainly ranchers worth millions in West Texas, but their attitudes were markedly different from Leopold's. She had faced arrogance and power, but Leopold had a flashy, white-toothed way of talking that heightened the arrogance. Every time he ran his hands down his well-tailored suit jacket or adjusted the sleeve of his shirt over the polished gold watch on his wrist, the actions appeared timed to draw attention. Josie couldn't imagine how exhausting that kind of life would be.

The first hour had nothing to do with Texas or anything Josie was interested in. The questions involved transactions that had taken place over a seven-month period and focused on three complainants who claimed he stole almost two million dollars from their retirement accounts. From the little Josie knew about the case, she didn't think much of what she was hearing sounded illegal: despicable behavior but not quite criminal.

Detective John Taub had said he would signal to Josie when he was about to turn the questioning toward Jezebel. Josie enjoyed watching Taub question Leopold. He was a master at playing up to Leopold, of allowing him the time and space to remain the center of attention. Leopold's narcissism was nauseating to listen to, but Taub appeared fascinated with the man's business acumen, smiling and nodding as Leopold explained the details of the transactions that he claimed were all perfectly legal.

Where it became interesting for Josie was as they closed in on the time period just before Jezebel's death. Taub glanced at Josie who was sitting at the interview table to Leopold's right. Josie tipped her head in return.

'Here's the problem,' Taub said. 'I have these two witnesses who say you took them out to the property two different times and showed them property lines that don't exist.' Taub pushed a calendar over to Leopold. 'I have those dates marked on the calendar for you.'

Leopold looked at the calendar and frowned. From talking with Taub, she knew Leopold had met the witnesses, but Taub was trying to get Leopold to place himself in Texas during the period Josie believed he was there, when Jezebel was killed.

Leopold grinned and shoved the calendar back across the table to Taub. 'Absolutely not. I wasn't even here on those dates! I was in Texas.'

'Come on,' Taub said, grinning. 'Where in Texas?'

'Artemis. A town the size of a traffic light in the desert. I have proof I was there – business receipts. Hell, I was there meeting with a senator. You can't have a better alibi than that.'

Taub laughed. 'No, sir, that's the truth. You can't have a better alibi than a meeting with a senator.' He nodded his head toward Josie. 'Actually, my friend here, Chief of Police Josie Gray, is from Artemis, Texas. She flew all the way from that one-traffic-light town just to talk to you.'

'Good afternoon. I have some questions about Jezebel Black. About your meeting with her in Artemis.'

Leopold stared at Josie for a moment as it dawned on him that he'd just been set up. 'I've had enough of this nonsense.' He scooted his chair back. 'Call my attorney with your bullshit questions.'

Josie considered the trip a success. She hadn't placed Leopold at the murder scene, but she had him in town the day Jezebel was murdered.

By eleven thirty, Josie was getting into the rental car with Jack for a quick beach lunch before they headed back to the airport. He'd already picked them up a to-go box lunch and found them a picnic table at one of the public access beaches. When they reached the beach, she changed into shorts and a T-shirt, and they ate with the sun warming their backs and the wind cooling their faces.

'Why would anyone want to live anywhere else?' she said. 'This is wonderful. Artemis is supposed to hit a hundred again this week.'

'There's definitely a beach vibe here. People seem a little looser, a little less suspicious.'

Josie handed Jack his drink and tried to keep her voice conversational. 'Speaking of suspicious . . . would you be offended if I asked you a question about Jezebel Black?'

'Usually when someone says, "no offense," they're getting ready to offend me. So given that you're asking that question, I'm probably going to get offended. But what the hell. Go ahead and ask. I just might not answer.'

'I'm not asking because I think your dad or uncle had anything to do with her murder, but I'm guessing you've heard them talk about her murder. You know that everyone in Arroyo County has an opinion about whether your uncle either did or didn't kill the woman. I would love to hear your take on all of this.'

'Out of curiosity or as an investigator?'

'Both.'

He nodded, taking a moment to finish a bite of his sandwich. 'All right, fair enough. Yes, they've talked about her murder extensively. My dad doesn't understand how my uncle could have gotten messed up with such a disaster of a woman. And that progressed to my dad accusing my uncle of thinking with his—'

Jack paused, and Josie took up the conversation. 'Meaning your uncle partnered up with Jezebel for the sex, not because she was a savvy businesswoman.'

Jack put a hand up. 'Those are your words, not mine.' He seemed to think about Josie's comment before speaking again. 'I think both of them thought she was talented at the art of the business deal. It wasn't like she was sleeping her way to a signature on a contract. From what I've gathered, I think she had a knack for making a deal. My dad's issue with her was that she was a mess. She seemed to move from one crisis to the next in her personal life. She had death threats at one point over the whole river-guide mess.'

'About what?'

'I don't know. It was too sordid to follow. Which was my dad's point. Uncle Mike could have found other people with less baggage who could have made the deals down south.'

'Do you know what kind of deals she was making?'

'Land deals. I think she and Mike were selling off plots of land around the racetrack.'

'Do you think she could have made enemies doing that? Maybe screwed over the wrong person and paid the price?'

'What makes you think they were screwing anyone over?' he asked.

Josie grinned and rolled her eyes, then realized he wasn't kidding. 'Sorry.'

'I wasn't offended before. But I might be now. Just because my family has money doesn't mean that they're not legitimate.'

'You're right. I apologize. I just can't figure out how Jezebel ended up with a six-figure deposit in her bank account, and two weeks later she was murdered.'

'Maybe she got the six-figure deposit because she was a better businesswoman than you're giving her credit for.'

TWENTY-FOUR

The day before the election, Josie met with Otto and Mark Jackson at the police department to discuss emergency plans. It turned out that Mark's fears about the election were well founded. They had credible information that animal rights activists were planning to shut down the polling sites to protest the greyhound track. Because of all the drama, Mark was able to find an abundance of people willing to work the polls, so volunteers were no problem; the issue was controlling tempers when the protestors arrived – and ensuring that the pollers weren't there to cause their own disruptions. Josie had received last-minute approval from the governor's office to receive National Guard troops to post at each of the polling places in Arroyo County the day of the election.

The night before the election, Josie drove out to Mike Striker's house to see how the senator was spending his evening. She found the house and grounds fully lit up with a dozen fancy cars parked in the driveway and along the winding road up to the house. The pool area was full of laughing people planning for a win. Josie parked her police vehicle on the road that wound down below the house, and she walked up the canyon drive, snapping photos of each license plate and car. She noted one old economy car amid the Benzes and Bentleys. Voices carried far along the dry canyon air, and she could hear snatches of conversations, most revolving around money or winning or both.

Josie stopped at a car with a license plate frame around it that said *El Paso Republican*. She sent a photo of the plate to the dispatcher on duty and asked for a driver look-up. Several minutes later, she discovered the car was registered to Kip Esposito, the political operator that Otto had mentioned. Josie looked around to ensure no partygoers had strayed over into the driveway. With no one outside, she shone her flashlight into the car and found stacks of papers in the front and back, with fast-food wrappers wadded up on the dashboard of the Jaguar. She used her phone to snap photos of the papers scattered over the seats and moved on to the next vehicle.

Once she'd taken photos of all the cars in the drive, she walked back down the hill to her SUV. She leaned against the side of her car and looked up to the back of the house. She noticed a man standing on the edge of the pool area by himself, talking on the phone. He was illuminated under a light used to spotlight a palm tree. Josie snapped a photo of him and left before she pushed her luck and received a complaint about a prowler lurking behind the senator's home.

Three miles away, she pulled off the road to download the photos on to her laptop. She started by examining the papers in the back of Kip Esposito's front seat. They appeared to be legal documents that didn't reference anything she was familiar with. But the backseat papers were more interesting. With the photos enlarged, she could see that one of the papers was part of a blueprint of a housing development that appeared to be surrounding a racetrack. Lying on top of the blueprint was a full-color photo of a plot with fully completed desertscape and a sticky note that read, *Plot 19 – Leopold needs five pics similar.*

Josie wondered if Leopold had sold five plots of land based on photos of land that appeared to have been fully developed but hadn't even been surveyed yet.

She quickly flipped through the other photos to the last one of the man in the spotlight and zoomed in to see that Jamison Leopold had taken his own red-eye flight to make it to her one-traffic-light town in time for the election the next day. Josie decided to crash the party.

She parked along the road with the other guests and rang the doorbell. Carla opened the door, and a range of expressions crossed her face, from friendly surprise at seeing Josie unexpectedly, to the realization that Josie was in uniform, to the dread of what lay ahead.

'I'm so sorry to stop by unannounced. I'd just like to

have a quick conversation with one of your guests. Jamison Leopold.'

Carla furrowed her brow as if that request was the last one she had expected.

'Of course, come on in. Jack's on the patio if you want to go say hello. I'll go find Jamison for you.'

'I don't want to interrupt the party. I'll wait out here.'

A moment later, Jack opened the front door, holding a beer, smiling and looking like a man enjoying a party. 'Josie, come inside.'

'No, really. This is fine. I'm here on business. I don't want to ruin the evening.'

'On business?' His eyebrows raised, and understanding lit up his expression. 'I see. I bet you're here to see Jamison. Was he the person you interviewed in Florida? I hadn't realized your trip to Florida concerned my family.'

Jack's words had the slowed cadence of someone who was approaching drunk.

'You didn't ask. And the interview didn't concern you. You even told me that you didn't want to hear anything about the police business I was on.'

He nodded slowly. 'Excellent point.'

A man appeared behind Jack, and Josie heard him say, 'Excuse me.'

Jack nodded to Josie and went back inside the house. She thought how odd it was to see him in this light, with people who were clearly not in Josie's social group.

The front door shut, and Jamison Leopold crossed his arms over his puffed-up chest. He appeared to sway, and Josie could see he had been drinking as well.

Josie reintroduced herself while Leopold remained quiet. 'I'm sorry to bother you this evening, but you didn't give me a chance to ask you any questions when we met in Naples.'

'Under false pretenses.'

'Not at all. Officer Taub just offered me the chance to talk with you while you were at the station.'

Leopold glanced away as if he wasn't even going to dignify her comment with a response.

'This isn't formal questioning. I'm just trying to understand what happened to Jezebel Black. We are struggling to find a motive for her killing. To date, the only thing that makes sense is that her murder had something to do with the large sum of money she had recently acquired.'

Leopold threw his head back and laughed. 'My money!'

'Can you tell me how much?'

'I have no idea. Whatever Mike Striker pays his real-estate brokers.'

'Jezebel was a broker?'

'I don't know. She was a smooth talker. That much I'm sure of. But she was also a walking disaster.'

'What do you mean by that?' she asked.

Leopold laughed again. 'Did you know her?'

'I did.'

'Then you know her life was a series of disasters. Do you know how Mike met Jezebel?'

'No.' Josie lied, wondering if his version of the story was the same as the one she had heard.

'She was walking down the road in the rain one night after she ran out of gas. In the middle of the desert. Does that surprise you?'

'It doesn't surprise me.'

'You know she left some woman behind on a river trip? Ruined a guy's business. Then Mike decides this is the woman we need breeding dogs and brokering land.'

'She must have done well, given the size of the deposit into her bank account,' she said.

Leopold turned back, apparently making sure the door was closed. 'Look. I don't know why you're asking me questions about this lady's murder. She was an attractive real-estate broker. End of story with me. You want anything deeper than that, go talk to her boss. For now, I have a party to attend.'

Josie drove home and stuck a bag of popcorn in the micro-wave for a late supper, and then sat at the kitchen table with her laptop to check the license plates from Striker's party. There had been one car that hadn't fit the guest profile. Josie clicked through the photos, found the photo of the Chevy

Spark and ran the plate. She leaned back in her seat, completely unprepared for the name that came up in the system. She couldn't have been more surprised, but at the same time, it all finally made sense.

Next, she called Otto and asked him to get hold of Carla and have her text him a list of guests at their party that night. She told Otto that she didn't need any family members' names, but a complete list of everyone else. Twenty minutes later, Otto forwarded the guest list to Josie – minus one name. The owner of the Chevy Spark.

Otto pressed for details, but with no evidence to back up her theory, she didn't want to discuss it just yet. She asked Otto to stay close to the PD in the morning, with voting opening at six a.m. She hoped to be back in town by eight.

At six the next morning, Josie called Sam Greene, former owner of the Rio River Guides, and asked him to meet her at the empty church in the ghost town of Ruidosa. She explained that she was the chief of police in Artemis, that there had been an accident and she needed him in Ruidosa as soon as possible. She didn't give him time to ask questions before hanging up. Then it was a matter of waiting, allowing him the thirty-minute drive to get there.

By seven o'clock that morning, she was sitting in the vacant church lot, watching as the sun pushed up over the horizon. She had timed it so that she and Sam would arrive at the site before other travelers attempted the trip, but she also wanted to ensure enough daylight so that she could watch his reactions.

When Sam arrived, he pulled in next to Josie's marked SUV and got out of his little Chevy Spark, with an expression of frantic concern.

'What's going on here? What's this about an accident?'

Josie held her badge out, and he barely glanced at it before looking around the deserted place for whatever tragedy he'd been called to. 'What's this all about?'

'I can explain,' she said. 'The accident is up the road.' She opened the passenger door to her police car, and he looked at her as if she was crazy.

'Please. We need to get going. It's just up the road.'

He climbed into the passenger seat, clearly uneasy about the situation, but Josie knew he couldn't walk away from the request. How do you walk away from a situation when a police officer tells you there's been an accident and you're needed?

She glanced over at him as she pulled on to Pinto Canyon Road. His eyes were wide and unfocused. He didn't ask Josie what accident she was talking about. He'd already figured it out.

'Tell me about your relationship with Jezebel Black,' she said.

He didn't speak. His hands were on his legs, his fingers white from digging into his thighs.

'I know you were angry with her over what happened with the woman on the rafting trip who died, but I'm curious about your relationship after the legal battle finally ended.'

'She destroyed my business. What kind of a relationship do you think we had?' he said. His voice was quiet and angry.

'Help me understand how she was responsible for that woman's death? People seemed to blame Jezebel more than the husband who probably killed her.'

'I never said she was responsible. But the way she handled it was against all rules. We have ways to communicate on the river. We talk with other guides, we have radios. Jezebel said nothing about what happened. Everything could have been avoided if she'd followed the protocol. And I would still have the business that I loved. The business I worked my whole life to build.'

'Would it have done any good? She still had to get the group back to shore. The woman was most likely already dead.'

'She didn't tell anyone about the lady not coming back until the police showed up at the guide shop the next day. They came into my office wanting to know why one of my guests never made it back. I didn't know anything about it. The media didn't just tear Jezebel up; they slaughtered me as well. And I had done nothing!'

'Is that why you continued to harass her? Sent her death threats? Posed as RiverRider on Facebook to taunt her over the racetrack?' Josie asked.

'What's all this about?'

'I was given a list that your Facebook pal Dugout put together. He identifies you as RiverRider.'

'Since when is posting on Facebook a crime?'

Josie ignored his question, and they drove the last mile up the canyon in silence, with Sam staring straight ahead, his hands still gripping his thighs.

She pulled her SUV off the side of the road and turned her lights and flashers on. Her car was pulled up against a pile of boulders with just enough room for her to exit the vehicle. Josie got out of the car, but Sam didn't. She opened the passenger door and motioned for him to follow. There was at least ten feet from the passenger door to the edge of the canyon. She walked toward the edge and was surprised when he followed her.

'This is the exact spot where Jezebel's body went over the edge. But you know that, don't you?'

He shook his head but didn't speak.

'Why kill her, though? How did that solve anything for you?' Josie asked, trying to engage him. 'She'd moved on with her life, had finally started a new business. Why didn't you do the same?'

He laughed. 'She had the nerve to try to sell me plots of worthless land from her new business. She mailed me a letter and a flyer. Bragged about all the money she was making. Made it sound like she was going to cut me in. I sat and looked at that letter for days. She'd ruined my life and now she was in business with some senator. Ready to bring a racetrack into the desert. See what else she could screw up.'

'So you went to her house and picked her up.'

'She said she'd show me the racetrack development, like she was doing me a favor. So I said yes, that I'd come pick her up. But the more I thought about it, the more it pissed me off.' He turned and narrowed his eyes at Josie, as if surely she could see how absurd it was that Jezebel had contacted him. 'So I picked her up and decided to show *her* something instead. I wanted to show her what it was like for that lady down the river. I was going to leave her here. I swear that was it. Let her walk home in the middle of nowhere. Let her see what it's like to be left.' Sam looked out across the canyon and grew quiet for a long while.

'You got out of the car when you got here. And what happened?' she asked.

'We fought all the way here. She tried to explain it all away. I was tired of hearing it. She knew something was up when we headed toward the canyon. She was trying to call someone, and I grabbed her phone and threw it out the window. She came unglued then, yelling at me. I finally stopped driving right here. I got out and she followed me, still yelling about how unfair I was being to her. I told her I wanted her to see what it was like. She came after me, hitting me with both fists, and I pushed her back.' He placed both hands over his eyes, but it felt to Josie like an act. She saw no sadness or regret in his demeanor.

'When you pushed her, did she fall off the edge?'

He nodded, keeping his head down. 'It was all a terrible accident.'

'I think it was more than that. I think you wanted to destroy Jezebel and her business, just like she destroyed you.'

Sam looked at Josie as if surprised by her comment.

'I saw your car last night, outside Mike Striker's home. But you didn't go in. You weren't invited. I think your goal is to ruin them all. Destroy Jezebel and her successful business. Take them all down.'

Sam bolted toward the car, just a half-dozen steps away. Josie assumed he was going to try to steal the vehicle, but he hit the car with his hands and pushed himself off, propelling himself back toward the canyon. She grabbed his arm as he moved by her, catching the neck of his T-shirt with her other hand, pulling back and down toward the ground.

He howled out as he hit the ground. 'Just let me end this.' His face dropped down on to the road, and tears now mixed with the dirt underneath him.

Josie dropped her knee into the center of his back and snapped cuffs around his wrists. She pulled him up and dragged him back to her vehicle before he could lunge again for the side of the canyon.

TWENTY-FIVE

As Josie was booking Sam Greene for the murder of Jezebel Black, she received a call from Otto.

'I guess you haven't seen Facebook,' he said.

Josie stepped back to allow the booking officer to escort Greene down the hall for fingerprinting.

'You know I don't have Facebook.'

'Well, maybe you should get it. In the meantime, get over to the courthouse. I'll show you mine when you get here.'

'What's going on?'

'Carla carried through with her threats,' he said.

Josie heard a crowd of people yelling in the background.

'Gotta go,' he said and hung up on her.

By the time Sam was in lockup, she'd heard the full story and seen the photos from several officers. Senator Mike Striker's bare backside was the focus of one of the photos, with his hand raised to spank the naked backside of the woman bent over in front of him. The caption on Carla Striker's Facebook post read, *Meet Family Man, my husband, Mike Striker*. Another photo of Striker in a different bedroom under similar circumstances was titled *Meet your new mayor, Senator Mike Striker!*

When Josie arrived at the police department, she found every parking space around the courthouse, and for blocks on all sides, taken with angry citizens – or those looking to watch the latest freak show. Josie made her way to the largest group of people and found Mark Jackson standing in the middle, calling for order.

Dozens of people were talking at once. 'This election should be invalidated immediately!' 'This election is a farce!'

'I can't invalidate an election that isn't even over,' Mark yelled. 'Enough of this! Go cast your vote, and we'll deal with the results when it's over. We will not stop the voting process because of social media nonsense. If we do it this time, then the same thing happens the next time. The election proceeds. That is all I have to say about this.'

Josie pushed her way through and ordered people to disperse. She escorted Mark to the police department where he followed her inside. His hair was disheveled, his tie askew, and he looked as if he'd barely survived a mobbing.

'My worst nightmare just came to life,' he said, sliding into a chair that Otto offered him.

'What do we do about this?' Otto said.

'Nothing. There's nothing we can do. Someone posting naked photos on the internet isn't illegal. Mike Striker may be immoral, but that doesn't mean he can't be mayor. If something was going to be done, it needed to be done long before today. And with that, I'm headed back out into this mess. I'll be at the elementary school, checking on the poll workers.'

'Call if you need us,' Otto said. He turned to Josie once Mark had left the station. 'Mike Striker and his crew are really off the hook for Jezebel Black? You're convinced Sam Greene killed her?'

'He confessed. He was eaten up with anger over Jezebel ruining his business.'

'I was convinced we'd have Striker and his brother on the hook for murder by nightfall.'

'Maybe his biggest crime is bad judgment,' she said. 'He doesn't seem to make good decisions when it comes to women.'

'You haven't heard the senator's other bad news.'

'I just saw the governor Tweeted that Mike Striker's political future is finished in the state of Texas. You have worse than that?' she said.

'I'd say so. The sheriff called. He said they have digital video from Betty Richardson's phone the night of the break-in here. She was in town that night helping her granddaughter film something for her high school English project.'

Josie laughed. 'And she ended up getting footage of the break-in?'

'Close. She was talking to Philips yesterday at the grocery and mentioned how she was astounded that the town of Artemis couldn't afford to keep the PD open at night. And how she saw some truck race out from behind the police station that night it got broken into. We have her phone footage that shows a truck both entering the alley and exiting the alley, at the exact time that the digital camera line was cut. No other vehicles were back there during that time.'

'Are you going to make me guess what kind of truck it was?' she said.

'Ford F-150 Lodge Edition. White. We got a partial plate and a rental car company sticker on the video, too. The same vehicle that Morey Striker rented when he arrived at the San Antonio airport. Morey Striker was picked up for questioning this morning. I haven't heard a follow-up,' Otto said.

'I'd say the senator's good luck just turned to shit,' Josie said.

The rest of the day was spent fielding calls about the election and whether it had been 'canceled' given Mike Striker's condemnation by the governor. Politicians both locally and in the senate at large were calling for his immediate resignation. The event that provoked the most outrage occurred the next morning when the results of the mayor's race were announced on Marfa Public Radio. Senator Mike Striker won the mayoral race in Artemis by a thirty-three percent margin. Given the outrage over the Facebook photos posted the day of the election, there wasn't a person in the whole state of Texas, Republican or Democrat, who believed the vote count was accurate. A news anchor from one of the San Antonio stations led the news story saying, 'Senator Striker facing his own spanking over charges of voter fraud today.' The memes were relentless.

Josie stopped at Manny's Motel on her way home from work that night. The curtains were open in Jack's room, and she could see him sitting up in bed with a TV remote in his hand. Josie tapped on the window, and he waved her in without getting up.

'Just checking on you,' she said. 'How are you holding up?'

He shrugged. 'My family has never shied away from media attention. But this? I just saw a photo of me presenting at some conference. The announcer claimed I was Jack Striker,

Senator Striker's son, and the man poised to take over the company if he does jail time.'

'Maybe you should turn that off.'

Jack hit the power button and pitched the remote on to the bedside table.

'How much trouble is my dad in?'

'I wish I could say. With a good attorney, probably not as much as you might think.'

'I'm ready to catch a flight back to the Congo. I had less turmoil there, in the most corrupt country in the world, than I've had working with my dad and uncle for a month in Texas.'

Josie said nothing.

'The worst part? I have defended them both my whole life. To my mom, my stepmom, my coworkers. Uncle Mike and the photos? No real surprise there. He has the morals of an alley cat. But my dad?' He shook his head and turned from her.

'Can I sit?' she said, gesturing toward the bed.

'Of course. I'm sorry.'

Jack patted the bed beside him, and she sat next to him, leaning her back against the headboard.

'This is what I do every day,' Josie said, 'so nothing that's happened here has really surprised me. I understand it's your dad so it's personal. But people make mistakes all the time. They're punished, they do their time, and they start over again. Life sucks for a while, but people move on.'

'It's not that cut and dried to me. I'm not sure how I forgive my family for this. And they aren't just family; they're my employers. How do I walk into the office in Manhattan and face my coworkers with my uncle's bare ass on every one of their phones, with my dad sitting in a jail cell?'

'I guess you walk into the office and tell them the truth. Whatever that truth is for you.'

Jack stared at the blank TV screen.

Josie got up from the bed and walked around to Jack's side, putting her hand out. 'Come on. We can't stay in this motel room.'

He shook his head. 'I can't. I can't carry on a conversation tonight.'

'Come on. I promise, you don't have to say a word. You were my travel partner, so I'll be yours tonight.'

Jack got off the bed slowly. 'I don't want to see people.'

'Not a problem. I'll grab us a twelve-pack of Corona and we'll go sit on the bank of the Rio Grande and watch the sunset. It'll be a much better view than a blank TV screen.'

'Then what?'

She put her hand out, and he grinned, taking it. 'We don't need to think that far ahead. I'll drive. We'll listen to some Elton John, spread a blanket on the sandbar, get a couple of Coronas in us, and what comes next won't even matter.'

The next morning, Josie was up early and, without putting much thought into it, she put her hiking gear on and took off from the house. It wasn't a planned hike, and she wasn't sure where she was going or how long she needed to be away. She just needed to be away. Her mind was numb from the loss of Marta. Her death brought back memories of the death of her father and the awful realization as a child that death was absolute and that nothing else would ever be the same. She vowed to find a way for her brain to process that another person she loved was removed from her life without her being able to say goodbye, or, more importantly, to say the things she wished she'd said but hadn't had the courage. Josie cried throughout the hike, crying for her father, for Marta and finally for herself.

She remembered an endless line of sad men coming to her house and speaking softly to her mom, a long parade of police cars, emergency lights flashing on the way to her father's gravesite. All the officers were dressed in pressed and polished uniforms. Bugles were played, rifles were fired, a man handed her mom a folded US flag, and then everyone left. And Josie knew the absence of what followed then was going to happen again. She knew that she had finally begun to mourn Marta's death.

Josie was unable to say goodbye or show the proper respect to Marta that she so much deserved. The best that Josie could do was attend the graveside service with Sergio, standing away from the family and partially hidden among the many other gravestones. She did not want to be a distraction for the grieving family, nor did she want to be a target of their anger. But she knew that she had to feel the sadness and grief and anger now or her brain would try to protect itself from those emotions forever. If she let that happen, she would lose another piece of who she was and allow sadness to further creep into her everyday life.

Josie heard the family's grief, she smelled the beautiful flower arrangements, she saw the crippling sadness that Marta's daughter Teresa was experiencing, and when the ceremony was over, she touched Marta's final place of rest. Josie knew it was not enough to honor Marta, but it was all she could do that day. She made a graveside promise to Marta that she would stay in contact with Teresa in the hope that she would accept her friendship and mentoring.

During the weeks that followed, Josie began the process of hiring a new officer to replace Marta. She and Otto spent many hours talking about the qualifications the next person needed. In the end, they both knew it was an impossible task, and that the best they could do was hire someone who was a good person. They would teach them how to be a great police officer. The night she posted the job opening, she arrived home to find a handwritten note on her door. It was an invitation from Dell, written on a torn piece of brown paper grocery sack, asking her to join him for a bonfire and a cold beer. She just had to bring her favorite chair.